REMEDIES FOR LOVESICK WEREWOLVES

SULA ALBA

Copyright © 2025 Sula Alba

Remedies for Lovesick Werewolves by Sula Alba

All rights reserved.

No part of this publication may be reproduced, distributed, transmitted, or used to train AI in any form or by any means, including photocopying, recording, or other electronic or mechanical methods, without the prior written permission of the author, except as permitted by U.S. copyright law.

The story, all names, characters, and incidents portrayed in this book are fictitious. Any resemblance with actual persons (living or deceased), places, events, or locales is entirely coincidental.

For you.

CONTENT NOTES

This paranormal romance book features on-page steamy scenes. It does also touch on several sensitive topics and themes. If you'd like to know more you can find a full list on my website: https://www.sulaalba.com/content-warnings

Take care and happy reading!

Chapter One

A painting dropped from its nail and landed on Molly's foot. She tried to soothe away the hurt, and would have chalked it up to one of her ghosts acting up, if it hadn't been the fifth portrait this week. Something was coming. She couldn't figure out whether it was good or bad. Avoiding it didn't exactly make things better, but after a long day of running her cafe, the last thing she wanted was to spend hours agonizing over something that she wasn't even sure was a problem yet.

So she settled on the couch, popcorn bowl in hand, and tried to ignore it and finish watching the movie.

A woman on screen without a hair out of place approached a rickety door that looked like cardboard.

"Don't go in there," said the little girl behind her.

She didn't heed the warning because characters in horror movies never did, and a furry claw broke through the fake door and snatched her arm.

A shrill scream echoed through Molly's house from the television. As she struggled with the comically giant paw, Molly laughed, fishing for more popcorn from the bowl.

The movie was Rosie's recommendation for their Friday roommate movie night. Molly had looked forward to an evening filled with cheesy B-grade horror. It would have been an enjoyable break from the unease she felt all day until she noticed Rosie and Lenore had replaced their pajamas with slinky satin dresses. Their outfits were far too revealing for a freezing February.

"Wait, that's tonight?" asked Rosie. She didn't even turn to Molly, as she was far too preoccupied with curling her black hair.

"We have scary movie night every third Friday of the month, you know that. You set up the schedule," said Molly.

"Shit, Molly. Listen," began Lenore, pulling her eyeliner away from her eye. "Sigma Chi is throwing their biggest party of the year tonight! We weren't going to go, but..." she glanced at Rosie, her hazel eyes full of embarrassment.

"Patrick Charles Manchester is going to be there, and Lenore is obsessed with him."

"Am not."

"You know only serial killers use three names, right?" asked Molly with a sigh. Perhaps this was a consequence of allowing college students to live in her home. In times like these, she remembered the silly things twenty-one-year-old girls would do for a glimpse of a crush.

Had she been that silly at that age? She took a glance at herself in the mirror as they preened. Her dark hair curled tightly around her head. Although she was older than her roommates, she couldn't help but still see her sixteen-year-old self staring back. She had the same dark radiant skin, high cheekbones, and full lips.

No, she thought, she hadn't been that silly.

"Look," said Rosie, "we can do horror movie night tomorrow. Or next week! But this is the biggest party right before everyone leaves for spring break!"

"Okay, okay," acquiesced Molly.

"I have an idea! You can come with us!" said Lenore. Rosie threw her a look as if Lenore had just invited their mother.

"Come with you? To a frat party? I think I'd rather drink poison."

"Oh, come on, Molly! No one will know you're older! You look great for your age!" said Lenore.

"I'm not old."

"I never said you were old! Just that you know, you're over thirty…"

"I'm thirty-four, and I'm not going to a party with a bunch of college students."

Rosie opened her mouth to protest, but stopped when she realized the curling iron in her black hair smoked. Molly sighed, exasperated by their frantic attempts at primping.

"Take care of each other, okay? And don't leave your drinks unattended," said Molly.

"Duh," they replied in unison.

So, she sat alone, watching a horror movie from the 1970s that Rosie had picked out. The movie bored her, and she checked her phone. It was just past 10:00 p.m., and she debated going to bed. She had to work at Books & Beans, her coffee shop, the next day, but she had told the barista to open for her. Although Lenore and Rosie had stared at her like she was a grandma, maybe an early night was what she needed.

No, so what if the girls left her alone? She would at least finish the movie. She reached down into the bowl again, only for her fingers to brush against hard kernels.

Molly got up and headed to her kitchen, turning on the lights as she walked in. She set another instant popcorn bag in her microwave and prepared some tea for later.

While she stood over her sink, filling the kettle, she giggled about the invitation Lenore had extended. She couldn't imagine herself at a frat party surrounded by twenty-year-olds trying to hit on her. Molly appreciated Lenore trying to get her out of the house, but her tone had suggested more. An inkling of pity laced her question. Almost suggesting staying home alone on a Friday night was pathetic. Molly didn't think so. She had a lot to do. Well, not a lot, but she could use the downtime to relax.

It had only been a month since the coven's last disaster. A dedicated and vindictive witch hunter stalked Violet and her boyfriend Scott, almost ending both their lives. The coven came out on the other side unscathed, but Molly couldn't help but wonder how long it would take for the next crisis to pop up.

It's not that the coven didn't have problems before Ellie joined, but Molly thought her introduction had caused a shift. She couldn't shake the feeling that something had changed, like finding the color of her house a shade lighter one day. Or as if everything had moved by just half an inch. No one else would notice, but Molly could sense it, and it unnerved her.

She poured herself a cup of tea, chamomile for calm, passion flower for sleep and relaxation, raspberry leaf for the flavor. As the popping from the microwave intensified, she stirred her tea clockwise, letting her intention steep along with the herbs. The worry swirled within her, mixing with the memories of finding Violet locked up in a little shed in some man's junkyard. A minute too late, and he would have killed her. She tried not to dwell on it. They had rescued her; she was safe. And yet she couldn't relax. Even weeks later, the fear of almost losing Violet kept her up at night. She wished she had asked Rosie and Lenore to stay home, but she couldn't keep everyone under her thumb. She had to let them live their lives and create the messes they needed to cause.

That was precisely the problem.

As the microwave finished with a loud *bing,* sirens wailed in the distance. They passed by her home, the swirling lights creating particolored shadows from her window. Molly thought nothing of it as she poured the popcorn into the bowl.

Crash!

Molly stood still, bag poised over her trashcan. Her house vibrated with the impact. The jars on her herb wall tinkled as they bumped into each other. She peered towards the door that led to the foyer. The crash had come from near the front door, but she didn't move. She waited, listening.

The sound of crunching glass reached her as someone walked over the broken shards. She tiptoed to the drawer by the oven and pulled out a ready-made potion. Hemlock, hellebore, wormwood, and wolfsbane. Not a lethal combination, but just enough to stun them. Unless she used more of it. The intruder made a mistake. He had caught her in her domain.

She raised the bottle above her head, knowing that as soon as the trespasser walked in through the kitchen door, the potion would knock him out. The footsteps neared, but something was off. A soft click followed each step, but it wasn't the click of heels. Her floorboards creaked with every movement. She stopped breathing as the sound got closer.

Something she didn't expect limped into her kitchen. A dog? No, not a dog, much bigger than a dog. A wolf.

She didn't throw the potion, feeling better about an animal in her home than a human. It was much larger than any wolf she had ever seen, with a deep warm brown coat and enormous claws poking from its furry paws. The wolf whined, and she looked down to see blood pooling beneath the poor thing's feet. She stepped closer, unsure of whether he would cower or attack her.

What is the protocol for rabies again? She wondered as she approached it.

"There, there," she said. The dog continued whining. The potion was still gripped tight in her hand, just in case. "Hey, buddy. I'm a friend."

She felt silly for talking to it, but it looked up at her, as if it understood. As she inched closer, the beast locked eyes with her, and her skin erupted in goosebumps. Was that normal? She didn't know. She had always been more of a cat person. Plus, she reasoned, dogs and wolves had little in common. Nobody looked at a pug and thought it came from a wolf.

The animal backed away, and Molly stopped approaching. The wolf peered at the hand that still held the potion. She racked her brain for what to do, cursing Lenore and Rosie for leaving her alone tonight. Molly slowly placed the bottle on the counter. The wolf followed it with his eyes. She stepped further back, wondering what to do next. It stared at the potion, and Molly thought the wolf appeared as if it debated its options.

"Don't be silly," she said aloud. "Dogs can't do that. It's just looking."

Molly's heart raced with panic as the wolf took a step forward. The animal looked her dead in the eyes, and she wasn't near her kitchen knives to defend herself if it pounced.

"Good dog. Back away now, please." She held her hands in front of her and tried to calculate the likelihood that it would chase her if she ran away.

The wolf stepped even closer, and Molly noticed a change. So minuscule, but it was there. A small bald patch appeared on its side. But there was fur there before? She was sure of it. The wolf took another step, and she stared in awe as the hair receded from the rest of the wolf's back. She grabbed her potion and raised it above her head. But the wolf didn't move, and the fur continued to disappear, revealing a broad back.

The wolf walked forward, this time hoisting itself to stand on its hind legs. He towered over her. His head nearly scratched the ceiling. He shrank a little, but not by much. The fur receded from his legs, and the claws retracted into his fleshy feet. Its arms followed, losing some of their definition. The torso shifted next, and Molly finally saw what was beneath the fur.

Bullet wounds.

The head was last. The wolf's snout shrunk into its face, and its teeth returned to normal size.

A naked man stood in the middle of her kitchen. His face was pale beneath shoulder-length shaggy chestnut brown hair, the same color as his fur. His eyes never wavered from hers, but blinked rapidly, trying to stay awake. Molly lowered the potion, but she said nothing. The man walked forward, his hand stretched out towards her. She reached out as he fell with a heavy thud on the ground.

Chapter Two

Molly stood still for a moment. Her heart hammering in her chest and her eyes stuck on the unconscious man's back. Her thoughts raced.

"Snap out of it, Molly," she said out loud, hoping to talk herself out of the shock. She kneeled next to him and gingerly touched him. His skin burned. The metallic scent of blood filled the air as it pooled beneath him. She struggled to get him onto his back, but he flopped over with some exertion. She counted six bullet holes and noticed fragments stuck in some.

"You need to stifle the bleeding," a voice said in her ear. Molly turned around and saw Camilla. She floated a few inches above the ground, her 1940s casual dress out of place in Molly's refurbished kitchen.

"Right," said Molly. She ran to the drawers and grabbed a few kitchen towels. She tried her best to put pressure on the wounds.

"What next?" asked Molly.

"You need to remove the bullet fragments. They don't look that deep. That's odd." The ghost kneeled, peering into the wounds. Camilla's liberty curls didn't move. "If you let him die, I wouldn't mind the company of someone so handsome."

"Forget it. The last thing we need in this house is more ghosts." Molly stood up and ran upstairs to grab some supplies. Some fragments would be too big for her tweezers, so she grabbed some pliers too.

Molly was thankful for the ghosts her home came with. The real estate agent told Molly the house was a steal because it needed repairs. But she knew that wasn't true. When she had first toured it, she had counted at least three ghosts. Now she wasn't sure how many spirits lived in her home. Some liked to come and go. Some of the coven members had ghosts attached to them and would only visit. Like Margaret, whose ghost never left her side until recently, that is.

After they had accepted her offer, she searched the history of the previous owners and realized that most people didn't stay longer than two years. No doubt the hauntings scared them away, but Molly liked them. She was never really alone.

"Okay," said Molly, placing all her supplies on the clean towel. "Now what?"

"I counted thirteen fragments. Most will be easy, but this one." She pointed to the wound closest to his heart. "This one is going to be tough. But I noticed something peculiar about him."

"You mean the wolf thing?"

"No, not that. He's healing."

Molly pulled back the towels and looked closer at the injuries. Sure enough, some wounds had stopped bleeding. Others were closing, pushing bullet shards from his puckered skin.

"It's not pushing out all the fragments. They're going to get stuck in his chest."

"More reason to do it fast, Molly dear."

Molly used some rubbing alcohol to disinfect the pliers, although she wondered if his healing would take care of any infection. She got to work, pulling each fragment. Some were stuck as the healed flesh adhered to the foreign object, and she grunted as she yanked them out.

The last piece of metal proved to be the most difficult, as Camilla predicted. The part curved, hooking deep within his flesh. Molly used her tweezers, and her hands shook as she struggled to pull it out. She gripped it as tight as she could and wrenched it out with some force. The wound started bleeding again, but the blood flow soon slowed. She dressed the wounds, taping gauze to his chest. A well-chiseled chest at that.

She inspected her handiwork while the man still slept. His brow relaxed, as if he was just taking a simple nap, and she hadn't just performed surgery on the floor. She didn't want him to stay on the kitchen floor, but she wondered how she would carry him. There was no real danger of hurting him further. He would heal. So she returned with a large quilt and laid out next to him. With a great heave, she rolled him onto it. She grasped two corners and pulled. He was a lot heavier than she imagined. The man didn't even stir as she almost fell over, pulling him towards the living room. The couch wasn't too far, but she groaned as she tried to lift his torso onto the couch. His legs must have weighed a hundred pounds each. He yawned, and Molly fought the urge to slap him awake to help her.

She gave up and grabbed her great-grandmother's crocheted blanket and tucked it around him. She lifted his head and slipped a cushion beneath it. The floor would have to do.

She placed her palm on his forehead, finding he was still running a fever. As she laid her hand on his cheek, he smiled in his sleep. Molly found it odd. He murmured something, although she didn't catch what he said, and he nuzzled her hand like he wanted to kiss her palm. Molly snatched her hand away like someone had shocked her.

Her work wasn't done for the night. She returned to the kitchen and wiped the blood off her floor. Next, she inspected the damage. She followed the broken glass and blood to her library. He had crashed straight through her window, destroying some of the original stained glass panes. She sighed. They were inconvenient windows that let the heat out during the winter, but they were beautiful. She wanted to keep the personality of the house when she first bought it. Sure, she had renovated some parts of the home, like the kitchen and the bathrooms. She wasn't above bringing some comforts of the twenty-first century into her home. But there were parts she kept intact, like the crown molding, stained glass windows, chandeliers, and the original wooden decorative elements in the staircase.

"What a shame." Camilla's voice floated behind her, and Molly turned to see the forlorn ghost's fingers gently brushing the shard on the floor.

"I know. Some things are just not meant to last, I suppose."

"I had these specially commissioned too."

"It's okay. I'll see what I can figure out."

"It's that damn dog's fault."

Molly wasn't sure what Camilla would do to the wolf, but if she had to guess, he had a couple of scares coming his way. Most of the ghosts like to keep to themselves, but there were some, like Camilla, that Molly preferred as a friend and not an enemy.

She would have to replace the window and doubted she could ever find the same stained glass again. Her fingers grabbed the bigger pieces off her floor. Its red roses and lush aventurine green leaves were still beautiful, even broken. Maybe there was another project she could repurpose them for. She drilled a wooden board she was saving into the wall to cover the gaping hole left by the wolf.

Molly stared at the boarded window, realizing she had brought this onto herself. Hadn't she just worried an hour earlier that she dreaded the next big mess? Well, the crisis came to her door. Her crisis was a six-foot-four man and a werewolf.

She grabbed her book of shadows and sat on the couch opposite the werewolf. He snored, unfazed by the sound of a broom sweeping up glass, or the buzz of a drill. Molly found the section about werewolves, but the one page lacked detailed knowledge. Under weaknesses, she read about wolfsbane and artemisia. But it didn't speak of their ability to heal quickly. She needed to ask the girls if their books had more information.

Molly yawned and stretched out on the small couch. She put the book on the floor and observed the sleeping man. His breathing was even and slow. He smiled again in his sleep, and Molly's eyes grew heavy.

Crisis indeed.

CHAPTER THREE

"He did not look at me!"

"Yes, he did! I'm telling you, Lenore! Patrick Charles Manchester was all over you! I even heard him asking Tiffany about you."

"I knew the rose hips would work!"

"Wait, rose hips?"

Rosie and Lenore opened the front door, and Molly startled awake. She glanced at the sleeping man on her floor. Not even the chatter of two drunk college students woke him up.

"Wait, are you telling me you spiked his drink with rose hips?"

"I didn't spike his drink! I may have cast a tiny spell last night and—who the hell is that?"

"Will you two be quiet?" Molly hissed at them. She stood up from her makeshift bed, swaying a little. She couldn't remember falling asleep. Molly thought Rosie and Lenore looked like they'd been in the middle of a mosh pit instead of a frat party. Both were barefoot, and given the slush outside, it was a miracle their toes hadn't fallen off from frostbite. The girls tiptoed towards the sleeping man.

"Who is he?" whispered Lenore.

Rosie picked up the edge of the blanket, taking a quick peek. "Oh my God! He's naked! Molly, what were you doing last night?"

"Shhhh," Molly grabbed them both by the arms and pulled them away into the kitchen.

Lenore started giggling hysterically, falling on the floor, over the same spot the werewolf had been unconscious only hours before.

"Great, you two are drunk," said Molly. She checked outside; the world was still dark. "What time is it?" she asked them. They shrugged. Molly peered at the clock on the oven: 6:06 a.m.

"Who is he, Molly?" asked Rosie.

"Did you summon a man?" asked Lenore.

They both started laughing, their bodies doubling over.

"I didn't summon a man!"

"Why?" asked Lenore.

"Yeah, why not? It would be good for you!" said Rosie.

"What do you mean by that?" asked Molly.

"Oh, come on, Molly…"

"No, please enlighten me."

"Come on guys, don't fight. I think I'm going to be sick," Lenore held her hand over her mouth, but she only burped.

"Yeah, and Molly, if I have to explain why it would do you some good, then it's probably been years since you've gotten some." The girls both laughed, and Molly tried to stop herself from smiling at her joke. Any little encouragement from her and she would hear naked man jokes for months.

"I can't handle you guys this early in the morning without caffeine. I don't know who he is, okay? He crashed through the library window last night." Molly shuffled to her coffeemaker and counted the spoonfuls of coffee grounds as she scooped them in.

"He crashed through the window naked?" asked Rosie.

"Not exactly. He was a wolf."

"You mean a werewolf?" asked Lenore.

"Holy shit, they're real!"

"I take it there is no information on werewolves in your book, Rosie."

"No way. I translated the whole thing. I would've remembered something about werewolves."

"Lenore?" asked Molly.

"I would have to double-check. I don't remember. But I could ask my mom to go through the family book." Lenore swayed a little. "Okay, now I'm going to throw up."

"Oh, ew, if you throw up, can it not be in our bathroom?"

Molly sighed, but the scent of brewed hot coffee was doing wonders for her patience. "You two head upstairs and sleep. I'll take care of the wolf."

"Wait, but what if he's dangerous?" asked Rosie.

"Yeah, we don't know this person. What if you're mis-remembering and it really was a naked guy that crashed through your window? What if he's a pervert?" asked Lenore

The giggling started again, and Molly pressed her hands to her face in frustration. Why did she let these girls live in her house? Something about the dorms being full. At least, that's what they had told her last year.

"Rosie?" asked Lenore. "How big was it?"

Rosie held her hands about a foot apart.

"No way!"

"I'm telling you the truth! He's huge."

"You flatter me, but that seems anatomically incompatible with women, don't you think?"

They all whipped around at once. The man leaned against the doorframe, a mischievous smile on his lips. He held the blanket wrapped around his waist like a skirt, and Molly thought he held it lower than necessary. Molly noticed the girls ogling his well-defined, albeit gauze-covered, chest, following the trail of dark hair that led down his hips. His fingers pushed back his long hair away from his face, flashing a brilliant smile. He walked towards Rosie first.

"Henry Marsh." He extended his hand to hers, which stayed stuck in the air, measuring his supposed size.

"Rosie," she said, blushing.

"And you?"

"Lenore," she squeaked. Her hazel eyes bulging.

He approached Molly. His gaze fixed on hers, but she wasn't easily intimidated.

"The homeowner whose window you busted," she replied. He smiled, almost embarrassed. His eyes flashed gold. It had happened so fast, Molly thought she might have imagined it. Maybe a trick of the light. A reflection from the rising sun peeking through the window.

"That's quite a name."

"Molly Brookes."

"Molly," he repeated. His attention didn't move, and she felt like he x-rayed her.

"Anyway..." said Rosie. "We'll be heading out." She grabbed Lenore, and they stumbled away, whispering all the way upstairs.

"Ignore them. They're children." Molly returned to the coffeemaker, unsure of what to say.

"This is your house?" asked Henry, bringing Molly back to him.

"Yes."

"I'm sorry about your window."

"Well, I'm sure you had little control over that."

Henry peeled off the gauze on his chest, wincing as the tape pulled his skin and chest hair. Molly noticed he didn't have a single scar. As if nothing had happened. As if she hadn't used pliers on him only hours ago.

"Did you do this?" he asked.

"Yes, but I don't think you needed it. You healed just fine." Molly stared at his large hands as he finished pulling off the rest of the gauze. "Can I ask what happened to you last night and why you crashed through my window?"

"I was being chased by what I'm guessing was animal control. And... I smelled you."

"Excuse me?"

"I caught your scent, and I followed it."

"And what exactly do I smell like?"

"Ripe figs, gardenias on a hot humid day, and amber."

"That's... very specific."

"Yes, it was." Henry reached over to the fruit bowl on her island, grabbing an apple. He took a big bite of it, and Molly got the sense that he ate it to avoid answering whatever questions she had next. And she had many.

"You weren't scared of my wolf form?" he asked mid-chew.

"I was."

"But you didn't freak out when you saw me? Most humans would at least ask some questions if they met a werewolf?"

"I'm a witch."

"Ahh," something clicked for him. She could see it in his smile, but his toothy grin made her uneasy, remembering the fangs she saw the night before.

"Listen, I'm glad that I could help you last night. Broken window aside—"

"I can fix that for you."

"No, thank you. I got it. I've renovated most of this house on my own. I can fix a window."

"You renovated this house? This kitchen too?" He walked over, his hands running over the cabinets.

"Yes. The only thing I don't mess with is plumbing. So I don't need your help. Thank you."

"So, you're a witch."

"And you're a werewolf."

"This is more perfect than I realized," he said, throwing his head back, as if talking to someone above him.

"What's more perfect?" Molly didn't like the glint in his eye or the smirk on his lips.

"I need your help."

"I'm sorry?"

"I need your help."

"Yeah, I heard you the first time. I helped you. Last night. So you can see yourself out now."

He clicked his tongue, and Molly wanted to slap the smile off of him.

"Aren't you supposed to help me?" he asked.

"What?"

"Yeah, isn't that part of the rules?"

"What rules?"

"You know, the witch rules or the witch's law...something like that." He scratched his head, and Molly hoped he didn't have fleas.

"What law?"

"You know the one..." he walked closer to her. Molly didn't move. This was her house, her kitchen. An overgrown dog would not run her out.

"Do no harm?" she asked.

"Nah."

"The threefold law?"

"Never heard of that one."

"Keep the balance?"

He snapped his fingers. "Yes, that's the one! Witches are supposed to help keep the balance between the magical world and the human world. Right?"

"I mean, not exactly. We just can't mess with the balance of nature." A lesson Ellie had to learn the hard way after she resurrected her boyfriend.

"Well, something has altered the balance, and I need some help to set it right."

"What are you talking about?" His face was a few inches away from hers. Molly felt like she couldn't move an inch. His warm eyes kept her locked on him.

"I need help to hunt a shapeshifter."

Molly's heart skipped a beat. Henry waited for her response, the apple in his hand long forgotten.

"What does that have to do with keeping the balance?"

"This shapeshifter has killed people throughout the country over the last couple of months. A magical creature attacking mortals would cause concern, wouldn't it?"

It would be, but Molly didn't want him to know that. She wanted him gone. "I can't help you with that."

"Why not?" he asked.

"I have to go to work," she said, moving away from him.

"I mean, I wasn't talking about getting it right now."

"You don't understand; I'm busy. I run a cafe, and I have a coven I'm responsible for. The last thing I need is to be running after a shapeshifter!"

"Have you ever seen a shapeshifter?"

"No."

"It's going to become your problem soon."

"What's that supposed to mean?"

"Like it or not, the shapeshifter led me here, and if it hadn't been for animal control last night, this wouldn't be your problem. But as I'm here talking to a witch, I thought you would be up for a challenge."

"You're talking to the wrong witch. I can't help you, but if there's somewhere I could drop you off, you let me know."

Henry opened his mouth to protest, but Molly stormed out of the kitchen, grabbing her coat and keys. She was still wearing yesterday's outfit, but she kept an extra pair of clothes at the cafe in case of accidents. She didn't want to argue, or explain, or apologize to the stranger in her home. Forced to justify her decision to a man who busted her window. All she craved was to put as much space between her and Henry. Between her and the next crisis, she wanted nothing to do with.

CHAPTER FOUR

Henry had one purpose. The pack. Protect the pack, do everything for the pack. The pack was his family, his friends, and his world.

Henry had first shifted when he was thirteen. A sprig of a young boy shot up three feet overnight. His muscles became well defined, he grew hairier, and an urge under his skin made it hard to control his ability to shift under a full moon.

An unfamiliar sensation accompanied his newfound power. Something no one had told him about. He felt a creature living inside of him. His wolf. It paced inside his chest. A constant companion reminding him of the creature he was always destined to be.

None of this was a shock to him. His older brother and his grandfather were wolves. The gene had missed his father and a few of his uncles; it was strange that way. But Henry had hoped that it would skip him. He wished to be normal, like his father, playing pool on a full moon at the bar, boring and human. Instead of running through the woods half naked, hoping he wouldn't have to replace another pair of jeans.

Yet one night his older brother Malcolm shifted for the first time in their childhood bedroom. He stared in shock as his brother screamed in pain. His body grew to twice its size. Malcolm's canines pierced through his gums, and he opened his mouth in a pained howl. Henry remembered his mother and father bursting into the room to find a fourteen-year-old Malcolm sitting on his bed like a puppy.

Even though his brother flourished with his newfound power, Henry hoped it wouldn't happen to him. But the gene that skipped his father took hold in his children's genetics. He had no choice. For twenty-two years of full moons, Henry found his limbs expanding, his fur growing into a warm blanket across his flesh, and claws sprouting from his feet and hands. He grew to not hate it. It was the most he could do.

Was being a wolf ideal? No, not in this world where they prosecuted witches. But the same fate hadn't befallen the wolves yet. Werewolves were still fairy tales. The kind whispered around campfires. Wolves and dogs for unsuspecting humans. They were safe.

The night before was different. As Henry picked up the shapeshifter's scent in the wind, he ran through the forest hell-bent on getting his revenge. In his wolf form, he was unstoppable. He would do it. He would reach the creature he'd been chasing for three months. The creature that he'd chase through most of the United States. The creature that killed Malcolm.

He had been so close. His teeth were near the beast's feet. It had taken its preferred shape. A large mountain lion, with paws the size of dinner plates and teeth so long they peeked from its jaw. Henry had seen it take different forms: lions, bears, even wolves. But it didn't smell like an animal. It smelled putrid. Its stench was as strong as it had been on Malcolm's half-eaten body.

But then the first shot rang through the still forest. A sharp, hot pain spread through his torso. Henry fell back an inch, but it was all that the shapeshifter needed to run ahead. He had lost it again.

He didn't stew in the disappointment for long as more shots burst the night's silence. The pain intensified, along with the searing scent of scorched fur. He slowed as each breath burned his lungs. One bullet wasn't enough to slow down a werewolf. He wasn't sure how many times they had shot him.

The footsteps grew louder, accompanied by frantic voices, and Henry panicked. He couldn't stay a wolf for long. Even as he hobbled through the forest, the wolf inside him pulled back into the unconscious space in his soul.

He needed shelter and quick. He started running again, knowing the more energy he used, the faster his wolf would slip away. But better to be caught as a human than a wolf. Werewolves would be worse off than the witches if he exposed them.

He ran; little else crossed his mind but safety. He took a deep breath, and then he smelled it. A scent so intoxicating, he nearly stopped in his tracks. A fresh floral scent with warmth running through it. He raced towards it.

Henry didn't understand at the time why. He wasn't even sure that anything good would've come from the scent. But he ran anyway. Fleeing from the forest and into a sleepy neighborhood. He passed a house with raucous noise and through a person's garden. He might have heard screaming, but Henry wasn't sure if he had imagined it.

A home painted the dark blue of early summer nights drew him forward. The scent was stronger the closer he got. He didn't think of knocking, or about how loud the sirens were in his ear, or how far he'd left behind animal control; he only ran.

The windowpane exploded around his shoulders as he crashed through the glass. By then, the pain was unbearable. He saw spots, but he walked towards the fragrance anyway, unaware of its source.

Henry used to have one purpose. The pack. So when a shapeshifter killed Malcolm, he didn't care what happened to him. He survived on three hours of sleep a night. He didn't remember the last time he had eaten a full meal. His mission and his reason for living since Malcolm's death was nothing more than retribution.

Now Henry had a new purpose. One he hadn't expected to have.

Molly.

He had heard the stories from his grandfather growing up. He told him the day would come when he'd meet someone. It could happen anywhere, with anyone. But his wolf would recognize them. His wolf would pick. He would meet the love of his life. No matter how devoted he was to another. This person would be his new reason for living. His everything.

Henry didn't accept it at first. Yet, he had watched as two of his pack mates found their wives. At a grocery store, at school. One day, they were waking up hungover in their bachelor pads, and the next they bought flowers and fell at the feet of their lover.

Henry rubbed his face hard, unsure what to think. Molly's scent lingered in the kitchen, toying with his senses and tempting him to follow her.

He didn't need this now. After months of chasing the creature through half the country, he couldn't just stop.

His mate was beautiful. Henry thanked his wolf. She had pretty, tight, curly hair that bounced around her lovely face as she moved. She had the most exquisite dark skin that Henry wanted to kiss. An innocent round face with high cheekbones, and wide giant eyes that pierced him. A gaze both steady and alluring.

Henry didn't know what to do after she left. He stood frozen in her kitchen, touching the dried orange slices she hung on the window. His mate. He found her. It couldn't have come at a worse time. Molly presented a complication and a blessing. She was a witch. He hadn't expected that. But then again, he wasn't expecting anything at all. Not after years of barely dating and loneliness.

He tried to focus, but his mind wouldn't be still. Even with Molly gone from the house, he felt pulled. His body urged him to find her. Keep her near his side. And yet, the voice he had followed for months. A voice filled with grief dragged him from her, compelling him to continue his hunt.

There were a few things he had to take care of first. He needed clothes and to get back to his car parked on the outskirts of town. The creature might have already left, but Henry wanted to call the pack and let them in on what had happened. He would figure out what to do about Molly later.

"Oh shit, you're still here." He turned and saw Lenore standing in her pajamas in the kitchen doorway. She had heavy bags under her hazel eyes. With every step, her loose bun of brown hair flopped around.

"Molly left for work."

"It's not like her to leave a stranger in her house." Lenore went to the cabinet by the sink and grabbed a glass, filling it with water. "Do you know any hangover cures, by the way? I'm about to have the worst hangover of my life."

Henry smiled. "Are you a witch too?"

"Oh, you know about that too, huh?"

"It's been an interesting conversation with your roommate."

"I bet. We're all witches. There's seven of us and two very attached annoying human boyfriends. But don't worry about them. They're cool with the whole witch thing. I shouldn't be telling you any of this."

"Why?" he asked.

"You're a stranger."

"But you guys know my biggest secret?"

"I guess that's true. Still, Molly probably wouldn't want me to tell you anything about us."

"Molly's secretive?"

"Molly protects us."

His mate was their leader. She had that quality about her. With that withering stare, he was sure, could make the most obstinate witch fall in line. He knew it well. Malcolm had the same look.

"A couple of slices of toast and you'll be good as new," said Henry, walking away from Lenore.

"Wait, what?"

"You said you wanted a hangover cure."

He walked to the library and inspected the boarded-up window. He needed to get a few things in order before he fixed his mistake. Molly wouldn't be easily pleased. He understood that now. He couldn't come out with the truth. She wouldn't take it well. He had to establish her trust first, and he would start with the window. A voice broke through his plans. Stubborn and angry. What he had to do was find the creature, not waste time fixing a window. Henry ignored it.

He walked back into the kitchen as Lenore put two slices of bread in a toaster.

"Do you have any clothes I can borrow?"

Lenore looked him up and down. "I'm not sure if what I have will fit you, but I'll give it to you anyway." She headed upstairs and came back with a pair of gray sweats and a t-shirt. Henry put the pants on and decided not to put on the shirt. The person the pants belonged to had been much smaller, but they would do.

He thanked Lenore and headed out. The icy February wind stung his lungs as he breathed in. His body didn't even have a scratch, but he had no clue what it had looked like last night. His healing would have taken care of every wound, but he still thought it sweet of her to dress them.

Henry ran barefoot through the snow, finding the cold comforting after the burning he'd experienced the night before. The wet snow was but a small bother to his hot skin. He worried more about stepping on a hidden nail.

Henry found his truck parked where he left it, outside of a supermarket. He dressed quickly and grabbed his cellphone under the seat. He dialed Mark and wasn't surprised when he picked up on the first ring.

"Henry! Where have you been? I've been calling all night!"

"I'm fine, Mark."

He saw Mark in his mind. Pushing his dark blonde hair from his face in his anxiousness, probably just getting home after a night out.

"Did you catch it?"

"No. I was close last night. But the thing got away."

"Where are you?"

"Close to home, actually. About an hour away."

"It's back then? To finish what it started?" Henry heard Mark's voice shift an octave lower, his wolf slipping through.

"I think it might. Listen, this thing has been playing with me."

"How so?"

"Think about it, Mark. It made me chase it through the country for the past three months, only for it to end up back here? What does it want?"

"To destroy the pack."

"If that's what it wanted, why would it have left in the first place?"

"I'm not sure, Henry. You're assuming this thing is capable of intelligent thought. It's controlled by its instincts to kill."

"Something just doesn't feel right about this, Mark."

"Are you coming back?"

"No." He debated how much to tell him about Molly. He didn't think Mark would have a negative opinion. It was just that Henry had no clue how he felt about it. He decided not to say anything just yet. "Listen, if I go home, I might lead it back to the pack. I don't want to put the young ones at risk." His pack mates, Brandon and Freddy, had families. He hated the idea of leaving their wives and kids vulnerable if something were to happen to them.

"So, what should we do?" asked Mark.

"I don't know," said Henry.

Malcolm had always been their leader. The alpha. Born into the role. A quality that no one questioned or fought against. Since his death, the pack was like a shell of its former self.

Meandering and weak without Malcolm's steadying presence. Nobody seemed eager to fill the position.

"I think you and Chris should come over. I don't think the shifter has left. I still picked up some of its scent."

"Wouldn't that leave Freddy and Brandon vulnerable?"

"Shit. I didn't think about that."

"Look, I'll come and I'll ask Chris. But he might not be up for it. He'll have his own plans."

Henry felt himself tensing, frustrated with the lack of coordination from the pack. They would all go their separate ways. He knew it. Without a leader who could organize them all, they were defenseless.

"See if you can convince him. If there had been more of us with me last night, we could have killed the bastard."

"Okay. Henry, take care."

Henry hung up the phone, stretching in his seat. His body felt agile and strong even after the previous night. Molly's face popped into his head. Her full bow lips and those eyes. He would tell Mark and Chris about her when they came. Well, he would at least tell Mark. There was no guarantee Chris would show up. He didn't want to keep her a secret. She would be left vulnerable if he did that, and he needed them to know he wanted to keep her safe.

His pants tightened uncomfortably. He looked down, seeing the imprint of his cock on his pants. Just the mere thought of her elicited such a reaction. He wanted to laugh. So, this was what his pack mates spoke about when they talked of mating for life.

He needed supplies if he was going to fix her window. Against the vengeance that had flowed in his veins for months, Henry drove to the nearest hardware store.

CHAPTER FIVE

Molly drove home in the dark after a hard day, made harder by her thoughts of the werewolf she had left behind in her house. She tried not to think about his problem. A problem he placed on her lap to resolve. She hated him for it. As if she didn't already do enough for the coven and for their boyfriends! Now she had to deal with a shapeshifter.

Absolutely not.

She pulled into her driveway and groaned at what she saw. Henry, clothed and working on her window. Hadn't she told him she would fix it? She stepped out of her car, and he turned and waved her over, a giant smile pasted on his face. He wore a simple black t-shirt and jeans, not looking at all bothered by the cold.

"Hello there!" his voice boomed throughout the neighborhood. Was the guy not capable of whispering? "I fixed the window!"

"I can see that," hissed Molly, getting closer to stop him from shouting her business to all the neighbors.

"I'm just going to finish out here and then I'll be down to dinner."

"Dinner?"

"Yeah, Lenore invited me." He raised an eyebrow, a smirk on his lips.

"Lenore?"

"Is that a problem?"

"No. Not at all. Excuse me." She left him and rushed in through the front door. She found Lenore and Rosie cooking. Dirty pots filled the sink, while Lenore nursed something in the oven, poking it with a fork. Rosie chopped lettuce, almost chopping off her fingers in the process. They were too busy to notice Molly seething at them.

"And here I thought you two would be too hungover to move today. What are you doing inviting Henry over for dinner?"

"We found some of your hangover potion in the fridge. Also, he fixed the window," said Lenore.

"He broke the window!"

"But then he fixed it. It's a nice thing to do, Molly," said Rosie.

"Wow, what is that smell? It smells delicious," said Henry, walking into the kitchen.

"Moussaka! I wanted to try out a new recipe," said Lenore, pulling out a dish from the oven.

Molly sidestepped towards the girls and away from him. He walked over to the sink to wash his hands, but his eyes stayed on

Molly as he did so. She shivered, busying herself with grabbing plates.

Henry offered to transfer the dish to the table, handling it as though it wasn't scorching hot. They settled around the table. Lenore and Rosie chatted away with Henry. But Molly didn't speak. She hardly ate either. He sat across from her, and she focused on not stretching out her legs too much, lest the guy think she was playing footsie. She found every little thing that Rosie and Lenore asked irritating. But Henry didn't seem annoyed at all, answering each question they threw at him.

"So, do you only shift during the full moons?" asked Rosie.

"We can shift whenever we want, but it's harder to control on full moons. When we're younger, we have no choice but to shift, but after a few years, it gets a little easier to control during full moons. But it's damn uncomfortable."

"Is it?"

"Imagine something like an itch, only it's internal and you feel you might explode."

"That sounds terrible."

"It is, but some months you can't help it. Werewolves have been on high alert since the mortals found out about witches. We can't always run wild like we used to."

"Were you bitten by a werewolf?" asked Lenore.

"Lenore," warned Molly.

Henry laughed it off. "No, I wasn't bitten. It's genetic."

"Submissive or dominant?" asked Lenore, with a smirk on her face. Molly kicked her under the table.

"Ow!" she yelped.

"Dominant. I like to be in charge."

"She meant *recessive* and dominant. Like the genes," said Molly through gritted teeth. She caught Henry staring at her.

"Recessive. There is no guarantee that our children will be wolves."

Our children?

Rosie cleared her throat, and a small giggle escaped from Lenore.

"My brother and I got the gene, but my sister didn't. My father isn't a wolf, but my grandfather was. Nobody understands why it skips generations. It's not like we're running to geneticists to get tested."

"Can women be wolves?" asked Lenore.

"I've met one."

"Is she part of your pack?" asked Rosie.

"No, she belongs to another."

"Are there a lot of werewolves in America?" asked Lenore.

"There are more in Canada, but there are a few packs here as well."

"So, how does it work?" asked Rosie.

"How does what work?"

"Shifting. What does it feel like?"

Henry rubbed his chin, reflecting. "Think of it like contracting and expanding. When I shift, everything expands. My bones, my muscles, my body, my nails and teeth."

"Is that all that expands?" joked Lenore. She had moved far enough away to stop Molly from kicking her, but Henry laughed, his hands gripping his stomach to steady himself. Lenore and Rosie joined in the laughter, but Molly failed to find it amusing.

"Oh, that's a good one. I'll have to tell Mark that one." He wiped a few tears from his eyes.

"Mark?" said Rosie, perking up. "Are there more of you?"

"There are six... I mean, five of us in total in my pack."

"All single?" asked Lenore.

"No two are very much married. But Mark and Chris are single." Rosie and Lenore looked at each other with a mischievous glint in their eyes. Henry noticed it too, because he laughed again.

"So, out of the five of you, do you guys have like an alpha or something?" asked Rosie.

The smile evaporated from Henry's face. He cleared his throat and smiled, but it didn't reach his eyes. Molly got the sense that he was trying to shield something painful. Wanting to stay the fun-loving guy he'd been only moments before. But it faded faster than he wanted it to.

"My brother was the alpha. He was killed."

"I'm sorry," said Rosie. Thankfully, she wouldn't quip about this. "I shouldn't have pried."

"It's okay."

"So your pack doesn't have an alpha?" asked Lenore.

"Not since he passed."

"Are you guys going to choose a new one? Is it a democratic process?" asked Lenore.

"Not exactly. My brother had a natural gift. He was just born a leader, I suppose. Now we're waiting to see who can step up to the plate."

They ate in silence after that, with a few questions sprinkled in every few minutes. Molly stole a look or two when she could. His hands eclipsed the silverware. They looked like children's toys in his fingers. She couldn't help but imagine what her hands would look like in his. He had his brown hair tied behind his head, and she could better see his features in the dining room light. His stubble-lined jaw had a hint of gray in it. He had a prominent nose; it looked elegant on him. Awake, he appeared much more tense and worried. Despite playing along with Rosie and Lenore's jokes, a sense of sadness remained. Molly saw it in the creased muscles in his forehead and his tight smile.

She glanced down at her food as he peered up. Her staring was a little too obvious. She excused herself and took her plate into the kitchen. Heavy footsteps approached, but she didn't turn around, running the plate in the sink.

"I'll be back tomorrow to finish the window. The sealant needs time to dry. Also, I was wondering if you could tell me the name of the paint you used for the library."

Molly turned around to face him, noticing his eyes flashing gold again. So, she hadn't imagined it after all. He was standing closer than she expected, and he towered over her.

"Thank you for fixing the window, but I got it from here."

"What?" he asked.

"I can paint a wall, you know."

"Why won't you let me fix it?"

"You fixed it."

"Yes, but why do you fight me on it?" He walked even closer, and Molly backed away, her tailbone hitting the sink.

"I'm not fighting you."

"Did I not crash through your window last night?"

"Yes, but—"

"So I'm going to fix this. Is this about the shifter?"

"What?"

"It's just since I've mentioned it, you've been cold towards me. Well... colder." His hands drifted too close to her face before he lowered them again. For a moment, it looked like he wanted to touch her, but she pushed the thought away.

"This has nothing to do with the shapeshifter," she said.

"Look, you don't have to help me with that. But let me at least finish fixing what I broke."

Molly didn't answer. She didn't know when he had gotten even closer, but his warm, spicy smell engulfed her. A strange, heady mix of wood and cloves.

"What's a shapeshifter?" Lenore stood in the kitchen, plate in hand.

Whatever magic transfixed Molly to Henry broke.

CHAPTER SIX

"It's nothing," said Henry.

"Lenore, don't worry about it," said Molly, stepping a few paces away from him. He hated that and wanted to pull her closer to him.

"Why?" asked Lenore.

"No, she's right. I shouldn't have assumed when I met you—"

"No, it's not that," interrupted Molly. "We've had a few incidents over the past couple of months that almost led to our exposure."

"No, I completely understand," Henry apologized. Of course, how stupid could he have been? He had placed a burden on her that wasn't hers to carry. He watched her as she argued with Lenore. His need to protect her grew with each passing second. This was it. He couldn't believe it.

His mate.

Since she came back home, he noticed how attuned his wolf was to her. He held onto every word from her mouth, even though she spoke so little during dinner. Her perfume engulfed his senses. Although she wore a sweet coconut, it only enhanced the natural magnolia of her skin. A strange urge took over almost all his senses. He wanted to kiss her. Well, do much more than a kiss, but he couldn't give in to the sensation while the others were in the room. And not while Molly still looked at him with suspicion.

"But wait," said Lenore as Rosie walked into the kitchen. "What happened? Why are you chasing after a shapeshifter?"

"A shapeshifter? What's that?" asked Rosie.

"Is it like a werewolf?" asked Lenore.

They outnumbered Molly, and Henry wanted to save her from them. "Not exactly. Shifters can take the shape of any animal."

"Are they people then?" asked Lenore.

"Yes," said Molly.

"You're familiar with them?" asked Henry, surprised.

"No, but I've read about them."

"They're humans that can turn into animals? That's pretty cool," said Rosie.

"So, why are you chasing a shapeshifter?" asked Lenore again.

"It killed my brother." A silence settled in the kitchen, and Henry heard only Molly's heartbeat in his ear. A steady drum for his own erratic heart to follow. "Three months ago, a shapeshifter came to my town. It killed several mortals, and then my brother."

Mentioning Malcolm brought everything back. He thought of his laughter, which used to fill their home growing up. The way he taught him how to fight and how to ask out girls. He remembered those first few shifts when his lanky body changed with the moon. Henry hadn't been afraid, because his older brother acted as a guide. Malcolm would tell him what was normal, and what wasn't. He trusted his leadership, as did the pack. Now they were scattered, as if he was the only glue that held them together.

He remembered finding Malcolm in the forest. Searching for him after he didn't come home. Henry picked up his scent along the way and followed it. Unaware that he would find his smart, funny, and loving brother dead. An open wound festered in his soul, and mentioning it to the girls reminded him of how much it still hurt. Nobody deserved a death like that. Nobody deserved to be made a meal of.

He noticed Molly staring at him. He wanted to reach for her, to keep her close to him. Fear and anger coursed through his veins as he remembered discovering only a head and half a torso in the woods. He wanted to tell Molly everything, of each painful lungful of air he breathed since finding his brother. But he had no right. He shouldn't have presumed her help, but he wished for it. He felt so lost.

Henry wanted Molly to say something. She looked sad, but he couldn't read more in her expression. Was she changing her mind? He didn't know, but he understood that one day he would know every thought that passed through that beautiful head. He wasn't sure how the magic worked. The connection came with gifts. He'd heard Brandon and Freddy talking about it once in hushed tones. They wouldn't let him in on the secret, only telling him he would understand only when his wolf chose. Some of those gifts would only come after Molly claimed him, but there was no saying how long that would take.

"Is the shifter here? Now?" asked Rosie.

"I believe so. I have been chasing it all across the country. We live not very far from here. It's returned to the area. I think there's something wrong with it."

"What do you mean?"

"It smells strange. Rotting almost. Its scent is strong, which is why I've been able to follow it for so long, but it doesn't smell like a normal shifter. That, and the victims I keep finding, are half eaten."

"Are shifters cannibals?" asked Rosie.

"I mean, are you still a cannibal if you eat people as an animal?" asked Lenore.

"I have no clue, but we might not be dealing with a regular shapeshifter," said Henry.

"What animals has it looked like?"

"Its favorite is a mountain lion. Although I've seen a wolf, bear, and falcon. Luckily, it can't hold on to its bird form for long, so it sticks to land animals, or else I would have already lost it."

"So, it's come back for a reason?" asked Lenore.

"I'm not sure. But I won't stop until it's destroyed."

"And you need help to kill it?" asked Rosie.

"No, I can kill it. But I'm having trouble keeping it in one location long enough for me to destroy it. I almost had it last night, but animal control is trigger-happy here."

"That's our fault," said Lenore. "One of our coven members brought her boyfriend back from the dead. He changed into this weird bird creature. Anyway, he killed a bunch of people, and they thought an animal attacked them. They don't know that the original creature they're looking for is already dead."

"It's probably not safe for your kind to shift while you're here," said Molly. Henry noticed it was the first time she had spoken since mentioning his brother. Was she worried about his safety?

"It's not safe for anybody here as long as the shapeshifter is in town."

"How do you know it's still here? It might have moved on?"

"I was afraid of that, but I ran into its stench this morning. I'm not sure how long it'll stay, but I called the pack to join me."

"And how many is that exactly?" asked Lenore with a hopeful and playful smile.

Henry laughed, thankful for her easing some of the tension out of the conversation. "Two. I asked the ones without families to come."

"Can you two finish cleaning up the dining room?" asked Molly, annoyed. The girls left, chattering and giggling among themselves.

Henry liked them and felt comfortable around them already. He hoped he would get the same reaction from the rest of the coven. From what Lenore had told him earlier, there were four more members he had yet to meet.

He wondered how Mark and Chris were going to react to them. Chris was always so serious; he would probably approach them with wariness. But Henry wasn't too sure about Mark. He was more easygoing than Chris, but he'd been much more reserved since Malcolm's death. With any luck, their wolves would choose them, so he wouldn't be alone on this journey.

He turned and saw Molly regarding him. God, he wished he could read her. He often got the sense from Brandon and his wife Whitney that they communicated without speaking. Their shared glances said more than words ever could. But maybe that wasn't a wolf gift, but a consequence of spending so much time with someone. He wanted to have that with Molly.

She turned around and placed the dishes in the dishwasher. "The paint color is called Azure Wave."

Chapter Seven

M olly stretched in bed, her limbs heavy with an uneasy sleep. She heard a skirt sweeping along her hallway. Followed by the tiny feet pitter-pattering against her hardwood floors. Somewhere in the house, Lenore sang off-key.

Her home. Molly had worked hard to build it. To create the secure space her twenty-year-old self would have wanted, she succeeded. With every new layer of paint and wallpaper, she created her perfect home. Even if she had to deal with a handful of ghosts and chaotic roommates.

Molly reached for her phone and decided it was early enough to get out of bed. She stretched, needing to hurry if she was going to buy breakfast in time from her grandmother's favorite spot.

Grandma Joni lived in an old folks' community about twenty minutes away. Molly didn't choose to have her grandmother live far away, but at ninety-one years old, she required more care than Molly could provide alone. It didn't seem to matter much to Grandma Joni, but it mattered to Molly. She wanted to care for her in her own home, and keep her near as she had kept

Molly close growing up, but her grandmother's health wouldn't allow it.

Molly rushed out of the house and was lucky the restaurant was still serving breakfast when she arrived. She picked up her grandmother's favorites. Coffee with more cream than sugar, scrambled eggs, and a croissant. She hurried as she drove down the long stretch of highway to reach her grandmother.

Molly counted herself lucky in a lot of respects. She grew up surrounded by love. She had a family that cared for her when times were good and bad. Although sometimes try as hard as she might, she could only focus on the difficult moments. Her mother died when she was eleven. Her father passed away at seventeen. But no matter how heavy those deaths had been, she had Grandma Joni. She wasn't alone in the world.

Molly knocked on her grandmother's apartment. The door opened immediately, as if she stood on the other side waiting for her. She shuffled in, carrying the bags full of food. Her grandmother's room was spacious. A large bed in the corner had a crocheted blanket on top. A wardrobe and a chest of drawers were on the opposite wall. Her grandmother had pictures everywhere, hanging around the room, and on every available table and surface. The familiar faces of Molly's parents stared back, frozen in time on their wedding day. Molly kissed her fingertips and placed them lightly on the frame. There were other unfamiliar people among the photos, and Molly only recognized them from stories. Grandma Joni had known them all, and she spent entire afternoons telling Molly who they were, when they met, and what they had meant to her.

Molly settled into the small dining room area of her home. "Don't tell the nurses," she said, reaching into the bag, "but I brought you two croissants."

Grandma Joni laughed, her eyes disappearing into her lovely, wrinkled face. "You always know what I need." Her hand reached up, and she pulled Molly down to kiss her cheek.

They chatted while they ate. Grandma Joni caught Molly up on the gossip of the community. Whose kids hadn't visited, who was kissing whom, the sex talk they had to have because of the gonorrhea outbreak among some of the old folks.

"Granny, you're kidding!" Molly laughed, almost choking on the coffee.

"They talked to us as if we were children. Can you imagine talking about condoms with us?"

"Were condoms invented back in your time, Granny?"

"Oh, hush!" Grandma Joni slapped Molly's leg.

"But how was there an outbreak?" asked Molly, wiping tears from laughing.

"Listen, when you get to be my age, and your husband is long gone. You don't get picky."

"Ugh, Granny!"

"Women live longer than men. You'll see."

"So, how many men are in the community?"

"Four."

"They get around then."

"And they spread it. Let me tell you—"

"Oh Goddess Granny, please don't!" Molly covered her ears, to which her grandmother laughed.

"Fine, I won't scare you about your future. Tell me about you. What's new, baby?"

Molly hesitated, hoping she wouldn't notice. "Well, work has been going well. People need coffee, so it never ends there."

"What about the coven? All good there?"

"Yes, things have settled since everything with Violet and Ellie. Nothing new."

Granny squinted her eyes. "But something's happened?"

"What? No."

"You can't lie to me. I took care of you since you were a baby."

"I know that—"

"So, you might as well tell me. Or I'll just have to ask your parents."

"Please don't disturb them. They deserve peace in their afterlife. The last thing I need is them checking up on me and popping up in my house somewhere."

"They wouldn't spy on you."

"They would if you told them to."

"Then tell me."

Molly sighed, knowing that resisting was futile. "What do you know about werewolves?"

Her grandmother's face lit up, and she whistled. "They're handsome."

"Granny, be serious."

"Has a wolf come into your life?"

"Crashed into it more like. But I was looking in the book to see if there was anything on wolves, but there wasn't much there. Did you ever meet one?"

"I didn't, but my mama did."

"Great-grandma Penelope?"

"Yes." Grandma Joni looked wistful.

"Did Granny Penelope write the pages on the wolf?"

"I would need to check the handwriting, but it was her favorite story to tell me when I was a child. I didn't like it so much."

"How come?"

"Well, it was a scary story. And it was real. It made me sad to think of my mama there in the past, all scared."

"Will you tell me?"

Grandma Joni caressed Molly's cheek. Her touch was soft and nurturing, putting Molly at ease. "She was a young girl, you see. Back in 1920, or perhaps it was 1930."

"Granny, you were born in 1933," reminded Molly.

"Oh, the years are blending together now." Grandma Joni patted her head. "The date is not important, but she must have been nineteen or twenty when this happened. My grandmother, your great-great-grandmother, wanted her daughter married to a respectable family. My mother wasn't so sold on the idea. But they introduced her to Benjamin Larsen."

"That's not the name of your father," said Molly.

"No, it is not. And for good reason. He was a charmer. A phony. He could fool everyone around him, making them think he was an upstart man. But it was far from the truth. That man had secrets her parents had no clue about.

"My mother had gone to meet up with a friend, and he was there along with some other men. My mother told me she wasn't sure why, but her palms itched real bad. But this was her future husband. There was no reason to feel like her bones wanted to burst from her skin and run. So she stayed.

"The night grew long. Her friend said goodbye. The others left too, and she found herself alone with him, unchaperoned. Again, she had no cause to fear him. They would be married within the fortnight, but her chest tightened. He talked and talked. Told her about the house he bought for them. The children they would fill their home with. It all sounded nice, but her intuition would not let her rest.

"She needed to run. Make an excuse and get out of there. Before she realized it, he had led her somewhere she didn't recognize. Some strange cliff side, talking about the view and how beautiful it looked, but nowhere near as beautiful as her." Grandma Joni rolled her eyes. His charm would never have fooled her.

"My mother came up with an excuse, but he insisted, pulling her closer and closer to the cliff side. And then he twisted her around by her shoulders until she was dangling over the cliff's edge."

Molly gasped. "What? Why?"

"He had found out that she was a witch."

"How?"

"He learned from a friend that they had seen her performing a spell."

"Was she really?"

"I don't know. Perhaps he got lucky, or she was caught. Either way, it didn't matter. He thought she had cast a love spell on him and his family. And he wouldn't let her have him.

"But before he dropped her, a growl came from the shadows. Benjamin looked back, and it gave my mother enough time to grab hold of the cliff side and struggle away from his grasp. He nearly fell over, but he stood up straight and turned back to the growling.

"Mama held on as tight as she could. But as she tried to pull herself up, Benjamin noticed and stepped hard on her fingers. She cried out, and it was in that moment that a wolf burst through the forest.

"She couldn't see him well, but Benjamin sure did. He had nowhere to run, and the wolf ran and bounced on his chest, sending him plummeting to his death."

Molly let out a breath, realizing that her hands were clenched. "And Penelope?"

"She held on, but her strength was failing her. She would fall along with Benjamin. But then two hands grabbed her wrists, and a man pulled her up."

"Was he naked?"

"Completely. And my mother looked for the wolf, of course, but didn't find it. The man led her to the road without saying a word to her. Finally, he turned and ran back into the forest. She was sure that he and the wolf were the same."

"You've never told me that story before," said Molly after a moment.

"Funny what you can remember if you just ask." Grandma Joni grabbed Molly's hand, smiling.

"Mama thought of the story as an adventure, but it upsets me to learn she suffered."

"Did she ever tell you whether she saw him again?"

"She never did. That was the last and only wolf she ever met."

"How did she get the information in the book, then?"

"I'm not sure. But she may have gotten it from other witches. Werewolves are secretive, but I don't blame them. You see what they do to us? I can only imagine what the mortals would do if they found out."

"Do you have any pictures of her? When she was younger?"

"Not when she was a girl, but I have some. Hold on." Her grandmother got up from her chair and walked towards the wardrobe in the back of the room. She returned, holding a photo album to her chest. She placed it on Molly's lap and flipped to the page she wanted, knowing where every picture was. She stopped at her wedding photo, and Molly stared at her grandmother's face. She looked prim and glowing. Her features were so like Molly's own. Grandma Joni's fingers brushed over the photograph, and she pointed to an older woman next to her.

"Is that her?" asked Molly.

"Yes, on my wedding day. Wearing her best hat." She looked somber in the way people were in photographs back then. "See this necklace here?" Grandma Joni pointed to a teardrop pearl necklace that glowed around her mother's neck. "I'm saving that for your wedding day."

Molly just sighed. "Well, you might have to wait a little longer, Granny."

"How much longer? I'm close to death already!"

"Oh please, I know that's not true."

"You're lucky I have good genes."

"Very lucky Granny," Molly leaned in and kissed her on the cheek.

The rest of the afternoon passed in conversation, and when Molly drove home in the evening, she couldn't stop thinking of the story. She understood why Grandma Joni hadn't enjoyed listening to it as a child, because Molly had become anxious as she retold it. Her hands grew clammy, as if she didn't know the ending. Her great-grandmother had to survive because Grandma Joni was here. Molly was here. Her line didn't end with her. Molly carried back a small photo of Granny Penelope in her pocket. Something for her ancestor altar, even if she hadn't met her while she was alive. Molly existed because she had lived.

She thought of the wolf in the story. Had he any clue that his actions would lead to Molly? Generations later, the family of the woman he saved still remembered him.

Molly couldn't wait for a savior like that to come into her life. It would be nice. Someone to take care of everything. She had had it before, as a child and adolescent. But the thing about parents and grandparents was they grew older, and she had no choice but to outlive them all. She had the coven outside of Grandma Joni, but she didn't have family like she used to. Slowly, like wilting flowers in late summer, they slipped from her life. Sometimes suddenly, like her parents. Other times, even if she knew it was coming, it didn't hurt any less. Each time someone passed, she felt more alone.

She tried not to dwell on it, remembering Grandma Joni was alive and she would spend more time with her. Molly felt proud of her home, her community, and that she supported herself and her grandmother. She was okay. It had taken a lot of work, and sure, she had made mistakes along the way, but it was her life. She did it alone, and she wouldn't be ashamed of that.

She pulled into her driveway and found Henry there again. He turned as she drove up, as if expecting her. She got out of the car and approached him. Her skin itched, wishing he would look away from her. But those deep brown eyes wouldn't even move an inch away.

"How's the window?" asked Molly. It looked good as new, well, except for the plain glass.

"Almost done. I also painted the room, so don't lean on the wall. But all the finishing touches are done." Henry wore his hair down. The waves brushed his shoulders as he pushed it back. It looked soft to Molly.

"You're great at that."

"Thanks. My dad used to renovate houses, so I know a thing or two."

"What do you do now?"

"I'm a data analyst."

"A data analyst?"

"You sound surprised?"

"I guess I just didn't expect that."

"I'm too ruggedly handsome for that?"

Molly rolled her eyes. "Sure, that's it."

"You seem to be in a better mood today."

"Do I?"

"Yeah... happier."

"I had a good day," said Molly.

His eyes flashed gold again, startling her. She stepped back, her foot slipping on the plastic tarp on the dried grass. Before Molly could gasp, Henry reached out, grabbing her by the waist and pulling her tightly against him. Molly's fingers curled around his biceps, her nails digging in a little. His grip on her was strong, and she met his eyes. Maybe she had been imagining the gold. They were brown now.

He kept his eyes fixed on hers, almost rooting her to him. There was something so comforting about his arms. Strong and warm, and yet the grasp on her waist wasn't uncomfortably tight.

Molly snapped herself out of it. Henry sensed the change and loosened his grip on her. Molly thought he did so hesitantly, as if he wanted to hold her longer.

"Thanks," said Molly, stepping away from him.

"Yeah, so..." Henry looked flustered. He brushed back the hair from his face. "I'm done with your window."

"Are you leaving?"

"The pack will be here tonight, and we'll stay in town until we kill the shapeshifter. I won't leave this place until it's safe for you."

"Thank you." She was stuck with him for a little while longer, and it made her nervous.

Henry started gathering his things while Molly inspected the window. She wouldn't want to admit it to him, but he had done a great job. Her grandmother's story replayed in her head. Maybe it was part of the werewolf gene that made them so helpful. It gave her an idea, but she wasn't sure if he would like it.

"Henry?" she asked.

"Yes." He turned so fast she thought it would give him whiplash.

"Do you know anything about plumbing?"

"Uh, I know a little. Why?"

"There are some pipes in the storeroom of my cafe that are leaking. Could you look at them?"

"I'll be there tomorrow." His smile was so wide, he looked beside himself with excitement.

Molly was unsure what to make of it, but she ignored the anxious sensation growing in her chest.

Chapter Eight

Henry rented a small cabin from a family north of the woods near Molly. He needed to be close enough to her, but far enough to track if the shapeshifter returned to his hometown. The creature would most likely cross through the forest, but so far, the air by the cabin smelled fresh. Nothing but pines and snow, but in town it was a different story. The city stunk, as if infested with rotten meat filled with maggots. If the shapeshifter didn't leave, neither would Henry.

Henry smiled to himself as he drove. Molly had asked him to fix the pipes in her cafe. He wasn't sure what had changed, or why she seemed comfortable enough to ask him, but he didn't care. The point was, Molly asked. He had overstated his ability to repair things, but he would look up a tutorial online if needed.

But his excitement quickly turned to guilt. How much time would he waste fixing her things? He could better use that time to track the shapeshifter. Find its path to predict where it would hunt next. Or hunt relentlessly for the next few days and kill it. Malcolm would never get distracted like this, but it was as if no matter how hard he tried, he wanted to only spend time with Molly.

He pulled into the cabin to find a familiar blue car parked in front. His relief vanished when he realized that, out of everyone in their pack, only Mark came.

He shook off the disappointment. If Henry were the alpha, Chris wouldn't have a choice. No matter how deep in his PhD program he was, even if he was mid-discovery, he would obey.

"Henry," called Mark, getting out of his car. He pushed his blond hair up from his face. Shopping bags in hand, no doubt filled with ingredients to make dinner. Henry hadn't even been thinking about food. His mind was too wrapped up in Molly the entire trip.

"How was the ride?" asked Henry.

"Not too bad if you don't pay attention to all the nagging."

"What?" As if on cue, the passenger door opened and Chris skulked out. "And here I thought you were too busy."

"I am busy. But you can't do this alone, can you?" Chris stood taller than both Mark and Henry. He was muscular, but he never seemed to bulk up like the other wolves. He stayed lean and fit, and Henry thought he looked like a praying mantis. All limbs and grace.

"What of the shapeshifter?" asked Mark. "What have you learned?"

"Not out here," said Henry, lowering his voice. Although the air was clear, he couldn't help but be a little paranoid.

He led them into the cabin, glancing behind them before he closed the door. Mark set the groceries down in the kitchenette, and Chris brought in their bags. Not that Henry had expected them to pack a lot, but seeing the amount they carried in made him more at ease. He wouldn't be alone anymore in his search.

The cabin was quite spacious, with two bedrooms, a living room area, and a small kitchen with a stove and a mini-fridge.

"Were you working on something?" asked Chris, peering down at Henry's jeans. The dark blue paint he'd used to patch up Molly's library walls had splattered on them as he worked.

"Yeah, about that. There's something I need to tell the two of you." He hesitated, unsure of how they would react. "I found my mate."

"What?" they asked simultaneously.

"I found her."

"How?" asked Chris.

Henry told them the tale, the chase, the shots, crashing through her window.

"She didn't freak out that you're a werewolf?" asked Chris.

"That's the thing. She's a witch."

"Seriously? Like a real one, not one of those fake ones on TV?" asked Mark.

"Yes, she's perfect."

"Oh God, it's begun," sighed Chris, as he laid down on the longest of the three mismatched couches in the living room.

"How did she take it when you told her?" asked Mark.

"I haven't exactly told her yet."

"Why?"

"I don't want to scare her away. She doesn't know about our customs, and I didn't give myself any favors after busting her window."

"Is she hot?" asked Chris.

"She's beautiful."

"Yeah, well, they all say that, don't they?" said Chris, rolling his eyes.

"That's true. We might have to look at her ourselves," joked Mark.

Henry's skin bristled at that. The unmistakable shaking of his bones worried him. If he wasn't careful, he would shift in the living room. He calmed his racing thoughts and tried to ignore the desire to tear out Mark's throat for suggesting such a thing.

"Whoa there, Henry. It was a joke. I would never steal your girl, on purpose at least," said Mark with a wink. That stoked his temper more.

"Wow, he's got a caveman brain already," said Chris, laughing.

Henry chuckled, deflating a little. "Well, the joke's on you two. I'm sure you're going to find your mate soon enough. I heard there are a lot of single women in this coven."

"Please don't curse us with your misery," said Chris.

"Yeah, come on, Henry. Chris will never finish his PhD if he finds his mate. He'll spend all day as his mate's lapdog," laughed Mark.

Chris tried to punch him as he walked by, but Mark dodged his fist. Chris was very sensitive about any comments about his PhD. Last time Henry had asked, Chris had told him he was almost done, but that had been three years ago.

"You two might laugh now. But you'll see. It's not misery. I can't even describe how it feels."

"Hungry?" suggested Chris.

"Happy?" guessed Mark.

"Horny?" asked Chris.

What Henry wanted to say was that he felt like he had noticed a hole. A hole he'd never known existed, deep somewhere in his soul where his wolf slumbered. He knew the hole would bother him until he had her. Until she made him hers. Until he was deep inside her, listening to her cry out his name. Then he would be happy. When she was asleep in his arms, satisfied and blissful. But he couldn't tell them that. They would laugh at him. Brandon and Freddy wouldn't, but they had their mates. They would understand, but they weren't here.

"I feel... ready," said Henry. And yet, Malcolm's dead body floated back into his head. In him there were two opposing forces: the need to run to Molly and make her his, and the second, vengeance. He was ready to be with her, but he understood she wouldn't be yet. Henry had never considered himself a patient man before, but his newfound love made him so. And the constant thrum of revenge flowing through his veins reminded him he needed to focus on that first.

"What about the shapeshifter?" asked Chris, bringing the mood down.

"It's still in town. You can't smell it here because it hasn't tried leaving. I don't think it wants to go back to our pack, at least not yet. I caught its scent this morning when I went for a jog. Its movement is erratic, and I can't make sense of it. When I was chasing it through the south, it almost moved in a straight line. Like it was on a track or something, but here, it just keeps circling around."

"Have you tried tracking it in wolf form?" asked Chris.

"Yeah, I did the first night, and I got shot at six times, remember?"

"But why are they so trigger-happy here?" asked Mark.

"The witches had some issues with some creature a couple of months ago. The creature is dead, but animal control doesn't know that. It's not safe for us to shift while we're here."

"That will make this a lot more difficult," said Chris.

"We need to be careful to not bring extra attention to the witches."

"It might help us too," said Mark.

"How so?" asked Henry.

"If we stay humans, the shapeshifter might not realize it's outnumbered. One wolf might be easy for it to kill, but three is significantly harder. We can surprise it."

"Thank you, guys, for coming," said Henry.

"Of course," said Mark. "We haven't been the biggest help to you. And I feel bad about that. Malcolm was our leader, too."

"We should've been there for you," said Chris. His gaze was directed towards the carpet.

"It's not as personal for you guys. I never held that against you. Believe me."

"Should we hug now?" asked Mark, trying to ease the tension a little.

"If we hug Chris, he might have a seizure," joked Henry.

"Ha ha, okay. That's the last time I ever tell you guys sorry." Chris was scowling, but his smile betrayed his knitted eyebrows.

They settled in for the night. Mark cooked an easy meal of pesto with garlic bread for them. Henry didn't realize just how hungry he was. For months he hadn't taken a moment to sit and relax. He'd grown used to hurried phone calls with the pack and lonely nights. When he had dinner with Molly and the girls, he forgot what it was like to talk to someone over a meal or even laugh. Being with his pack mates again brought him a level of comfort he missed.

As he lay in bed, falling asleep to the soft snores emanating from Mark, he realized it was the first night he had felt somewhat peaceful in months. He pictured Molly, her tight curls bouncing in front of her face, as he held on to her. Afraid that she would slip and break something. She felt so small in his arms. Fragile. The thought scared him. As if her bones were glass and one squeeze from him would shatter her.

He'd wanted to lean in and kiss her. Her soft waist was firmly in his grasp, and her sweet scent filled his nostrils. The only thing that stopped him was the realization that she would hate him for it. Henry could feel his boxers getting uncomfortably tight. He couldn't believe he was hard just imagining kissing her.

Brandon and Freddy hadn't prepared him for this. This yearning. The pain of sleeping miles away, wondering if she was safe, or happy, or in danger. He had to talk himself out of checking up on her twice through the night. He reminded himself that he would see her tomorrow and that he could be strong for just a few more hours.

And as he drifted asleep, he realized it was the first night he didn't sleep to images of his ripping apart the shapeshifter.

CHAPTER NINE

"Take a break," said Molly to an exasperated Violet and Ellie. They both sat crammed in a corner of Books & Beans. Notes, textbooks, and tablets with flashcards splayed out in front of them on two tables. They looked tired, with their dry-shampooed hair in twin braids down their backs.

"We can't take a break, Molly," said Ellie. Molly refilled her mug but noted the dark circles lining Ellie's brown eyes. Last she counted, this was Ellie's sixth cup of coffee in three hours, and Violet was on her eighth. But the warm and comforting smell of coffee seemed to perk them up again.

"We take a break and we fail," whined Violet, as she rubbed her eyes. She fiddled with her hair, twisting the tail end of her black braid.

"You two won't fail," said Molly, trying to reassure them, but at this point she worried more that she was giving them a caffeine addiction.

"Yes, we will. You don't get it. Contracts are so fucking boring. It's so weird. I hear the information, but then it slips out. Right out of my brain, like I never learned it!" cried Violet.

"You two have been here all week. You're going to be fine! I would hate to see you two when you guys take the BAR."

"Ugh, do not mention the BAR. I don't even want to think about that!" cried Ellie.

"Fine, I won't mention it again. Anyway, don't your boyfriends miss you guys?"

"Why do you think we're here?" asked Violet. "They can't stand us when we're like this."

"Here, have something to eat, at least. You're going to get holes in your stomach on coffee alone." She went to the pastry shelf and grabbed two eclairs for them.

The girls thanked her, and Ellie bit straight into her eclair without peeling her eyes away from her textbook.

"Molly?" asked Violet slowly.

"Yes," Molly could already tell she wanted something.

"Is there anything," Violet lowered her voice, "herbal, you could give us?"

"Wouldn't that be cheating?"

"I'm not saying something that will give us the answers, but like a little herb that might, I don't know, boost mental acumen or help us concentrate?"

"Hmm," Molly pretended to think about it. "Would that be very fair to the rest of your classmates?"

"Oh, come off it, Molly. It's not like you're going to give us the questions or anything. It's just something to improve our memory."

"That still sounds like cheating," Ellie singsonged.

"Please don't you act all noble."

"Not that I'm condoning this request, but I may know of a little herb that could help."

"Thank you, thank you, thank you. I promise I'll never ask for anything else."

"Oh sure you will," laughed Molly.

The door opened, the little bell making them all turn. Molly froze seeing Henry. He leaned down as he entered, to not bump his head on the frame. He scanned the place, taking everything in, but he only lingered on the bookshelves for a second before his eyes fell on her. He waved when he saw her, his face lighting up like a lantern.

"Hello, Molly," he said, toolbox in his hand. He looked down at Ellie and Violet, their concentration finally taken away from their looming test. Henry glanced back at Molly, a questioning expression on his face.

"Right, sorry," said Molly, flustered. "This is Violet and Ellie. They're umm," she lowered her voice, "members."

"Nice to meet you," said Henry, shaking both of their hands. Molly watched the girls, afraid that they were going to act like foolish children the way Lenore and Rosie did, but they reacted more awed than anything else, unable to close their mouths.

"So those pipes?" asked Henry.

"Right. This way." Molly led him to the counter and opened the door to the storeroom. The space was small, but with Henry's large body in there, she thought the room shrank by a couple of square feet.

"This here," she squatted down, and pointed to a pipe poised over a bucket. "It started doing this two days ago. I'm not sure how it started, but I shut the water off at night because I'm worried the leak will grow."

Henry kneeled down next to her, his body pressed between her body and the wall. Molly wanted to shuffle a few steps away, but she didn't. He didn't seem to notice how small the space was, or even that she was there. He concentrated fully on his work, but up close, his scent overwhelmed her. Cedar, but there was a waft of citrus like a pomelo. She swore that his skin radiated heat, and Molly could see herself melting into it. She bet he would make a nice pillow in the winter.

"It looks like rust, but I need to take a few things out to make sure," said Henry, bursting the little moment that held Molly to him.

"Okay, I'll leave you to it." She stood up a little too quickly, feeling her head whoosh. Maybe Rosie and Lenore were right; here she was sniffing a guy. It might have been too long since she'd had sex, or been alone with a man for any prolonged period, if being this close to him made her weak in the knees.

She walked out of the storeroom and found Ellie and Violet waiting by the counter, their grins wide like painted clown faces.

"Is that him?" asks Ellie.

"Him who?" asked Molly.

"Come on, Molly! Rosie and Lenore have been blowing up the group chat," said Violet.

"Of course they have." Molly sighed and grabbed a mug to dry, needing something to do with her nervous energy.

"So is it true, then? That he's of the *dog* variety?" asked Violet.

Molly looked at the customers. All of them had their headphones on and seemed too busy to pay attention to them.

"Yes, he is."

"Whoa, did you see him change? Lenore said you saw him change?" asked Ellie.

"I did."

"What was it like?"

"It was... weird. That's the only way I can describe it."

"Lenore also said he was naked," said Violet.

"That Lenore," sighed Molly.

"So is it true?"

"Of course it is. This isn't a movie. He wasn't a dog wearing pants." Molly remembered his wolf form. The soft brown of his coat, matted with blood. Those long claws clicking on her hardwood floor. It made her shiver.

"He's really hot," said Violet.

"You have a boyfriend," reminded Ellie.

"So do you! Didn't stop you from almost drooling back there."

"I know," said Ellie, biting her bottom lip. "He's just so..."

"Big?" suggested Violet.

"I wonder where else he's big," joked Ellie.

"You two better stop. I swear, you guys are just as bad as Rosie and Lenore."

"We're only joking, Molly," laughed Violet.

"And you're right, we have boyfriends, but you don't," said Ellie.

"And what is that supposed to mean?"

"Molly, he gave you a look," said Violet.

"What?"

"You didn't see it?" asked Ellie.

"He did not give me a look," said Molly, the mug almost falling from her fingers.

"Yeah, he did! Violet, show her," said Ellie. Violet hooded her eyes and squinted.

"You look constipated," said Molly.

Violet laughed. "I know you don't see it, but it was a look! I think he likes you."

"Don't you two have a test to study for?"

"We're taking our break, like you told us to," said Ellie.

Molly huffed and turned to the coffee pots, but there was nothing else for her to do. They were filled to the brim. She had already dried and washed every mug near her. She needed to occupy herself and take her mind off Henry. Violet and Ellie's snickers kept making her turn, paranoid that they were still talking about her.

If she dated Henry, would that be the worst thing in the world? She shook her head as if to rid herself of the idea. He would be an inconvenient addition right now. She already had a lot to do, and so much to take care of. Add a boyfriend and an entire wolf pack to her to-do list, and she would crumble, and not just because he would quite literally crush her beneath his weight.

Finding no suitable distraction in front of her, Molly realized she needed to go to the storeroom to grab some supplies. As she turned to leave, she crashed straight into Henry as he walked out. He grabbed her by the waist again, his feverish hands grasping tightly to steady her. She looked up at him and found his head already bent, his eyes inspecting he didn't hurt her. He was built like a wall. Hard as one, too. His eyes flashed gold again, and it startled her enough to step away from him. He loosened his arms around her, but Molly sensed a hesitation.

So, she hadn't imagined it after all. His brown eyes changed to gold near her.

Henry cleared his throat, his face turning a bright red. Molly swore she could sense the girls' eyes burrowing into her back.

"This is the part that's causing the problem." He showed her a rusty bit of pipe. "I need to go to the hardware store to replace it."

"Fine," said Molly with a heavy sigh. "That sounds fine." She struggled not to gaze directly at him, afraid of what she would find.

Henry left, and Molly tried not to turn around to watch him leave; instead, she pretended the espresso machine needed some cleaning. Again.

"Well," she heard Violet's voice sing. "Looks like someone's in denial."

Molly whipped around, her curls snapping in unison. "I swear to all that is holy, if you two don't get back to studying, you can kiss my help goodbye for your test."

Violet and Ellie giggled and skipped back to their table. Molly knew their whispered conversation was about her, but she tried not to think about it. While she cleaned up around her, she touched her waist beneath her sweater. The skin felt hot to the touch.

CHAPTER TEN

Henry waited in line to pay at the hardware store. He craned his neck and almost audibly cursed as he realized the old guy in front was trying to pay by check. The line inched forward, and Henry was sure he would leave the store fully gray. He fought the urge to run back to Molly's cafe without the pipe he'd promised to get.

He imagined her alone, refilling coffee and looking like a goddess while she did it. But he also saw her unprotected. The shapeshifter could be anywhere in the city, and what if it transformed into a mouse and sneaked beneath the door? What if she went to the storeroom by herself, where the shapeshifter lay in wait for her?

He sighed, unable to do much else, when a scent like rotten meat under heat wafted in. He gagged as the putrid smell took over all his senses. However, looking at the others in the shop, no one was reacting at all. The shapeshifter had to be near. There was no other explanation for it.

He got out of line, putting the pipe down to leave the store. The air stood still; no breeze helped to push the scent away, and the rancid odor drenched his surroundings.

Henry ran towards it, the heavy stench causing his eyes to water. He had caught trails of it before now, but this thing was close. Too close. It wasn't too far from Books & Beans, and his earlier fears flooded his mind.

He ran faster; the aroma making him want to cover his nose. But if he did so, he would lose the trail. The odor disappeared after he dashed a mile south. Henry took a lungful of air, but without shifting, the subtler notes were too faint for him to pick up.

For a moment, he almost shifted. Right in broad daylight next to a woman pumping gas into her car. Exposure would add more complications, so instead, he called Mark and Chris.

"It's here," said Henry. "By the north side out of town, about a mile and a half away from the hardware store."

"That can't be true," said Mark.

"What? I just found the trail."

"But I followed it here on the east side."

"Well, it's over here in the south by a park full of old people playing chess," said Chris.

"How is that possible?" asked Henry.

"Is there more than one?"

"Shapeshifters are not pack creatures. They're solitary," said Mark.

"But that doesn't explain why the scent is strong in multiple parts of town."

"It's not leaving," said Henry. "That's why the stench is everywhere. There's something here that it wants."

"So, what should we do? We can't catch it as humans. We're going to have to shift to track better," said Chris.

"It's too dangerous," sighed Henry. Although he had no scar to prove it, his chest ached from the memory of the bullets.

"Well, what else can we do?" asked Mark.

Henry didn't have a clue, and it frustrated him. Malcolm would know. Malcolm always knew exactly what to do. He would've told Henry and the others to split up and search for the shapeshifter as wolves. Or maybe tell them to stick together and investigate as humans. Or some other third option they didn't even think about. Whatever he chose, Henry trusted him. His plan would work. They would be safe because Malcolm would make sure of it. Now Henry was more lost than before. He couldn't trust his choice without wondering if the other was the right one.

"So we shift tonight?" asked Chris.

"Yes," agreed Mark.

Henry didn't answer.

By the time Henry got back to Books & Beans, the sun was almost gone, casting a weak orange light amidst the clouds.

He brought the supplies in and found Molly at the counter speaking to a customer. He approached them and seethed when she slapped the man's arm, laughing. She threw her head back and covered her mouth while she giggled. The man was tall, with dark hair, wearing scrubs and holding a cup of coffee. He laughed along with her, and Henry wanted to pounce on him.

He reached the counter, and Molly's smile faded. "Hello," said Henry rather short.

"You're back," said Molly. Henry raised the plastic bag, and she nodded. She turned to the man in front of her. "River, will you join us?"

Henry's bones shook under his jacket. His wolf snarled in his chest. Why did she invite him along? Henry had sensed the tension in the storeroom together. He had heard her heart drum. The air between them became charged with a power he had only just begun to explore. He thought he'd done the right thing by ignoring it to not make her uncomfortable. Had he misread the signs?

Henry followed them both, his temper and patience with River shortening all the while. His mind replayed what he had seen only moments before, but his brain added more to it. Had River touched Molly? Had he kissed her just as Henry had entered, only he hadn't noticed? Molly closed the door behind him.

"Henry, this is River. Remember Ellie from earlier. This is her boyfriend."

"Right," said Henry, feeling his bones immediately still. "Hi." He shook River's hand. He could have torn this man's throat out in a second. What was wrong with him?

"Nice to meet you. So you're the guy Rosie and Lenore have been talking about in the group chat."

"The group chat?"

"Don't ask," said Molly quickly. "River is a medical examiner."

"Molly told me about your shapeshifter issue, and I think that might explain some of the recent bodies we've been finding."

"Bodies?" asked Henry.

"Police found two half-eaten bodies yesterday." Henry's blood ran cold. "The thing is, we would normally mark these as killed by an animal given the marks. However, not all the bite marks resemble an animal. There are human bites as well."

"It's feeding," said Henry through gritted teeth.

"As a shapeshifter? Or as a human?" asked Molly.

"Maybe both."

"River, can you mark the deaths as animal attacks?" asked Molly.

"If it were just me, I would have, but that was before I knew about the shapeshifter, so I marked it as a homicide. It's not conclusive. We turned in our findings to the police already, and they're on the lookout for both an animal and a person. I believe they might look for a cannibal with large dogs."

"That should narrow it down," said Molly.

"Also, you won't like this, but they're looking into witches as well."

"Of course they are," sighed Molly.

"Witches are known cannibals?" asked Henry.

"No, but Brian, my coworker, thinks they are. And it doesn't take much to convince the police force in this town that everything is related to witchcraft. Plus, I learned from another cop that Officer Wharton's disappearance is being looked into."

"Who's that?" asked Henry.

"A witch hunter we had the misfortune of running into a couple of months ago. He's dead, but it's another thing we have to worry about," said Molly, rubbing her head. "Any more bad news for me, River?"

"The witch theory didn't convince everyone, and some think it's an animal. They're leaving all their options open. I'm sure the idea of people being eaten by a cannibal is too wild for some of them, so they don't believe it. I mean, if you saw how much was left on those bodies, you wouldn't want to believe a human could do that."

Henry didn't need him to elaborate; he knew. He had seen it.

"So, you can't shift," said Molly to Henry.

"We have to. I detected the shapeshifter when I was out, only I lost the scent. When I called my pack mates, they told me they also smelled it in other places. The whole town stinks of it now. It'll be hard to find it as humans. We need to shift if we're going to narrow down its location."

Molly opened her mouth to argue, but a ping on River's phone stopped them.

"That's work. I've gotta go."

"Another body?" asked Molly, worried.

"It's always another body, but I'll let you know if we find more shapeshifter kills," said River. Molly gave him a hug before he left the storeroom and Henry had to take a deep breath to not yank him from his collar away from her.

Henry breathed easier once he was gone. Girlfriend or not, he hated another man near his mate. Molly's brow stayed furrowed in worry, even after he left. She bit her nails, her mind clearly rushing. Henry wished he could say something to make her feel better, but he had spent so little time with her he was unsure what would help.

"This complicates things," said Molly, pacing in the small room.

"I know."

"You can't shift. You or your pack mates. They're looking for anything that killed these people. And three giant wolves are conspicuous."

"How else can I track it?"

"We can track it."

"What?"

"I can ask River to see if he can get some sort of sample from the shapeshifter, and we'll use magic to find it."

"So you're helping me, then?"

"I guess I am."

"What's changed?"

"They placed the blame on us witches again. Whether I like it or not, if it involves the town, it involves the coven." She sighed, sitting on a small chair by the door.

He wanted to reach out and hold her. Tell her he would take care of it. She didn't have to worry, but he got the sense she would push him away. The thought made his chest hurt.

The sensations were so different from what he expected. Even the idea of rejection made him want to die. He wasn't sure if he could trust anything he did now, even his revenge. His heart, his mind, his soul entangled around her.

"I won't leave town until that thing is dead," said Henry. "I might have driven it here when I chased it. It's my fault."

"It's not your fault," she said, shaking her head. "You have no more control over that thing than we do."

"Still, I won't leave you to deal with it alone."

"Thank you. If the cops are looking for witches now, they'll be on the alert for anything magical, and I'm worried what will happen if your pack shifts."

"The full moon is a few weeks away," he reminded her.

"You can't control it then?"

"We can, but it's difficult. But I won't leave until you're safe. I can't leave you unprotected."

"Me?" asked Molly.

Henry cursed himself in his head. He hadn't meant to say the last part out loud. "The coven, I mean," he blurted.

"We can protect ourselves. It's the humans I'm worried about." She stood up and took a deep breath. "We'll figure out something, I guess." She said it more to herself than to him.

She left him alone to return to work, but Henry couldn't concentrate yet. The storeroom smelled like her, and after spending the afternoon drenched in the shapeshifter's stench, he reveled in her scent.

He now understood Molly would take time. More time than they might have. But she opened slowly, like soft rose petals. They were unfurling in front of him. She agreed to help him. Another in. He'd get there if the shapeshifter didn't get him first.

Henry kneeled down and got to work, but surprisingly, his knees ached the longer he kneeled. His body felt strange to him, sore and tired, after having to exercise so much self-control to not shift because of River. He'd never felt this weak before.

Chapter Eleven

Molly finished cleaning up the counter, throwing away some empty oat milk cartons in the trash. She pulled the straps of the trash bag closed and hoisted it out with some difficulty. She walked out of Books & Beans through the alley door in the back and carried the heavy bag to the garbage between her cafe and the flower shop next door. The wind brought a chill that gave Molly goosebumps. She heaved the bag, missing the garbage can. Maybe this was something that Henry could help her with, but she was done asking that man wolf for favors. With a heavy sigh, she groaned as she threw the bag in with some difficulty.

The notes were low at first, as if blown by the breeze. She would have missed it if she had still been struggling with the trash. The whistled melody made Molly's stomach flip. She hurried inside, slamming the door behind her. The whistling stopped, but her heart raced anyway.

She had imagined it. She was imagining all sorts of things lately, like Henry's eyes changing color. Maybe she had misheard it. The theme song belonged to a sitcom from the fifties. It was a popular show. Anybody could have whistled that tune.

It couldn't be him. It won't be him. He's dead.

"Molly?" Henry burst through the storeroom, startling Molly enough to shoot her heart rate even higher. She pushed herself away until her back hit the espresso machine. Henry reached out anyway, misreading her intentions. Even though Molly wanted to push him from her, his warm hands cupping her face brought an odd sensation of comfort. His hands snaked down as if taking stock of all of her.

Molly's good sense snapped her out of her fear, and she side-stepped to the other end of the counter away from him.

"What's wrong?" he asked.

"Nothing. Nothing's wrong. Why would you think something's wrong?" She was sure she looked scared. Her breath was only now slowing, but she wasn't about to tell Henry about what had happened. He was a stranger, and just because she had seen more of him than she would have liked, it didn't mean they were close.

"I heard your heartbeat from the storeroom."

"You heard my heartbeat?" Henry opened his mouth but shut it tight. He wanted to say something more. His brow furrowed in guilt, but he stopped himself. "What aren't you telling me?" she asked.

Since meeting Henry, life had seemed off. She couldn't place it. It was like being dizzy all the time, unsure which step would tilt her towards the earth with nothing to cushion her fall. He'd been lying from the start, and she wasn't letting him get away with it anymore.

"Molly," he began, but the bell at the front door stopped him. Two men walked in; one had to stoop to avoid hitting his head on the door frame. Their large bodies were imposing and threatening in her small cafe.

Molly turned to Henry, but he didn't look worried. Although his body still appeared tense. They were both tall, although the one who had to stoop towered over both Henry and the other man. He seemed annoyed to be there, a scowl etched into his thick eyebrows. The other appeared much more curious as he studied her.

"Molly, this is Chris and Mark. They're my pack mates."

"Right," said Molly. She reached out her hand to shake theirs. They examined her with interest. Almost like they dissected her, scanning from her shoes to her head. She felt self-conscious under their gaze. What was up with wolves? Did they all stare like that? Or was it just with her? Henry hadn't even looked twice at Violet and Ellie, although he had stared down River.

"You ready?" asked Mark. His hair was the same length as Henry's, but a darker blonde. He kept a close-cropped beard, and he scratched it nervously as he avoided her gaze.

"Ready for what?" asked Molly, turning to Henry.

"Right, uh, change of plans, guys, we can't shift. They found two bodies, and it would be too dangerous to shift now. We have it on good authority that animal control and the cops are looking for an animal. We'll be too noticeable."

"What? If there are more victims, it's going to kill again. We have to shift," said Chris.

"We can't," repeated Henry. "They're suspicious that it may be witches. If we're caught, we might expose ourselves, and we could put all werewolves and witches at risk."

"So, what do we do?" asked Mark.

"Yeah, I mean if we can't shift, there is no way we're going to find this thing as men." Chris sighed, crossing his arms.

"We're going to track it with magic," said Molly.

"What? Come on, Henry, you can't be serious," said Chris.

Henry puffed up, getting defensive. "I get this is frustrating for you guys. Trust me, it's frustrating for me too. The last thing I want is for the creature to be out there killing more people, but if the shapeshifter doesn't kill us, the police and animal control will."

"So what? We're going to let it run wild until we can find it *magically*." Molly picked up Chris wasn't a very patient guy. His dark hair fell on his face, but he seemed too pissed to brush it away.

"I think we're wasting time," said Mark. "How many people will die before all this can happen?"

"The full moon is a few weeks away. If we can't track it magically by then, we'll shift."

"Henry, I don't think that's a good idea," said Chris.

"Do you think it's safe to shift in this town?" asked Henry.

"Well, no, not after what happened to you—"

"Then we can't shift. If one of us gets hurt or worse," his voice caught, "we'll have fewer resources to kill it."

Something in his voice made the other two listen. The air, which had grown thick during the argument, lessened somewhat. They would accept it, but Molly realized Henry had no proper authority. They were unfocused and indecisive. They would listen, but for how long?

Mark and Chris left, deciding to drive around to see if they picked up the scent again. Henry assured them he would join them after he finished with his work. The other two studied him, as if questioning his motives. Molly ignored their looks, wondering what else they thought Henry would do. But their smirks made her cheeks grow hot. They acted like Henry was about to get lucky.

He turned to her as soon as the door closed and she walked ten paces away from him on the other side of the counter. She busied herself picking up books customers left on the tables and placing them back on the shelves.

"I'm sorry about those two," said Henry, walking behind her. "They're good guys, I swear. They're just a little tense right now."

"I hope they're not too mad."

"They'll get over it."

"What were you saying earlier?" Henry looked away, his face turning slightly pink.

"I should get back," Henry turned to leave, but Molly wasn't finished.

"No, wait." Her hand wrapped around his arm. He turned to her, his eyes flashing the now familiar gold. "What is that?"

"What's what?"

"That thing, with your eyes."

"What thing with my eyes?"

"You don't know? They turn gold, but it's only for like a second and then they go back to normal."

"Shit." He turned away from her again, this time rubbing both of his palms on his eyes, as if he could change the color back to their warm brown. "I didn't know they did that. Believe me, Molly."

"Why are they doing that?" He didn't answer, so Molly continued. "What did you mean earlier about hearing my heartbeat from the storeroom?"

He stared at her apologetically, and it made her stomach drop. "I had hoped that by now I would have figured out a better way to tell you this."

"Tell me what?" she started panicking. She didn't understand why, but she felt like she was going to hate whatever Henry told her next.

"Werewolves," he started, walking back towards her, "have a strange custom. We don't choose our mates, not in the traditional sense. Our wolf chooses." He waited, but Molly both wanted and didn't want him to continue.

"We mate for life. And our wolf chooses the perfect mate for us. Nobody understands how it works. Some people know each other for years, and then one day the wolf chooses that person. But sometimes, you know as soon as you see them. The wolf knows before we do. And my wolf," he walked even closer, closing the space between them by half, "my wolf chose you."

Molly felt rooted to where she stood, not quite grasping what he said. "Your... wolf," she began trying to set it straight in her head, "your wolf chose me?"

"Yes, you're my mate." He sounded relieved that she understood, but she was more confused than ever before.

"I'm sorry?"

"It chose you."

"Yeah, I heard you the first time." She paced in front of the bookshelf, her head spinning. Why couldn't her life slow down for one goddamn moment? "Are you kidding me?" she asked to no one in particular, but Henry answered anyway.

"If I am honest, out of all the ways I imagined this going, I didn't think this would be your reaction."

"Oh please," scoffed Molly. "And what exactly did you think my reaction was going to be?"

His cheeks flamed red. "I don't think it will help my case if I told you."

"Right, well, fuck you," she said, fuming. He smiled, and she wanted to slap it off his face. "Is there a way to reverse it?"

His smile faded, replaced by shock and anger. "What?"

"Can we make your wolf choose someone else?"

"No, of course not! You're mine!"

"Excuse me?" This was worse than she had imagined.

"And I'm yours," he quickly added.

"I don't want you! Would you have even looked at me twice if your stupid wolf hadn't chosen me?"

"You can't ask me that."

"Yes, I can. It's a valid question!"

"You," he moved right in front of her, walking so fast she nearly walked into him mid-step. She wanted to move away, but she stayed put. She refused to let a werewolf make her run. "You are the most beautiful woman I have ever seen." His eyes darkened, holding her gaze in a stare she was too angry to break.

"That's the wolf talking," she spat.

He growled, grabbing her hand and placing it on his chest. She tried pulling it away, but he gripped it tight like a trap. "It's not my wolf. It's me, the man. I thanked my wolf the moment I saw you. The moment I realized you were mine." His eyes turned gold and stayed gold. "You don't realize this yet, but I was made for you."

Molly felt his heartbeat beneath her hand. Flustered and unsteady, like hers. This close, his smell was overwhelming. Cedar, pomelo, and a musk she couldn't name. He leaned in, his face inches from hers. Molly wanted to fight, to push him away, to slap him, to find a spell that would undo all of this. Yet, a small voice, and she couldn't have been sure it was hers, said something completely different. *Kiss him and let him taste you.*

Just then, the bell on the front door jingled again. Like being shocked by a thousand volts, Molly pushed him away, but he didn't budge very far from her. He hesitated, letting go of her hand, but she didn't. She snapped around and saw Lola skip inside. Her hair was faded blue, and she was bundled up in three sweaters and a coat.

"Hi," she said apprehensively. She hurried towards Molly, sensing her unease.

"Hello," said Henry, trying to smile, but it didn't reach his eyes. "I'll just get my things," he said, heading back to the storeroom away from them.

Lola gave Molly an inquisitive look, but Molly shook her head. Not here. If he could hear her heartbeat, their conversation wasn't safe. She poured Lola tea to give her something to do, and to calm her down. Henry appeared a few moments later with his toolbox. With a rushed goodbye, he almost ran out of the cafe.

Once gone, Lola whipped towards Molly. "Is that the werewolf from the group chat?"

Chapter Twelve

Molly woke up to the sound of footsteps by her bed, but didn't stir. She had no reason to feel unsafe in her own home. Lenore was somewhere in the house singing off-key again.

She yawned, stretching her limbs and arching her back. She thought she would feel better in the morning. Maybe wake up and realize it had all been a dream. Henry hadn't confessed to her the truth of his glowing eyes, or the weird connection they had together. Everything was as it should be, but of course it didn't work. Although she and Lola had spent most of the night dissecting everything he had said, she felt worse.

Hours later, she still flipped between anger and confusion. There he stood, at six foot three and muscular beyond reason, her soulmate. And she didn't even get a choice.

The footsteps got louder, and she opened her eyes to see Camilla near her. Her blue eyes were striking even in death.

"Why are you still in bed?" asked Camilla. Her feet creaked on the wooden floor as she neared.

"It's my day off. Can't I sleep in?" asked Molly, sitting up. She rubbed her eyes, and Camilla came into focus.

"You never sleep in, and anyway you'll waste your day." Camilla sat on the bed.

"I won't waste my day, it's only," she flipped over her phone and balked at seeing it was ten till eleven. "Shit." She couldn't remember the last time she had slept in that late.

"What's wrong?" asked Camilla. She appeared as prim and pristine in death as she did in the photos Molly had found of her in the attic.

"Nothing's wrong."

"Clearly something is, and if you don't tell me, I'll assume the worst. So you might as well tell me."

"You're so pushy," groaned Molly.

"Tell me," Camilla repeated. Her stern tone managed to settle stubborn soldiers during the war, and it worked on Molly too.

"Did you ever fall in love? When you were alive, I mean?"

"Of course," said Camilla, her gaze softened.

"What happened to him?"

"He died in the war."

"Right, sorry. I shouldn't have asked."

"Is this what this is about? You're in love?"

"I'm not in love, but someone has shown... interest."

"Why are you moping? This is a good thing. Is it not?"

"Unclear."

"What's the problem?"

Molly didn't know how to respond. The problem was she hadn't asked for this. The problem was the last guy she dated broke up with her over six years ago, and since then, she had no interest in dating at all. Not when dating meant introducing a random mortal man to her life of witchcraft. Not when it could have led to her exposure or that of the coven. The problem was she would have kissed Henry last night. Her body screamed at her to do it. She wasn't sure what to make of that.

"Is it the werewolf?"

Molly could only nod in response.

"Do you not like him? Is he not suitable?"

"I don't understand what you mean by suitable? He seems nice enough."

"Is he from a good family?"

"That's old-fashioned of you."

"These sorts of questions were important in my time. Perhaps not so much now."

"No, they're important now, too. I don't know a lot about him."

"Get to know him then. He could surprise you."

Molly heard rustling near her, followed by a drawn-out yawn. Lola stretched her arms above her head, and Camilla disappeared.

"Are we talking to the spirits again?" murmured Lola. Her eyes were still closed, and her faded blue hair knotted around her like a rat's nest.

"I was," sighed Molly.

"Sorry, I forgot yours are shy." Lola sat up. "Are you getting advice from your ghosts now?"

"What's wrong with a little more feedback?"

"Did sleep help you decide?"

"No, I'm more confused than last night."

Lola pulled out from under her pillow a rumpled and wrinkled piece of paper. She unfolded it and tried to smooth it out. The words **PRO CON** glared in the morning light.

"Did you sleep with the pro-con list under your pillow last night?" asked Molly. Lola was eccentric, but what was this?

"You've never slept with things under your pillow?"

"Yeah, a sachet with lavender and wild lettuce for better sleep, but not this."

"Well, if I ever need more information or I'm lost and I need some guidance, I'll sleep with something related to my problem underneath my pillow. I can dream the solution or get a message."

"Wow, you meant sleep on it literally."

"Exactly," smiled Lola.

She yawned as she studied the list. Molly reviewed it, too. Under PRO: handy, looks strong, knows about magic and didn't freak out about it, cute smile (that had been hard to admit), and strong enough to help rearrange furniture. Under CON: a werewolf, probably sheds, could get shot by animal control, and might get lice.

"So, what did your dreams tell you about him?" asked Molly. Rereading the pro-con list did nothing to help her decision.

"Well, they told me something that just might tip the scales. But I'm unsure which way."

"What is it?" asked Molly, dread bubbling up.

"He's really hot." Molly slapped Lola on the leg. Lola fake-yelped and laughed. "Oh, come on, Molly. It's going to be okay either way."

"How? How is any of this remotely going to be okay?"

"Well, if you say no, you'll just have a shadow, but I doubt he'll try to force you to be with him."

"I'm not so sure about that. He gave me a look last night, like I shouldn't even bother fighting. Like it was inevitable."

"Do you really expect he's the kind of guy capable of doing something so horrible?"

"I don't know him, Lola."

"But what does your gut tell you?"

Molly hesitated. "It tells me no. He wouldn't do that."

"So if you say yes, you'd get a boyfriend. And is that so bad?"

"I wouldn't get a boyfriend, Lola. He's *it*."

"So you'd get a husband! Isn't that better anyway? To always have no matter what, this man who would do nothing to hurt or betray you? I can think of worse things in life than a loyal man."

"I know," sighed Molly. She lay back on the bed, covering her face with a pillow.

"Listen, we can make all the pro-con lists in the world, but you're still going to have to talk to the guy."

"Ugh," said Molly beneath the pillow. She could hear Lola's muffled giggle, and she pulled the pillow off her face after a while. "You know what's the worst?" asked Molly.

"What?"

"I almost kissed him last night. I wanted to kiss him before you interrupted."

Lola's smile grew. "Just kiss?"

Molly threw the pillow at her, but Lola just laughed harder. Molly plopped back onto the mattress, bringing the duvet up to cover her face. "As if I need something else to go wrong," she sighed.

The laughter on the other side of the bed stopped. "Are you okay?" asked Lola.

"Hmm?"

"It's just you've been extra — I'm not sure how to say this..."

"Mean?" suggested Molly.

"Uptight," corrected Lola.

Molly sat up again and realized Lola looked sorry to have suggested it. "Have I?"

"You know I love you..."

"Mmm, you always say that when you're going to say something I don't want to hear."

"I've noticed that since Ellie joined the coven, you've been more nervous. Like you're clinging to us for dear life. As if one minor mistake will lead us to be discovered."

"Do you blame me? After what happened with Violet?"

"But Molly, everything turned out okay. We got there in time, and Violet's safe. We're all safe. Nothing bad is going to happen."

"I'm not doing it on purpose."

"I get that," said Lola, grabbing her hand. Molly felt a wash of relief flood her then. Lola's specialty, she oozed calm.

Molly often wondered how Lola did it after everything she'd been through. Her mother had been one of the first women prosecuted under the new anti-witchcraft laws of the country. Even after having to endure weeks of court days and constant speculation in the media, she still seemed to hold on to a positivity that was endless.

"When everything is chaotic and out of my control, it freaks me out," said Molly.

"I know."

"I just need everything to go back to normal, and I'll be okay. This werewolf isn't helping much."

"I get you can't see it now, but it's all going to work out somehow."

Lola always believed in everything working out for the best. Molly wasn't sure how. For Lola, the universe had logic, order, a plan. She could fall and trust someone or something would catch her. For Molly, much of the world seemed uncertain. She worked hard to create her peace and to make her life as uncomplicated as possible. Since Ellie and Violet's problems, life just wasn't rearranging itself into the peaceful existence she had before.

"So what are you going to do?" asked Lola.

"We're going to help the wolves kill the shapeshifter. We can't ignore that problem away, especially since it's not leaving."

"And Henry?"

"I'll figure that out later. That's as much as I can promise."

Chapter Thirteen

Molly asked Rosie to call Henry. She tried to reason with herself that she didn't have his number, and Rosie had the foresight to ask him for it when he was over for dinner. But the reality was she was too scared to call him herself.

Rosie set up a meeting between the pack and the coven. Molly dreaded it all day, but when she opened the door and saw Henry again, her heart leaped anyway. His eyes flashed gold, but it no longer surprised Molly. She felt the heat warming her face, and she only hoped that Henry and the others didn't notice her nervousness.

Mark and Chris shuffled in after him. Mark was kind and attentive, complimenting her home. Chris looked uncomfortable being there, his eyes scanning the space and everyone there, like he was trying to scope it out.

The coven's collective chatter and laughter stopped as soon as the wolf pack entered the kitchen. This was going to be more awkward than she had realized. Henry watched his pack mates closely. Molly understood what he was looking for. Were they going to fall in love at first sight of one of the coven members?

What if they chose Ellie or Violet? They had their boyfriends, and she didn't think they would be so keen to leave them. Or worse, what if their wolves chose another single coven member? Then she could never get rid of them.

Molly panicked about whether it had been a good idea to bring them together like this. She didn't wish her confusion and problems on any of her coven family, but desperate times left her no choice.

After quick introductions, where Margaret turned bright red, Rosie and Lenore giggled hysterically, and Lola, Violet, and Ellie gawked, they got to work. Molly pulled out a map of the city and set it on the kitchen table.

"Where have you been smelling the shapeshifter the strongest?" she asked. The wolf men pointed them out. Molly planted a pin at each location. When they finished, they had placed thirty pins all around town.

"Concentric circles..." said Margaret as she leaned over the map, her red hair brushed over Mark's hand.

"What?" asked Violet.

"Do you have a pencil?" asked Margaret. Lenore ran to a drawer in the kitchen and handed her a mechanical pencil. "Look," she connected the dots. First starting in the outer layer, the points farthest from town. She then went into the next layer, following the pins to complete a second circle inside the other one.

"It's circling the town," said Mark, leaning in. His arm brushed Margaret's, and she blushed so red her freckles almost disappeared.

"There's something here that it wants," said Violet.

"But what?" asked Chris. "I mean, if it wanted the pack, it would have gone back to our hometown. Why did it kill Malcolm then?"

"He wasn't the intended target," said Henry. His voice sounded strained, and while Molly had tried to stand far away from him, the pain in his voice almost compelled her to get closer to him. "Maybe he was just in the wrong place at the wrong time."

"That's so shit," said Chris. "The thing never wanted Malcolm, or the pack. Whatever it wants, it was always here. You chased it off course."

"I delayed what it wanted, but it doesn't think I'm a big enough threat to it now."

"How do you kill a shapeshifter?" asked Ellie.

"The way you kill any other magical creature, I guess," said Violet.

"What so like stabbing it?" asked Rosie.

"Stabbing, beheading, pulling out its heart, fire. All of it would work," said Henry.

"What animals does it change into?" asked Ellie.

"A mountain lion, but I saw it change into a wolf only a handful of times."

"A werewolf?" asked Violet.

"No, it was a normal wolf. They're smaller than we are."

"Have you ever seen it as a human?" asked Ellie.

"No, it's always an animal."

"We've figured out where it'll circle next." Mark circled the imaginary line with his finger under the inner circle. "We follow this, we might get it."

"We should split up," said Rosie.

"Bad idea," said Chris.

Rosie rolled her eyes. "Excuse you, you didn't let me finish."

Chris raised an eyebrow, curious about her, and Molly worried it was happening again. She glanced at Henry to see if he saw it, but found him only staring at her.

"We should split into groups of three. A wolf for each team. The next area that it'll be in still covers an area of 100 miles all around. We'll never catch it if we're just one enormous group."

"You're right," said Molly. "Mark, Lenore, Ellie, Lola can be one group. Chris, Rosie, and I will be another. Henry, Violet, and Margaret will be the last group."

"I don't like that," blurted Henry.

"What?" asked Molly, flustered. She thought she was being sneaky about it, too.

"You and I need to be on the same team."

"Well, I already made them so."

"I can switch," squeaked Margaret.

Molly couldn't argue, not in front of everyone. Not without arousing suspicion from the coven. She wasn't quite ready to tell everyone about Henry's dating proclivities.

"Fine," she said through gritted teeth. She saw out of the corner of her eye Rosie, Lenore, and Violet giving each other confused looks. Great, another thing she would have to explain away later.

The night drew to a close, and the coven members left one by one, well, the ones that didn't live with her. Molly tried to busy herself with the girls, but they all soon left. She tried to waste more time with Lenore and Rosie, but they gave her a look like she couldn't fool them. They wouldn't let her stall any longer, skipping away on the pretense of finishing homework.

"Hey," she heard behind her as soon as they went upstairs. Molly turned to see Henry keeping some distance between them. It made her feel better that he was learning she didn't like him being so close. "I need to apologize for last night. I shouldn't have sprung that on you like I did."

"It's the truth, isn't it? It's always better to speak the truth."

"Still, I shouldn't have done it like that. Or scared you how I did."

"Well, thank you for apologizing." It all seemed so formal to keep her at arm's length after everything that had happened the night before.

"Have you thought about what I told you last night?" He asked after a moment.

"I... I can't be with you, Henry. At least not in the way you need me to be."

Henry hung his head and nodded. "I understand. I would never force this on you, Molly. Never."

"I need more time. This was just too much. I mean, I know nothing about you, or you me. Not really, anyway. I get your wolf is saying it's me, but can you understand why I'm not so convinced?"

"I get it, Molly. Believe me, I do."

He turned to leave, but stopped. Molly panicked when he looked back. There was no anger or malice in his brown eyes, but the pain was clear enough to see. It made her want to escape upstairs, and pretend that this problem wasn't hers to figure out.

"When you're ready, I'll be waiting." With that, he opened the front door and left. Molly only stared at the door as it shut.

Chapter Fourteen

Henry lay on the couch, staring at the wooden ceiling of the cabin. Mark had fallen asleep, but Chris was still awake, scrolling on his phone on the adjacent couch. Molly's face kept poking through Henry's mind.

The sad look in her eyes, the furrow of her brows. He had focused on her lips as she spoke during the meeting. The deep red of her lipstick highlighted the bow of her upper lip. He wanted to kiss her, and for a moment in Books & Beans; he thought she wanted to kiss him, too.

Molly felt further away from him now. Any distance from her brought about a cold in his soul that left him heartbroken and empty. Yet he understood where she was coming from. He cared for her and would exercise patience, as she asked. He sighed, and it hurt.

"Oh my God," Chris said near him. "Stop it, Henry."

"Shut up," said Henry, kicking him from where he lay and knocking Chris' phone from his hand.

Chris growled and stooped to pick up his phone. "You've gotta stop being such a big baby."

"So I take it you didn't find your mate tonight?"

"Of course not. And thank God for that, as if I have time for it right now."

Henry was about to make a snide remark about Chris and his never-ending PhD, but he needed a friend tonight, not an enemy.

"I had hoped that one of you would. I could use some help."

"Molly said no?"

"She didn't say no. She just needs more time."

"More time for what?"

"Romance and seduction, I guess?" sighed Henry.

"You don't have time for that. Doesn't she realize the longer she waits to claim you, the weaker you'll get?" Henry didn't answer, and Chris sat up, eyeing him. "You didn't tell her, did you?"

"I won't coerce her into claiming me."

"It's not coercion; it's the truth!"

"You think me telling her, 'Hey, if you don't claim me, I'm going to get weaker and weaker until I can't shift,' isn't coercive?"

"Yeah, you forgot to add you'll die. You'll get weaker until you die!" Mark snored louder from the bedroom, and Henry shushed Chris.

"It doesn't matter. She needs more time, and I'm going to give her that."

"Henry, we can't have you weak before we fight the shapeshifter," said Chris through gritted teeth to not yell and wake Mark.

"You won't get it until it happens to you. Whatever she wants, I'll give it to her. I can't fight it."

"And if she says no?" asked Chris, massaging the bridge of his nose.

"Then I'll die," shrugged Henry.

"Fucking hell, man. Are you serious? I hope I never find my mate. If it makes you like this, I don't want it."

Henry wanted to defend himself, but there was no winning Chris over. He didn't get it. If he called Brandon and Freddy, they would understand. They had lived it; they had fallen in love, and they had the privilege of being near their mates every day. Henry wasn't afraid. He believed in the magic, in the tales. He believed he wouldn't die.

When he watched Molly in her element, her commanding presence with her coven, it filled him with such pride he could almost burst. When he saw her smile and laugh, he knew that one day he would be her happiness and she would be his. His moon, his life, walking among the living. She would accept him, and he was sure of it.

But first, patience.

Two days later, Violet and Molly piled into Henry's truck. Violet sat between Molly and him, and he tried not to convince them to switch seats. They headed to the west side of town. They had divided the section of land into three. Molly held her phone in her hand, ready to call the others if they spotted the shapeshifter.

"So, Henry," said Violet. He sensed her cool gray eyes on him as he drove. "How long have you been a werewolf?"

He smiled. The one thing he had learned from being near the coven was that these girls were curious. "I first turned when I was thirteen."

"Wow, did it hurt?"

"A little but, it doesn't hurt much anymore."

"Anyone else in your family?"

"Just Chris. He's my cousin. I had a couple of uncles as well. Most of my family carries the gene."

"What about the other wolf boys?"

"Wolf boys," he repeated, laughing. "Well, Chris had a sister, and she wasn't a werewolf, but she's gone now." He didn't elaborate, not that he wanted to, but it wasn't his story to tell. "But Freddy and Mark are brothers. No one else in Chris' family was a wolf except his dad."

"So it skips a lot, this gene?"

"It seems like it, but we don't understand how it works."

"Magic isn't an exact science."

"Yeah, well put."

"Molly always says that," said Violet, turning to look at her.

Henry wished to see her face. He didn't want to drive. He wanted to just stare into her eyes all night, but since he had shown up at her house to pick her up, she had been deathly silent. Her scent filled the car, and Henry had to roll down the window to not forget to sniff for the shapeshifter. But the car was heavy with the scent of figs, warmed by Molly's skin. The grassy-sweet aroma made his mouth water. He craved to kiss her throat. Let his tongue linger on her warm skin and drink her in. Curious to discover whether her perfume emanated from deep within her.

He forced himself to concentrate. He had a job to do, and if he didn't focus, there was no way he could exact his revenge. The last image he had of Malcolm played in his brain, surging the anger in his body and forcing him to stop thinking about Molly.

As he drove through sleepy neighborhoods, he took deep breaths to catch a whiff of something. Passing well-lit garages and children making snowmen out of the last snow of the season, he soon drove out of the residential neighborhoods. Still, the only scent his nostrils picked up was Molly.

Perhaps she was right to suggest they would be better off on separate teams. He could never be a leader. At the thought of being away from her, at not being able to protect her from harm, he made his team practically useless. Malcolm wouldn't have made that mistake.

Henry wondered if that was the reason Malcolm had never found his mate. Malcolm had someone, but it wasn't the same bond. He tried his best not to hurt the poor woman, so he always kept her at arm's length. Maybe if he had a mate, he wouldn't have been an effective leader. They would become his weaknesses and would've made him second guess his decisions the way Henry did his. He wasn't sure, since Malcolm never let him into that part of himself, diplomatic and headstrong as he always was. Henry realized just how easy he had it before.

Maybe that was why Henry was so crap at being a leader. Molly became his vulnerability the longer he waited for her to claim him. He didn't feel weak yet, but he wondered how long he had before he noticed the effects of a delayed claiming.

An odor wafted through the window, cutting through the scent he had been relishing. It made him hit the brakes, and Violet and Molly held on to the dashboard.

"What is it?" asked Violet.

"I smell it. Can you guys?" Violet sniffed the air and shook her head.

"Where is it coming from?" asked Molly.

Henry took a deep whiff, even though he would rather have held his breath until he died. The rotten stench made him nauseas. He continued driving, following the stink as it grew stronger. Buildings along the road disappeared. Long-abandoned manufacturing warehouses replaced the strip malls and big box stores. The strength of the odor made Henry's eyes water.

"Tell Mark and Chris where we are. It's here. I know it is." Violet's nails tapped on her phone as she messaged someone in the coven.

Henry eased up on the speed, trying not to miss it. His instincts were on high alert, his muscles tense in his seat. He turned right, but found himself at a dead end, with a chain-link fence blocking his way. A graffiti-laden building with blown-out windows lay behind it. He shut off the engine.

"Is it in there?" asked Molly.

Henry breathed in again. "Yes. It's so strong here. I'm surprised the two of you can't pick it up."

"We don't smell anything," said Molly.

It made Henry feel a little better. His senses were more attuned than those of a human, even if he couldn't shift. He unbuckled his seatbelt and opened his door. Violet and Molly did the same.

"What are you guys doing?"

"We're going with you. Duh," said Violet. Molly also opened her door, ready to step out.

"Wait," said Henry, panicking. "You guys can't come."

"Why?" asked Violet.

"Henry, you can't go in on your own. We can protect each other. We're not powerless," said Molly. Her eyes were sharp and determined. He wouldn't be able to change her mind.

"Fine, but be careful."

They all climbed out, and Violet spotted a bent portion of the chain-link fence. Violet and Molly crawled through with little trouble, but Henry struggled and ended up having to pull the fence further apart. Henry stood in front of them protectively, letting his senses lead him. Violet and Molly used their phones like flashlights, but he didn't need them. Even as a human, his eyesight was keen in the dark.

Tall weeds covered most of the ground, and they walked around the litter strewn about. The whole place looked deserted, and Henry's ears only picked up the scurries of rats within its walls. When they reached the graffitied doors, they found them open. The metal chain and lock lay broken on the dirt.

"Stay close," said Henry. "And stay with me." He said it to Molly, although he would protect Violet too.

His wolf growled inside him, upset at leading his mate into danger. As much as Henry wished to calm the beast, his instincts were right to be mad. He wasn't positive how all of this was supposed to work, but knowing Molly, she wouldn't have stayed in the truck. What's more, he wasn't sure what was worse, bringing her with him, or leaving her behind with no guard. His wolf was just going to need to deal with it.

They entered the derelict building, more graffiti and litter covered the place. Whatever they had used it for didn't leave much of an impression on the remaining structure. The shapeshifter's stench overwhelmed Henry's senses. It was everywhere. He couldn't track it like this. It could be anywhere in the enormous building, and they were running out of time and being put in danger.

"Listen," Henry turned to Molly. The light from her phone made her brown eyes appear softer. "I need to shift. I can track it better."

"Okay," she replied.

Henry turned from them, a self-consciousness he'd never experienced before taking over. He took off his shirt, followed by his pants. He debated for a moment if he should take off his boxers, but he wasn't sure how many pairs he had left in the cabin. And he hoped Molly watched.

He peeled off his underwear and closed his eyes. Breathing in, his own heartbeat thrummed in his chest, and then he picked up another heart. Beating like a tiny drum in search of a rhythm. He smiled to himself. She was watching.

His bones throbbed, and he breathed through the excruciating pain of his muscles stretching. Followed by the blissful warmth of his fur covering his skin. The ground moved beneath his feet as his center of gravity changed and he fell onto his four legs. He opened his eyes, the world brighter and the smells so much stronger.

Violet stared at him, her mouth open in shock. The fear from the first night he shifted was gone from Molly's face, and in its place was curiosity. She had watched him shift into a man. She had never seen him turn into a wolf.

Henry tried to concentrate. In his wolf form, his nose burned with the stench. All his senses were heightened, and he knew from experience his thirst for revenge would multiply as well. The stronger the odor became, the more hatred he felt coursing through his veins. What he didn't expect was for Molly's scent to consume everything around him.

He found his need for her almost unbearable and wanted to take her away from this place. Every second they stayed there, the more danger he might put her in, and he realized his anger at himself eclipsed his thoughts of revenge.

But he couldn't abandon the plan. He knew where it was and started leading the witches towards it. He needed to run, but they wouldn't be able to catch up with him, so he kept a brisk pace. Their footsteps echoed along the empty building. Echoing off broken glass and windows covered in tarp. But he couldn't pick up anything else. If it was in the building, he would hear its soft padded feet reverberating through the walls. Or the pant of an animal who'd spent weeks running. But the building stood silent, except for the three of them.

Another scent intermingled with the others. Metallic and all too familiar. He found the room. Up six stories, four doors to the left of the staircase. He pointed to the closed door. Molly pushed it open, and the stink made him want to run in without another thought, and sink his teeth into the shapeshifter's neck. But he wouldn't leave Molly's side unless he knew it was safe.

He walked in first, his senses on high alert. Although the odor hung heavy in the room, it appeared empty.

"Is it in here?" asked Violet.

"Shhh," shushed Molly.

Henry was thankful to Molly for silencing her. Violet's voice echoed through the room, covering every other noise. He waded through the large room, sniffing all the while. The further in he went, the odor intensified, until his nose touched something fleshy. He peered up and whined.

"Henry?" asked Molly. He heard her footsteps approaching before she gasped.

"What?" asked Violet, but her steps soon stopped too.

They all stared at the half-eaten body. Henry could make out a leg with a still-attached foot, but that was it. The rest of the body was a mess.

Somewhere behind him, Violet wretched. He turned and glanced at Molly. Her eyes weren't on the body, and she looked only at him. He shook his head. He hoped she would understand.

"It's not here, is it?" she asked. "At least not anymore."

"But its dinner is," said Violet.

"Should we call Mark and Chris and call them off?"

"I think so," said Violet. "Unless Henry can you follow it?"

He ran out of the room and down the stairs. They struggled to keep up with him. But his anger made him run faster. He was always too late. Too late to save Malcolm. Too late to save anyone.

He stopped in front of the building and sniffed. But the stench only came from the warehouse. Every other direction offered nothing but fresh, although polluted air. It was here; it had to be.

Figs and amber overpowered his nose. Molly stood by him, breathless and watching what he did next. The fragrance was much stronger in his wolf form. He had no clue how he had resisted it for as long as he had. It was quickly pushing away the shapeshifter and his task from his mind. His self-control was working overtime. Already, he could see his body looming over hers, her lips on his.

"Anything?" asked Molly.

Henry turned to her and shifted back. His skin burst out in goosebumps as his fur receded. His bones shook again as they shrunk, and he watched as the world became less bright, darkness engulfing and deadening his senses further.

"Holy shit," said Violet behind him. "That's so cool!"

"It's a remarkable thing," said Molly. Henry grew hot with pride at her saying it.

"I lost the scent. It's all over the building. I think it may have been its hideout."

"It's not anymore?" asked Molly.

"Outside of that room, its scent wasn't as strong."

"So what now?" asked Violet. "You can't detect it leaving this place, can you?"

"No. The trail ends here."

"That person..." said Violet.

"I'll call River. We'll need to leave an anonymous tip," said Molly.

Molly approached Henry, his clothes in her arms. She handed them to him, avoiding his gaze. He turned to change, but he swore he caught Molly glancing down towards his bottom half. He grinned, pretending that he didn't notice.

They climbed back into the car. Violet yawned from her middle seat, and Henry checked his phone and realized it was half-past one. After a few minutes of driving, Violet's head rested on Molly's shoulder.

"We should stop for the night," said Henry.

"Are you sure?" asked Violet, sitting up straight again. "We can keep looking. I mean, can you pick up the scent anywhere else?"

"Its scent is everywhere, but not strong enough to lead me in the right direction. I'm sure the others will pick it up, too. We're not gonna find it tonight."

The reality that he would need to hunt the following night hit him in the chest. Another night where another person could find themselves as the shapeshifter's meal.

Chapter Fifteen

Henry dropped off Violet at her apartment and waited until she entered the building to drive away. He stretched, finding his muscles sore and tired. Shifting exerted a lot of energy, but normally he would be fine ten minutes later. But today his eyes drooped, heavy and glassy, and all he wanted was a nap.

So, the weakening began. He assumed he had more time. None of his pack mates waited this long. He remembered Brandon's wife claimed him in a few hours. Freddy in two days.

"Are you okay?" asked Molly.

"Well, seeing that we found another dead body and didn't find the shapeshifter tonight, I thought I would feel worse, but I'm just tired," he said.

It wasn't just the night's events, or his strength weakening, or the past couple of months running and chasing the shifter. His life had lost all sense of order since Malcolm's death. He'd been tired for months. Expecting Molly to make him whole wasn't fair to her. She couldn't fix half of the things he needed.

"When you were talking earlier about your brother," began Molly, "I was wondering, did he ever find a mate?"

"He didn't."

"Why is that?"

"Magic isn't an exact science," said Henry. He turned towards her and saw her smiling softly. It made his heart swell. "I'm not sure why he never did. But in some ways, it was a clean cut that way. He didn't leave anyone behind."

"He left you behind, and the others in the pack."

"It's different."

"He was still your family, your leader. It still hurts, I'm sure."

"If he had a family outside of the pack, it would have just been more heartbreaking. The way Brandon and Freddy are with their families, their wives would break without them. I don't know how they would carry on without their mate. Chris' dad was a wolf, but his mom wasn't his mate, and yet she wasn't the same after."

"Much deeper than a breakup?" asked Molly. Her voice was unsteady and hushed.

"Much, much deeper." He couldn't elaborate. Not in the way he wanted, he only just realized how his own heart broke every moment he wasn't with Molly. He couldn't think of losing her without being filled with an unfathomable grief.

"What did their wives think when it happened to them?" asked Molly.

"Brandon and Freddy's wives?"

"Yeah," she said. "Did they accept it?"

"Their families also had the wolf bloodline. So they understood what it meant."

"Do wolves only mate with people who already carry a gene for lycanthropy?"

"Most do, I think. I met a couple in Texas, where his mate is human. She has no lineage to werewolves."

Molly stayed quiet for a moment, staring straight ahead of her. Henry stole a glance, wanting to see her reaction.

He couldn't stand the silence anymore and asked, "What are you thinking about?"

She smiled. "Can't you tell with your super wolf's senses?"

"Reading minds is not one of the gifts of mating."

"Gifts of mating?" She turned towards him, and it took everything in Henry to focus on the road.

"There are some things a couple gains from mating. But that will only happen after you claim me."

"Claim you?" she asked.

"Yes."

"And how exactly do I claim you?" Henry's cheeks grew warm. He imagined himself on top of Molly, his cock poised to enter her. She laughed at seeing how red his face turned. A full belly laugh that made her throw her head back. "Right, stupid question. So what are these gifts, then?"

"We gain the ability to sense each other's presence, even if we're not in the same room. I can do a bit of it now, but you would gain it too. I can hear your heartbeat now, but it's not the same thing. Brandon once described it to me like he had two heartbeats in his chest. His and Whitney's." His hand touched his chest, and the steady thrum of his heart pulsed beneath his skin. It felt oddly lonely.

"What else?" asked Molly.

"I get stronger, and I'm only guessing here, but I think your magic would, too. It's rare, but there are stories of wolves being able to heal their mates when they're wounded." He didn't want to tell her the rest. He wouldn't reveal how weak he felt now without her in his life. Or how the bullet wounds from a few nights before throbbed in his chest.

"Anything else?" asked Molly.

"That's it."

"That's it?"

"Yup."

"You're lying," she said.

"We don't have that gift yet," he countered.

"I don't need a gift. You're as red as a tomato. Spill it." She turned her whole body, and he became keenly aware of her scent. He was almost at her house, so he slowed down, not wanting the conversation or the night to end.

"Well, just remember I was trying to protect your dignity," he laughed.

"My dignity? And what exactly can my dignity not handle?"

He licked his lips. "I've heard that the sex is incredible."

A soft, "Oh," escaped her. He didn't turn to look at her. He couldn't trust himself, not when she was this close and her scent played with his senses.

"I've heard nothing feels as good as slipping between the legs of your chosen mate. No pussy tastes as sweet, no body was made more for each other than that of chosen mates. When a wolf is first claimed, they won't leave the room with their mate for days. When Brandon found his mate, someone had to be brave to enter their house to make sure they were still alive. We had to be careful, because there is a possessiveness that wolves develop over their mate. There are old stories of people leaving with their throats torn out after entering the home of a newly mated pair."

"Did Brandon cut off your head when you went to check on him?" asked Molly. She sounded a little breathless. Henry tried not to read too much into it.

"I didn't check; Malcolm did." He laughed at the memory. Brandon had been the first. Henry hadn't believed Chris when he told him. Brandon? The guy, who had only ever been asked out once as a joke by a girl in the seventh grade, found his mate? Already? He had no game, no sense of flirting, and was thicker than a safe when it came to understanding women. Yet, he discovered Whitney. She had a wide smile, and a snort-filled laugh, and on seeing her one day in college, he knew.

"Brandon was missing for three days," explained Henry. "The need to have her was so intense and sudden that he hadn't bothered calling the rest of us to tell us where he was. So Malcolm followed his scent to her home. He went alone, but he didn't have to walk into the house because Whitney's cries carried to the backyard."

A fresh perfume broke through the memory, lingering under his nose. Making his mouth almost water. He focused on Molly. Her pulse was erratic, her breath shaky, and then he realized where the perfume came from. She was aroused. Her wetness pooling between her legs, making her panties slick. Henry gripped the steering wheel harder, feeling himself grow hard in his pants.

"I shouldn't have asked," said Molly with a nervous laugh.

Henry didn't answer, but he turned and gave her a tight smile. He made a mistake. Her pupils dilated, and her mouth parted just a little. He mustered all his willpower to not stop the car. He wanted to open her passenger door and nestle in between her legs and slip his tongue through her slick folds, breathing in the bouquet that now saturated the car. Wanting nothing more than to let his tongue travel to the little bud that he knew would drive her wild. He needed to hear her moan his name and beg for more.

He couldn't. Not yet. Not after she told him she needed more time. With a deep breath, he squashed down his disappointment. But his wolf thrashed in his chest. He'd never sensed it so distressed before, but he had to concentrate and ignore the animal.

Her house appeared much too soon. Molly unbuckled her seat belt, and Henry climbed out of the car, too. They walked to her door in silence. He contemplated whether he should kiss her. He needed to. The need was so overpowering, he almost felt like his skeleton would jump out of his skin to do it. Just as he knew that him giving her head wouldn't go well, he thought a kiss would be just as bad. She needed space. He could give it.

Molly gave him a soft goodbye as she unlocked the door and entered her home. Henry made sure to hear the click of her lock before he returned to his truck. He sat there for a moment, waiting for his hard-on to go down, but it was stubborn. The scent of Molly's skin and arousal lingered in the truck, not helping matters, and made the drive back to the cabin painful.

Chapter Sixteen

The pressure of his lips on her neck made Molly's skin erupt in goosebumps. His lips grazed her skin until his teeth found a hint of flesh to bite. Molly, on instinct, arched her back, but his hands pushed her down, keeping her pinned beneath him. He swallowed her whole. There wasn't an inch of her body left uncovered and cold. He growled in her ear. The sound should have scared her enough to push him away, but it had the opposite effect. It excited her even more.

"Right here, baby?" he asked, slipping a finger between her legs. But it wasn't Henry's fingers that found her clit, but her own. Her thumb circled it, and she melted further.

She didn't want to picture Henry. She tried not to. Any man would do, but it was Henry's warm eyes, staring down at her as he plunged his fingers inside of her. Or his large, broad chest, hard against her own soft breasts. His strong, yet gentle voice encouraging her to come on his fingers in her ear. His tongue was on her neck and on her lips.

Their conversation the night before replayed in her head. *I've heard that nothing feels as good as slipping between the legs of your chosen mate.* Her feet stayed rooted to the floor, unable to leave the front door when she got home. She wished he had kissed her. The craving for it shocked her. She would have kissed him back, and she wasn't sure if she would've stopped it there.

"Molly?" A tentative knock on the door made her sit up straight. Her blood pounded in her ears.

"Come in," she said, hoping they had heard nothing.

Lenore and Rosie entered, their smiles mischievous and suspicious. Lenore carried two mugs of coffee and offered Molly one.

"So," began Rosie, sitting on the bed, and tossing her black hair off her shoulders, "how was last night?"

"Fine," said Molly, unsure where she was going.

"How was Henry?" asked Lenore. She sat crisscross on Molly's bed with a look of genuine curiosity on her face. Her brown hair was in a floppy bun, and she looked like she had just gotten out of bed and wasted no time in coming and interrogating Molly.

"Fine."

"More than fine?"

"What are you two getting at? And don't think you can bribe me with coffee." Molly sipped her mug and recoiled. Lenore was the worst at making coffee in the house. They could have at least let Rosie make it if they were going to warm her up.

"Come on. We all saw the vibes during the meeting. Rosie and I had our suspicions, but we didn't want to say anything."

"Yeah, but then Violet told us what happened last night," said Rosie.

"And what did Violet tell you about last night?"

"Just read the group chat. It'll catch you up," laughed Rosie.

Molly groaned. Great, now everybody knew. Knew what, though, she had no clue.

"What's going on between you two?" asked Rosie.

"Nothing is going on between us."

"Look, we know you probably told Lola, but she won't tell us anything," said Lenore.

"Yeah, you can trust us. We won't say anything either."

"Yeah, right," said Molly, taking a sip of the coffee. She tried to remind herself why she had liked them in the first place.

"Listen, we all saw how Henry was looking at you," said Rosie.

"Like what?"

"Like we were all in the way of him banging you on the kitchen table," laughed Lenore. Rosie almost spat out her coffee.

"Okay, I'm done with this conversation," said Molly, standing up. She walked into her closet to change.

"Wait, wait, Molly, I'm sorry," said Lenore, but how sorry could she be in between giggles?

"What about you two? You were both all over Mark and Chris." Molly tried to throw it back on them, but they didn't seem embarrassed by it at all.

"Well, funny you should say that," started Rosie. Molly's stomach dropped. Oh no, had it happened to her too? Was she stuck with a love struck werewolf? "I might have a shot with Chris."

"A shot?" asked Molly.

"He plays a little hard to get, but I can seduce him."

Molly's pulse settled. It hadn't happened for them then. She was sure that she didn't need to seduce Henry at all. "I'm afraid to see what that even looks like."

"It's like one of those bird mating dances," said Lenore.

"Shut up," said Rosie.

"Listen, I have to get ready for work. Are you guys done?"

"Yes," Rosie rolled her eyes. "But Molly, you can tell us about you and Henry. We won't tell the others if you don't want us to."

"We won't put it in the group chat. We all like him," said Lenore. "And he's very cute and kind. Now that I'm saying it, why don't you want to date him?"

"That's not important right now, but I promise the second something happens, I'll tell you."

"Okay, ew, not right after it," Lenore faked gagged.

"Get out," said Molly. They rushed out of the room after that. Molly went into her bathroom and turned on the shower.

Henry's behavior was obvious to everyone. They understood only a certain version of events, and they wouldn't be able to guess all of it. She didn't know how to explain any of it to the coven. Who knows how they would react? She still couldn't quite make sense of it herself.

After a day of almost dropping every mug onto the floor, and non-stop rushes, Molly wanted nothing more than to enjoy an evening alone. But that wasn't the plan. It was another night of shapeshifter hunting, and Molly's nerves wouldn't settle, knowing Henry would soon arrive. She tried her best anyway to make the most of her late afternoon in her library, but thoughts of him slunk into her attention.

"Come in!" yelled Molly after the doorbell rang. She hoped her voice would carry to the front door, but if it was who she believed it to be, he would have no problem hearing her. A few seconds later, she confirmed her suspicions.

"Hello Molly," said Henry. His voice was tender, a little too familiar, and it flustered her.

"You're...um... early," she said without removing the book from her face.

"I was anxious."

"I didn't know wolves could get anxious."

"We can heal quickly, but we can still feel anxious."

"I'm sorry, that was dumb," she said, lowering the book. Henry stood before her, all muscle and warmth. His face relaxed as she looked at him. "We're you worried about tonight?"

"Yes, and no." He sat on the plush armchair opposite her. The deep-maroon upholstered chair was an antique, and it creaked beneath him. Molly stopped herself from telling him to sit on the floor. "I was anxious to see you."

"My opinion hasn't changed," she said, nervous to observe his reaction.

"I didn't think it would. I just wanted to see you. Make sure you're still alive. It's taken a lot of self-restraint to not park outside your house every night."

"My neighbors might call the police if they saw you do that."

"I don't doubt it."

"I'm okay, you know. I've set up protections and wards on my home. You don't have to worry about me."

"I shouldn't, but I still do. I can't turn that part of me off."

"Is that normal?"

"I'm not sure. Maybe? But I've never met anyone who's waited this long to be with their mate."

Molly didn't have a response to that. Something like guilt surfaced in her, but she was unsure why. She needed time. She needed to figure things out. Henry could wait. Love or lust could wait. She neglected that part of her life long enough. It was almost second nature not to think about it. But looking at Henry's forlorn gaze made her uncomfortable.

The silence grew long and awkward, and Molly needed to say something quickly before Henry made another comment that caused her to feel strange. "Who are your parents?"

"My parents?"

"I got told off by someone because I know nothing about your family."

"Who?"

"Just... someone." She didn't quite want to expose Camilla and all her ghosts so soon.

"They're both teachers. My mom is an eighth-grade social studies teacher, and my dad teaches high school English. My dad likes to fish, and my mother loves to bowl on the weekends with her friends. They have a bowling team. They've been married for over forty years." Henry stopped, an amused look on his face, and a smile on his lips. "What else do you want to know about them?"

"Did you like them growing up?"

"I did. My mom was very strict with me, though. If my grades were anything less than an A, I would get in trouble. But I guess that's just what happens when your parents are teachers. Malcolm was a kiss-ass. I swear he never did anything wrong. His grades were always perfect."

"It sounds nice."

"It was nice. I'm sure my teenage self didn't believe it was very nice, but I'm thankful for it now."

"Your parents are still alive?"

"Yes."

"You're very lucky."

"I don't always appreciate that."

They were quiet again for a moment, but Molly didn't sense the awkwardness as she thought about what he'd said.

"Did that satisfy a bit of your curiosity?"

"Some. I think the person who told me to ask about your family would want more."

"And who is this person?"

"Camilla."

"Camilla?"

"A ghost."

"What?"

"She lives in this house. She was just curious."

"I can't tell if you're being serious right now."

"Oh, I am serious."

"Can I meet her?"

"She'll meet you if she wants to."

"So, do I get any information about your parents?"

"Uh…" Her heart rate shot up, and it surprised her how much that made her nervous. But then she remembered Henry could hear her heartbeat.

"You don't have to tell me," he blurted, sensing her unease.

"I'm sorry."

"Don't apologize. Ask me more questions. I'll answer them."

She was thankful for that, but she wasn't sure what else she wanted to know. Every new piece of information brought him closer to her, and she wasn't sure if that was a good thing.

"Henry, have you had a girlfriend before?" What if that was the problem? Perhaps this man had never been with someone. His love sickness was nothing but an issue of experience. Of course, he'd be obsessed with his first crush.

But he dashed those thoughts with a hearty laugh. "Yeah, I've had girlfriends. Are you asking if I'm a virgin?" His laughter filled the small room.

"No! I—"

"Would you like me to prove it?"

"Henry—"

"I'm only teasing," he laughed.

"It was a dumb question."

"No, it wasn't dumb, just funny." His laugh died down, but a sigh replaced it. "You feel different from them."

"Different how?"

He opened his mouth to speak, but shut it hastily, shaking his head. "You wanted time. I'm going to give it to you."

"So you won't tell me?"

"I've told you enough."

"Hardly. I keep thinking you'll wake up and it'll go away and everything will go back to normal."

Henry followed the pattern on the armchair with his thumb, and she got the sense she really hurt him. "Is that what you want?"

"Would you give it to me if that's what I asked for?"

Henry didn't hesitate. "Yes."

Molly couldn't escape the pain in his voice.

"Your heart is beating very hard," he said.

"You can hear that?"

He nodded.

A terrible thought sprang up in her mind. *Tell him to go. Tell him you'll never consent. You'll never be with him. You can't be with him. TELL HIM!*

"Henry, I—"

"Oh my god, there you guys are," Violet's voice cut through the tension and Molly's courage. "Why are you guys in here? I thought we were supposed to be gone by now. And here I was worried I was going to get in trouble for being late."

"You're not late," said Molly, standing fast. "Let's get out of here."

Violet left, but before Molly could follow, a warm hand grabbed her, swinging her back. Henry's firm grip didn't scare her, but it was like touching a live wire. The energy was enough to shock her into silence.

"What were you going to say?" he asked.

She shook her head vigorously. "Nothing."

He didn't seem convinced, but remained silent as he let her go.

Chapter Seventeen

Molly bobbed next to Violet as Henry drove through town again. The cold air from the window made her shiver, but she didn't ask Henry to roll it up. He needed it open. She glanced at her phone periodically, making notes of the area they were in.

The coven and pack had moved further into the city by twenty miles. They each had to cover an area of 80 miles. The closer the shapeshifter got to the heart of the city, the more worried Molly became about exposure. Keeping a coven of witches and a pack of werewolves hidden was already challenging, but with a shapeshifter driven by hunger, it felt like they were toying with fate. Someone would slip up and alert the authorities to their door.

Henry had already stopped at three locations. The scent was strong, but they didn't detect the shapeshifter. Molly lost hope they would find it tonight. The others hadn't texted either.

As Molly came to terms with another wasted night, Henry slowed the truck.

"What is it?" asked Violet.

"It's close."

"Are you sure?" asked Molly. They were on a busy street full of bars and clubs that college students frequented. She had a hard time imagining a shapeshifter being able to blend in well.

"It's here," repeated Henry.

Anxiety churned inside her, making her keep Violet closer to her. Abandoned warehouses were one thing, but her magic would be tough to hide if she had to use it here. The crowded street presented another complication. Henry wouldn't risk shifting in front of mortals. He had no choice but to rely on his human senses. Although they were stronger than Molly's own, she now understood the pack's frustration with her when she told them not to shift. Seeing Henry in his werewolf form the previous night made her see just how much more powerful he was.

Henry led them forward, his nostrils flaring as he tried to take in as much of the scent as possible. It was a busy night with college kids everywhere braving the cold in their skimpiest outfits. Molly thought they looked silly, walking behind a large man sniffing the air, but everyone was too drunk to pay them a lot of attention. Henry stopped in front of a club, his eyebrows knitted in concentration. He motioned to Molly and Violet.

"In there?" asked Violet.

"Yes."

"Are you sure?"

"Only one way to know."

Molly and Violet passed by the bouncer with no issue, but he looked Henry up and down. Intimidated perhaps by someone much larger than him, he let him through without a word.

The music blared, and Molly wondered how Henry was going to find the shapeshifter in the chaos. The pumping music overwhelmed her senses. People yelled over the noise; the lights flashed overhead. Alcohol and strong perfume intermingled with sweat. It was like every other club she had been to before. Nothing seemed out of the ordinary, but these were the worst conditions for shapeshifter hunting.

"SEE ANYTHING?" yelled Violet. Molly shook her head.

A warm hand on Molly's waist beneath her jacket made her jump. She looked up and saw Henry bending his head towards her. "I'm going to check the back rooms and bathrooms. Stay here." His voice in her ear caused her to shiver.

She leaned into him, her nose brushing his hair. He stiffened as she got close to him. "Do you want us to come with you?"

"I'll be fine," he said, but his voice was harsh.

He left Violet and Molly in the middle of the club.

"DO YOU WANT A DRINK?"

"NO. WE'RE ON A JOB VIOLET."

"I DON'T THINK WE'RE GONNA FIND THIS THING IN HERE!"

Just then, Henry came back, looking dejected.

"ANYTHING?" asked Violet.

"NO."

"SO WHAT SHOULD WE DO?"

"IF WE DRIVE ANYMORE, WE'LL HIT THE AREA THAT MARK'S TEAM WAS SUPPOSED TO CHECK. I THINK WE'RE DONE."

"DRINKS!" yelled Violet, clapping her hands.

Henry laughed and motioned for them to wait. He joined the throng of people by the bar while they found a small booth at the back. Violet swayed to the music, enjoying the sight before her, but Molly fidgeted in her seat.

"HE'S SO CUTE," yelled Violet. Molly shushed her, pulling Violet down to her lips.

"He can hear you!" said Molly in her ear. Violet laughed and winked at her.

"Maybe I want him to."

"I read the group chat! Stop telling the girls about my business."

"He likes you. He looks at you like a little lost puppy, no pun intended."

"It's a bit more complicated than that."

"What do you mean?"

Molly contemplated telling her. Lola knew already anyway, so why not tell the rest? She knew why. It would make it real. Her silly daydreams and fears would be out in the open, and she would have to deal with it. She would handle the shapeshifter first, and Henry's weird wolf mating would have to wait.

Henry came back and passed out the drinks. He sat uncomfortably close to Molly. He didn't seem to notice her unease and missed Molly kicking Violet under the table after she gave her a wink. The booth was too small for the three of them, and his leg pressed against hers. He was so warm, and she fought the urge to lean into his chest. She noticed Violet's snide smile, observing her and Henry. Henry watched the people dancing, tapping his foot to the beat of the music.

"HEY, I CALLED SCOTT AND HE'S COMING TO PICK ME UP!"

"WHAT?" asked Molly. She panicked. Violet couldn't leave her alone with Henry.

"I'M TIRED AND I HAVE TO STUDY TOMORROW FOR A TEST. MY PROFESSOR WON'T LET ME USE SHAPESHIFTER HUNTING AS AN EXCUSE."

Molly tried to keep her composure in front of Henry, but she worried Violet wouldn't see her panic behind it. Not to mention, no matter how many deep breaths she took, she couldn't stop her heart from beating hard in her chest. Even with the deafening music, she knew Henry listened to it.

Violet soon got her text and left with a mischievous grin on her face. Molly doubted she had a test. More like an excuse to irritate her into Henry's arms.

Henry leaned into her ear once she was gone. "Should we go?" he asked. She didn't know what was worse: being stuck with him in a noisy, sweaty club, or going back to the truck alone with Henry. Her skin flushed, her heart beat faster as the scent of cedar emanated from his skin. She wanted to kiss him; she wished to do so much more. She wanted time, right? Why was she so horny for him?

"Let's stay for a bit," she replied. Enough time to cool down, at least. Her lips accidentally pressed against his ear, and he inhaled sharply.

"This doesn't seem to be your kind of place." His knuckles tensed around his drink, and she worried the glass would shatter in his hand.

"It's not, but what's wrong with a little change?" She didn't trust what she would do alone in the truck with him. Without her buffer, she worried about the conversations that could happen. Henry nodded, leaning away, but a part of her wished he wouldn't.

Something was happening to her. She couldn't explain it. Her magic boiled inside her. It was like a hundred fireworks exploding at once. She'd learned long ago to control her emotions. All magic was tied to emotion, but although nothing was going on, it thrashed inside her, threatening to fry the lights.

Henry's heat emanated from him, making her sweat even though they weren't touching. She fanned her face with a napkin, but it didn't help. Henry tensed next to her as she waved it.

She pulled off her coat and took another sip of her drink, watching the people dance and trying to ignore the wolf to her left. Her drink was stronger than she thought it would be. It almost tasted like battery acid, but it loosened her control. She glanced at Henry, only to find him staring at her. His warm eyes looked intense in the dark. Hungry. She leaned back towards Henry, and he stiffened at her side.

"What's wrong?" she asked.

"Nothing's wrong."

"You seem tense."

"That's because of you."

"Am I making you nervous?"

"Yes."

"Are you afraid I'm gonna run?"

"That wasn't at the top of my list."

"What is then?"

"If I tell you, I'll be going back on my promise to you. I said I'd give you more time."

Molly leaned away, finding his lips mere inches from hers. She couldn't bring herself to pull aside completely. Around him, she noticed her magic building. It was almost like a high rising to her head. She was sure with one small flick of her wrist, and very little energy, she could make all the bottles behind the bar explode.

"Do you dance?" she asked, trying to change the subject.

"Are you asking me to dance, Molly?"

"No!" His answer cut through her buzz, and the magic fizzled inside. "I was... I just.. I just meant..."

"You want to dance?" he pulled away, his smile broadening wide.

"I..." he stood up and offered his hand. Molly stared at it as if it would bite. She downed the rest of her drink, and Henry laughed, but it did little to ease the intensity of his gaze or the determination in his stance.

Against her better judgment, she took his hand. Her whole body shook, and she knew it wasn't from fear. It was as if his power flowed through her. It made her skin tingle, and she swore the ends of her fingertips were numb.

He led her to the dance floor, his grip on her tight, as if he wanted to stop her from escaping. The music blasted through the speakers; the bodies crushed against each other, and Molly's blood rushed.

She stood awkwardly, unsure of what to do. Henry leaned down until his face was inches from hers. "Do you need help?" he asked.

"I know how to dance," she scoffed.

"Prove it."

Henry's hands gripped her hips, and he turned her around. He pressed himself behind her. He swayed, and she bit her bottom lip as she moved with him. Letting herself enjoy the feeling of his body against hers. He was so solid and hard against her own soft body. She leaned her head back, so his chest supported it. She swore she sensed a soft vibration in his chest, but maybe that was the alcohol. The girls always teased her for being a lightweight, and right now she was glad for it. She wanted to test him. Feel him. If his wolf was so sure about them, then shouldn't she feel it, too?

Henry's grip tightened, turning her around. His eyes glowed yellow, and she wondered if the others noticed. His eyes glowed for her, and the idea sent a jolt through her. But it didn't scare her, and that was a surprise. He crushed her to his chest, and the pressure was marvelous. She wanted to feel more of him.

She stopped dancing, and so did Henry. Frozen in place, watching what she would do next. A soft smile spread across her lips. He waited for her. Waited for her to take the initiative. She loved a man who could follow directions.

She stood on her tiptoes, but her lips only reached just below his chin. He leaned his head a little, and she stretched herself out, holding on to him for support, until her lips crushed his. He bent down further, and she fell back onto the soles of her feet.

Blood rushed to her head as he kissed her deeper. His tongue slipped through her parted lips. She kissed him back hard, his hands grasping at every part of her body. Her hips, her back, her hair. Desperate for much more than a kiss.

If she didn't hold on to him, she was sure she would fall. She wanted nothing more than to push him down and take him there on the floor. In front of everyone in the club. Let them know he belonged to her.

Goddess, what was wrong with her?

She pulled away, her breathing heavy. Henry stared at her as if she were the best thing that had ever happened to him. His smile grew wider and wider the longer he looked.

Molly stepped back a little, noticing Henry's bruised lips. There was magic in that kiss. In their being together. She understood it now.

"It's true," she said.

"What is?" he asked.

She ran away from the dance floor, her head spinning. She wished to be alone. The cold air hit her square in her face. She breathed in as deeply as she could, but her lungs didn't get enough air.

Henry followed her out with her coat. She shook her head when he offered it to her. She let the breeze cool her down and, although she trembled from it, it steadied her.

"Are you okay?" asked Henry. He sounded scared, as if he had done something wrong.

"You weren't lying."

"About what? My wolf choosing you? I never would have lied about that."

"I know. I just... I think I had hoped..."

"That it wasn't true?" His eyes betrayed his hurt and pain.

"I didn't want it to be real."

"You felt it then? When I kissed you?"

Molly didn't answer. She couldn't; it would tell too much.

"It's different, isn't it? From all the other people you've kissed. It's never been like that. Right? Like your skin is on fire? Like if you don't have me right there and then, you might do something you'll regret?"

Molly looked away from his intense gaze. Henry grabbed her hand, bringing her to him. She still couldn't look him in the eye. Instead, she focused on the dirty concrete.

"Claim me, Molly. Why are you holding back? What haven't you told me?"

She peered up, his eyes gold. The warmth in them melted something in Molly's heart. A small piece of a much larger structure she created to keep her safe.

As Molly opened her mouth to answer, she heard a faint whistle. The melody drifted past the clamor of the club and froze her to the spot. Henry noticed the marked difference immediately.

"Molly?" he asked. His voice sounded far away.

The haunting tune continued, and she turned, expecting to see him there.

Bruce.

But he was dead. She'd seen the flames engulf him. She had gotten rid of the only evidence that she'd been there. The key buried outside her grandparents' home in Arizona. She had entombed it deep in the soil, breaking the caliche with a pick. Her sweat had fallen onto the dirt as she hit the hard deposit over and over until it gave way. But she needed every shred of evidence gone.

"Molly?" Henry grabbed her arm, but she pushed him away, following the song.

But there was no way to follow it. It engulfed all her senses, unable to tell her which direction it came from. The whistling stopped after a moment, and she wanted to throw up.

"Did you hear that?" she asked. She needed to know that she hadn't imagined it.

"Hear what?"

"The whistling?"

"Yeah, I did. Molly, what's going on?" His hands floated to her face, and the shock of his warmth brought her back to him. He wrapped his arms around her, bringing her in for a tight hug. Her body warmed to the core, and her magic surged again, making her lightheaded. But it wasn't enough to knock the fear out of her.

He led her to the car. Molly stole furtive looks over her shoulder, but she could only see people stumbling drunk through the streets.

Henry opened the car door for her, and she stepped in. The door closed behind her, and she jumped. He climbed in after and turned on the car, waiting for it to heat up.

"Molly, you need to tell me what happened back there." He held her shaky, freezing hands in his.

"I'm fine," she lied.

"You're not fine. I've never seen you like this. Please," he begged, kissing her hands. His breath warmed them a little, but not enough for her to feel better. "Please Molly. I know you're terrified. Your heart is pounding so fast. Just tell me. Trust me with this."

Molly turned to him. The truth played on the edge of her tongue. Tempting her to tell him. To let it go. Free herself from its clutches.

"Take me home," she said instead. Henry deflated, with a pained expression in his eyes. "Please, Henry. I just need to go home." Her voice caught between a sob and a hiccup.

Henry nodded. His right hand held both her freezing hands as he pulled out of the parking lot. He wouldn't let go of her hands the entire ride. But the urge to pull them away disappeared. She couldn't get warm enough. Henry focused on the road, but his whole body stayed tense.

When they finally reached her house, he hesitated before letting her go. He walked to her door, and Molly rushed to unlock it as fast as she could. She didn't say goodbye to Henry; she didn't have the heart to do so.

Molly locked the door behind her and ran to the kitchen. The ward she kept on the windowsill appeared undisturbed. It was a simple bowl of water and herbs mixed in. Nothing grew. No mold, no strange spikes. It looked the same as last week when she had placed it. She was safe.

For now.

CHAPTER EIGHTEEN

Henry woke up with his head pounding. He found it strange to experience a headache. He rubbed his temple and was surprised when it failed to ease the pain. His muscles ached and popped as he rose from his bed. He groaned, waiting a moment before he stood up. Were all these aches and pains normal for a human? How did they live like this?

He stumbled out of his room to see Mark eating breakfast, too engrossed in his book to notice Henry limping into the kitchen. He grabbed some eggs still left warm in the frying pan and sat next to him. That seemed to get his attention, as he dipped the book away from his face.

"Morning," said Mark cheerily.

"Morning," mumbled Henry.

"Bad night?"

"Bad week." He didn't elaborate, not that he needed to. Mark gave him such a pitying look, Henry almost wanted to tell him to stop it. "Where's Chris?"

"Not here."

"Where is he?"

"He didn't come home last night."

"What? Where are the witches that were with him?"

"Calm down. They're all fine. Although I expect one of them is better than fine," laughed Mark.

"What are you talking about?" asked Henry, his headache growing progressively worse.

"Chris was, how do I put this politely? Taken by a certain witch."

"Which one?"

"I think her name is Rosie. Strange name for someone so serious. She always gives me this look like she wants to beat me up, although now that I think of it, so does Chris. They might be a perfect match."

"She warms up to you. So, did his wolf choose her?"

"Please."

"Chris would never sleep with her. There's no way he'll do it. The day he breaks his monk's celibacy will be the day that hell freezes over."

"Grab a thermometer," joked Mark.

Chris was a lot of things — haughty, serious, quick to anger, and slow to trust. It made sense for his personality to keep girls at arm's length, the same way Malcolm had.

Everyone had their own idea of dating with fated mating looming over their heads. It made most dates a little more awkward, knowing that the first second mattered more than the rest of the date. While Malcolm and Chris dated infrequently, and almost never stayed with the same girl for very long, or didn't date period. Some, like Mark, just liked to have fun and not stick around for longer than necessary.

If Chris really had slept with Rosie, maybe more things were changing in the pack than their lack of a leader.

"Anyway, forget about Chris. How was your night? You came home late. Things settled between you and Molly?"

"No, if anything, they're worse," said Henry with a sigh. "I can't reach her. No matter how hard I try, those walls keep getting thicker and thicker."

"She'll yield. You'll see."

"I don't want her to yield. I want her to *want* me. If she just gave in, it wouldn't feel right." Henry sighed, his head falling to his hands.

Last night had been both the best and worst night of his life. He still felt the imprint of Molly's body on his. The feel of her ass pressed against him. The softness of her tongue on his. He could have lived the rest of his days in that tender moment. Blissful and unaware of the world around them. The shapeshifter was gone from his mind.

Then the cold shock. The walls that he wished he could tear with his claws. The ice he yearned to melt on his tongue. The woman he wanted just to hold.

She lied to him last night, and it stung. It was a bitter reminder that he wasn't there yet. That their fledging relationship couldn't hold them up. It crushed under the weight of Molly's secrets. Henry believed that pushing her on it would only crush it further.

"I'm going to check up on her," said Henry.

"You said yesterday we were going to work on a plan to catch the shapeshifter."

"And we will. I just need to see her for a minute. I'll come back, I promise."

Mark gave him a look like he didn't believe him.

"What?"

"Henry, I don't think you should go."

"Why?"

"We have work to do. I'm sorry, but you can't keep hanging around Molly and wait for her to change her mind. You can do that after we catch this thing." Mark didn't sound angry, only frustrated.

"I can do both. I have to."

Mark sighed, and it became apparent that nothing Henry said would change his mind. But he couldn't dwell on it. He'd visit Molly first and take care of the rest later.

Henry's headache pounded as he stood. "Do you have any ibuprofen?" asked Henry.

"Ibuprofen?" asked Mark.

"Never mind."

Henry left a bewildered Mark and got ready.

CHAPTER NINETEEN

Henry rang the doorbell of Molly's home and waited with an anxious heart. His ears perked to pick up any sound in the house, but the wind chimes tinkling covered any noise. The discordant melody aggravated his headache. If she ever did claim him, he would have to insist on getting rid of all the wind chimes.

He waited for a moment, but nobody answered. He tried not to panic and rang again. This time, he heard footsteps approaching the door. He had his speech in his head and had practiced on the ride over.

Molly. I know you have secrets, and you don't want to tell me. I get that. But if you're in danger, you need to tell me. It's up to me to keep you safe.

He repeated it under his breath. It sounded good in his head, but he recognized with one look, a squint of her eyes, or a wobble of her chin and he would forget it all.

The door opened, and Chris stood shirtless on the threshold. His face grew red, and the line between his frowned eyebrows dented further in.

"Chris?" asked Henry. "What are you doing here?"

"Chris, who's at the door?" Rosie skipped down the steps, wearing his hoodie. "Oh!" She placed her a hand over her mouth and giggled.

Henry smirked, and Chris looked like he wanted to kill him. So Mark had told him the truth, but he still had to see it for himself to believe it.

"Is Molly home?"

"No, she's not here," said Rosie. She pushed her black hair away from her face as she approached them and wrapped her arms around Chris' waist. He stiffened at her touch.

"Do you know where she is?"

"She might be at work," suggested Rosie.

Henry nodded and said goodbye. As he turned to leave, he saw Chris give him a scowl. His anger was palpable, but Henry couldn't tell if he directed it at him or Rosie.

Henry didn't have time to think about Chris' sex life. Whatever he did last night, he would have to deal with it now on his own. He had more important things to worry about.

He drove to Books & Beans, but when he asked the barista where Molly was, he told him she wasn't coming in. The news made Henry's stomach sink.

It wasn't safe for her. The shapeshifter was one thing, but there was something else in town that scared her. Something tied to the whistling they had heard the night before. Henry ran back to his car. He panicked, unsure of how he was going to find her.

He took a deep breath, trying to steady himself enough to come up with a plan. But his worry wound around his throat, threatening to choke him. He called Chris first.

"What?" spat Chris.

"What's wrong?"

"Nothing's wrong," he lied. "You called me. What do you want?"

"Does Rosie know where else Molly might be? A place she frequents or an errand she had to run?"

"I'm not with her."

"What are you talking about? I left you guys like ten minutes ago."

"Yeah, and I'm not with her anymore."

"Forget it." Henry hung up the phone. He didn't have time for Chris and his temper. He called Mark and explained the situation to him, and Mark told him he would call Lola.

Henry waited in the car. His pulse wouldn't slow down. Why hadn't they all exchanged numbers yet? Better yet, why wasn't he on the group chat he kept hearing about? His mind wove strange and frightening tales into his head. That was new, too. He never thought of himself as an anxious person, but it was as if, once it started, the stories wouldn't stop.

Molly was somewhere alone in the forest calling for help, and he had no clue where. Or she was already dead, in a ditch with a mountain lion chewing on her bones.

Mark called him, pulling him back from the brink of losing it. Henry answered on the first ring.

"Hey, so I talked to Lola, and she messaged everyone else. They're not sure where she is."

"Shit." Henry gripped the steering wheel, his knuckles turning white.

"Do you think she's in trouble?"

"I'm not sure. I'll call you back."

Henry hung up and took a deep breath. He wouldn't be able to find her if he panicked. But panic was giving way to anger. Not at her, but at himself. Wolves protected the pack. Not just the alpha, everyone. They were a community, and they were supposed to take care of one another. But Malcolm had died alone. What good was he as a werewolf if he couldn't even protect his brother, let alone his mate?

An idea crossed through the black hole that engulfed his mind. He could follow her scent. He had found her that way before. Following the intoxicating aroma of figs and amber that her skin emanated. But it would be impossible as a human.

His head hurt worse now than in the morning. Could he shift? He tested it, his bones and muscles vibrating under his skin. It would take a lot out of him, but it didn't matter. Not when it came to her.

He drove back to Molly's house, parking in her driveway. He stepped out of the truck and breathed in the air. The sun warmed the ground, and the snow melted in the streets, soaking the world in a humid blanket. Even then, Henry caught her scent, so familiar and inviting, he wanted to get lost in it. He walked to the forest on the edge of her property. The expanse of trees hid a walking trail. He wandered on the trail for a few feet before veering off it enough to hide in the shadows. The last thing he needed was surprising a hiker as he shifted.

It took more strength than he realized, and he panted as his four feet touched the earth. His legs shook under him. It was an odd sensation. Usually, shifting made him feel powerful. Unstoppable. But now, he wanted to shift back to a human and take a nap.

But he had a job to do. He breathed in, and her scent danced on his tongue. He imagined her walking along the paths in the evening in late summer. Her hands brushed against old trunks and blooming flowers.

He ran. Fast, even though his lungs burned. He didn't care if it required more energy. He didn't care about watching his steps as the soft padding of his feet scraped against jagged rocks. His breath came out in strangled huffs, but her scent took him further south, miles and miles away from her home.

He needed to find her, and quick, before the wolf in his soul skulked off. Before it reprimanded him for letting Molly out of his sight. Before, it left him entirely.

Would that be his end? A mortal once more. No longer strong, or wrapped around Molly like it was his life's purpose. If he was lucky, that would be all that would happen to him.

He followed the scent for twenty miles out of town. He was confused. What was out here? Was this part of her secret? His journey soon ended as the scent led him to a community center of some sort. He found some bushes near the entrance and hid.

He scanned the area. It wasn't a community center. It was an old folks' home. The wind carried her scent. He followed it, trying his best to keep to the shadows and bushes.

He found her outside, sitting on the patio furniture. Her radiant face turned to the sun, letting it warm her. Henry noticed someone sitting next to her. An older black woman with a wrinkled face and hands twisted from arthritis. She had a shock of white hair piled atop her head. A light smile on her lips erased years from her face.

"That sun!" exclaimed the older woman. "How I miss the sun!"

"You still miss the heat?" asked Molly.

"The hundred-degree weather, the sandstorms, the flash floods. I miss it all."

"Well, I like it here. We have all four seasons."

"I can live without snow. But I cannot live without you."

Molly smiled, turning to the older woman, and kissing her cheek. It clicked for Henry. It must be her grandmother. He could see the resemblance even through the creases. The same sharp jaw and delicate nose. He was sure they would have the same eyes, bright and intense, framed by the long lashes that tickled his ear the night before.

"So, I take it you didn't surprise me today to just lay in the sun with me?"

"Of course I did, Granny."

"Tell me the truth, baby."

Molly hesitated, biting her bottom lip. "Have you noticed anything weird or out of the ordinary lately?"

"No, why?"

"Nothing."

"You can't lie to me, baby. I've known you since you were this big." She held up her thumb and index finger.

"I'm not lying. I just want to know you're safe."

"What are you hiding?"

"Nothing, Granny, honest."

"You came here to make sure I was safe?"

"Yes. And I'm going to reinforce the protections in your home."

"I can set my own wards."

"I know, Granny, but it would give me peace of mind if I added some of my own."

"Okay, baby." Her grandmother pulled Molly in for a hug. Henry saw her melt into it, holding onto her for dear life. "You take such good care of me."

"I love taking care of you, Granny. Don't praise me for the bare minimum."

"You never do the bare minimum, Molly. You give too much." Molly smiled, looking out at the dried garden around them. Henry stiffened, afraid she would catch him, but her eyes passed through him.

"So, can I check your wards?"

"Whatever you need. But what are we going to do about the wolf?" Henry wasn't sure if he heard her correctly.

"What wolf?" asked Molly, her voice betraying her panic.

Granny pointed towards where he hid, her aim perfect. There was no use hiding, and he wanted to be closer to her anyway. He didn't glance at her; he knew she would be furious.

He sat by her, laying his head on his paws at her feet. "Interesting," he heard her grandmother say. "Does he just stay like that?" she asked.

"I'm sure he's staying a wolf because he doesn't want to be naked in front of you," said Molly with an angry sigh.

"Nothing I haven't seen before," laughed Granny.

Henry wanted to laugh too, but he thought it would be better not to.

"Henry, wait in the woods close to my car. I'll be out soon." Her voice was stern, as if he really were a dog. She stood, helping her grandmother up, and with one more glare sniped at him, they left for the building.

He did as she asked, sneaking back into the forest and waiting for her return. His mind turned to excuses and explanations. The anger in her eyes hurt him. All he wanted was to keep her safe. Why couldn't she understand that?

He waited for about thirty minutes before he saw Molly step outside. Her curls bounced around her head with each quick stride. She opened the passenger-side door for him, and he hopped in. He shifted as she walked to the other side. He could barely hang on to his wolf for much longer. The wolf faded from his consciousness, returning to the cavernous expanse within him. He stretched out his aching back as she closed the door.

Henry looked behind him and spotted a sweater in the back-seat and threw it over his lap.

"Can I ask why you followed me out here?" She wouldn't look at him, and Henry's heart sank.

"I was looking for you this morning, and I couldn't find you."

"So you stalked me?"

"No—"

"Because this seems like stalking."

"No one knew where you were, so I followed your scent. I wasn't chasing after your car like a dog."

Molly scoffed. "Isn't that what you're supposed to be doing with the shapeshifter? Sniffing it out? Not wasting your time following me!"

"I'm never wasting my time with you. And anyway, you can't just leave town and not tell anyone where you're going."

"You mean not tell you," huffed Molly.

"Well, yes, I am included in that. You don't even know what's out there, and you're risking your life like it is nothing."

"I'm not risking anything visiting my grandmother. I don't owe you a thing. And I'm fine. I don't need you to follow me like a shadow. I can take care of myself."

Her brow furrowed as she stared straight ahead of her as she drove. Henry wanted to apologize, but his anger took root. She was so stubborn. His wolf wanted to challenge him with their choice. And yet, through that anger, he needed to reach out and pull her into his lap. He wanted her to melt against him, like she had with her grandmother. He felt farther away from her, even after the kiss they shared.

"So," began Henry. He would get nowhere with her if they kept fighting. He needed to ease the tension and get her back on his side. "That's your grandmother?"

"Yes."

"Do you pay for her to stay there?"

"I do."

"Isn't that hard? I mean, that place was pretty swanky. It must cost a small fortune."

"Fortune and a half, but I make it work."

"Does nobody else in the family help or pitch in?"

"There is nobody else. It's just me."

"I'm sorry."

"There's nothing to be sorry about. I count myself lucky."

"Were you raised by your grandparents?"

"Not exactly. My mom died when I was nine, so my dad raised me after that. My grandparents helped him out a lot. Everyone else is gone now, though. I have a few aunts and cousins in Arizona, but my granny is all I have left of that life. I've been taking care of her since I was twenty."

"That's pretty young to have all that shouldered on you."

"I made it work. I think there comes a time when we're all turned into the caretakers of our parents and grandparents. My turn came a little sooner than most people."

"That must have been very difficult for you."

"I did what was right."

Henry watched her closely. The sharp slope of her nose and her long eyelashes framing her eyes made her appear much more delicate and naïve than she really was. He sensed the pride she had as she spoke about caring for her grandmother. Her family was everything to her. He liked that about her, but telling her that felt like trying to navigate around a landmine.

"You're not off the hook, Henry."

"What?" She turned towards him. Meeting her eyes for the first time that afternoon made his breath catch in his throat. God, she was beautiful. Even though her gaze was angry and upset, he didn't care as long as she focused it on him.

"You still followed me like a creep today."

"To keep you safe."

"You still don't get it."

"Get what?"

"I've taken care of myself all my adult life. I don't need your protection."

"You might not *need* it, but I can *give* it."

Her heart beat fiercely in his ear. Something about what he said scared her. Could he explore it without her running away again?

They reached her home faster than he wanted. Molly parked next to his car, but she didn't rush out. They had another round of shapeshifter hunting tonight. He doubted she would stick around long after they were done. This might be his only chance.

"I've noticed something about you, Molly."

"Oh?"

"We've only known each other for a short while—"

"You can say a week," she interrupted.

"A week." Her face was curious about what he would say next. "I've known you for a little over a week, and I've noticed you really care for your coven."

"Of course I care about the coven. They're like family."

"It's the way you care for them, Molly. I've seen the way you act around them. The way you make sure they're safe. If they've eaten. You take care of your grandmother. Hell, I even saw you ask Mark if he needed a sweater when he was here."

"He looked cold," said Molly defensively.

"We run hot," he laughed. "He didn't need a sweater."

"What's your point?" She was losing patience, and her heart rate hadn't slowed. It ticked like a clock in fast forward, reminding Henry of how little time they might have together if things didn't go the way he hoped it would.

"My point. Who takes care of you?"

Molly said nothing, taken aback by his question. He almost didn't think she would answer, but after a moment, she did. "I take care of myself. The coven takes care of me too, in their own way."

"Not in the way you take care of them. Does anyone carry your burdens? Would you even let them?"

She turned away, and Henry saw her eyes become glassy with tears. He struck a sensitive spot. The center behind her wall. He held it in palms and he stared at it, terrified of harming it further. It hurt to see it.

"No one's ever asked," she said.

Henry reached under her chin with his fingers, pulling her face up to him.

"I can take it. If you let me."

Molly sighed, a single tear falling from her eyes. He brushed it away lightly, to not leave an impression. Her pain in his hands, the fluttering of her lids as she tried not to cry more, the sound of her sniffling away the hurt — all of it built upon Henry's heart, leaving him yearning to kiss her deeply. Hold her against his chest and never let the shadows of her past touch her again.

"Your sweet Henry," she said. She pulled away from him and, as much as he wanted to hold on, he let her go. "My burdens, my problems, my life, even your strong shoulders couldn't carry it."

"You won't even let me try?"

"I can't risk you like that."

Henry wished he could understand what she meant. But like many things before, he knew that whatever secrets she held behind her wall, inside the sinewy gristle of her wound, she would eventually tell him.

He had to believe that.

Chapter Twenty

Molly laced her brown boots and put her curls up into a ponytail. She checked herself in the mirror, taking stock of her shapeshifter hunting outfit. After a few nights of failed attempts, she had perfected the balance between comfortable and functional. It was a small win that she could run and not freeze to death out there, but that was about all that was going right.

Five nights and they were no closer to catching the shapeshifter. On some excursions, the scent was too faint in their area to lead them anywhere, and a quick call to Mark or Chris told them they had found nothing, either. On other nights, according to Henry, the stench was so powerful it burned his nose, and yet they would return home dejected.

Molly stretched her muscles as she remembered the previous night's disappointment. They had followed a lead for ten miles, but somewhere along the path, Henry lost the scent again. In frustration, he had left a large boot-sized dent on the side of his truck. Grief had a funny way of changing people, because both Chris and Mark had stared at the dent in surprise when they arrived home. Neither of them made a comment, and Molly sensed Henry appreciated them for their silence.

She didn't sleep that night. Her thoughts kept her up. Henry didn't say that she was one of his frustrations, but she couldn't help but think that she wasn't helping. She dwelled on their conversation for days, feeling self-conscious that he had noticed anything about her at all. The pain and embarrassment of having someone know her was almost too much to bear. What else did he see when her guard was down?

Molly walked to her ancestors' altar by her window. She replaced the burned out candles and waved some incense over the images of her mother, father, grandparents, and great-grandparents. Her energy couldn't settle in her. An anxiousness crawled over her skin and made her chest tight. She tried to wave the sensation away with the smoke from the incense, but she couldn't shake the feeling. Something would go wrong tonight.

Her instincts were rarely wrong, but she ignored them. They were running out of time. They had only a week before the next full moon. If they didn't catch it by then, the werewolves would be at risk of animal control confusing them for the creature killing everyone. She needed to get a move on and leave. She only hoped the emotions would go away soon enough.

They had narrowed the circle yet again. The shapeshifter was getting closer to its intended target. It unnerved her to think about how systematic the creature was being, stalking around its prey.

She had discovered some information in Ellie's book about them. From what she gathered, shapeshifters were human, but the longer they stayed an animal, the more of its characteristics they would gain. It made her think that the shapeshifter they hunted must be more animal than human now. They hadn't discovered more dead bodies since the warehouse, but it was only a matter of time until the shapeshifter's hunger struck again.

River also couldn't provide a sample for them to use. Not even a speck of skin, blood, or hair was found on the bodies, only bite marks. Which left the coven no choice but to continue on their hunts.

The werewolves were getting restless. She noticed Mark and Chris especially grew annoyed that they didn't shift to hunt. They weren't as understanding as Henry, but then again, he acted like any instructions she gave were law. It wouldn't matter soon enough. They would take advantage of the full moon, whether or not she wanted them to shift.

The doorbell rang as she made her way downstairs. Rosie opened the front door, and on seeing Chris, flipped around, slapping him with her ponytail. Molly thought it strange, but she had no energy to confront her. Chris appeared bothered, but said nothing as he strode in. Henry followed, and he zeroed in on Molly like he had sonar.

Molly pretended not to notice and instead helped Violet with her hair, braiding it down her back. She couldn't stall forever, and they all climbed into Henry's truck. Violet sat between them again. Not that Molly gave her much of a choice. But Violet didn't seem to detect the awkwardness between them, chatting away as always.

"Where to first?" asked Violet.

"Chris told me he detected it when he went out to lunch today at a park. We'll go there."

Molly stayed quiet, her eyes on the road. Luckily, Violet filled the silence. Henry, for his part, didn't let the discomfort stop him from replying. Molly paid little attention to their conversation as the tightness in her chest grew.

But then Henry ceased talking. The air shifted, and Molly had to hold on to the dashboard as he stopped the truck.

"Is it here?" asked Violet.

"Yes," said Henry, as he unbuckled his seat belt.

They followed him and his constant sniffing. Molly thought he looked almost comical if their task wasn't so serious. The few houses around the park had most of their curtains drawn. There were no people out, yet Molly found it strange to find the place so empty even at night. Apart from a handful of raccoons searching for food in trashcans, there was no one else.

Molly shivered. Something was wrong. Her instincts flared, making her stomach sink.

"UP THERE!" shouted Violet.

Molly turned, and her breath caught at the sight. The shapeshifter hung from a lamppost. But it didn't look like a mountain lion. It didn't resemble any animal, but a strange combination of ape and wolf. Its arms stretched above its head as it swung from post to post, eyeing the three of them with eyes that resembled a goat's pupils. Short dark gray fur clung to its torso, but the fur on its arms was orange and long. Its teeth were sharp, jutting out of a canine-like face.

It pounced towards them, claws outstretched, and Henry shifted. His clothes ripped to shreds around them. The thing skipped past Henry and flew straight towards Molly. She reached into her pocket, grabbed a spell bottle, and threw the contents into the thing's face. It fell back, its clawed hands making ribbons of its own face as it tried to wipe off the potion. Thin lines of smoke floated off it.

Henry jumped in front of Molly, growling so low that it made her chest vibrate. Henry pounced on the shapeshifter before it could move again. Violet ran towards Molly, pulling her away from it. Henry's teeth gleamed in the dark. His canines bit down on the shapeshifter's fur. It screeched. The sound made Molly's ears ring.

The shapeshifter snapped at Henry, lacing its fingers around his neck. Molly watched in horror as the shapeshifter yanked him off of it by his throat. Henry flew, landing with a heavy thud on his side ten feet away.

The thing turned around, its beady eyes searching until they landed on Molly and Violet. Molly pulled a knife from her boot as it ran towards them. A hunter's knife, which she had boiled in hemlock and mandrake. Violet grabbed hers. The shapeshifter ran faster, and Molly didn't hesitate. She swiped the knife through the air. She thought she had hit something as the point of her knife met some resistance. A hot sting on her cheek made her fall back an inch, but the shapeshifter whipped away, holding on to its side. It hissed and stood again. Its eyes wouldn't move from her.

"Molly," said Violet. Fear laced through her voice. "What do we do?"

Molly glanced at Henry, but he lay still. *Please don't let him be dead.*

"Something's not right," said Molly. "Why is it still here? Why isn't it running away?"

The shapeshifter circled Violet and Molly. After all that talk about how much the shapeshifter stank, she now understood. It smelled purely of rot. The wind pushed its scent towards her, choking her lungs. Molly pressed her back against Violet's. Her heart beat wildly. The shapeshifter stopped circling and screamed. Violet covered her ears.

"What does it want?" asked Violet.

"It wants to eat."

The shapeshifter lunged, and Molly stood still, knife poised. But then the shapeshifter crashed sideways as Henry jumped onto its side. They rolled on the grass. It was hard to make out Henry amidst the mess of fur. Only Henry's teeth and the shapeshifter's claws shone in the dark. Henry pulled away long enough to howl. The shapeshifter answered in its own ear-splitting screech.

The shapeshifter's claws struck Henry, and he let out a whiny yelp. The rolling stopped, and the shapeshifter stood up straight, leaving a human Henry on the ground.

Molly stayed in front of Violet. She wouldn't move. She would fight. Her eyes darted to a lifeless Henry, hoping that the healing process had already begun. The shapeshifter seemed pleased with itself, kicking Henry once more with its hind legs.

"STOP IT!" yelled Molly. She waited, her hand on her knife. Her whole body shook. The shapeshifter noticed it. The lampposts swayed, and the ground beneath its feet quaked. "Come on, you piece of shit. COME ON!"

"I don't think taunting it is going to help us!"

As if it heard Violet, the shapeshifter stepped towards them, but it was exactly what Molly needed. With one quick breath, the nearest lamppost fell on top of it with an unsettling crunch. The thing unfurled its lips, exposing its sharp teeth. With some difficulty, it pulled itself from the wreckage, growling all the while and never breaking eye contact with Molly.

Instead of being on all fours, it stood on its hind legs, human-like. The fur receded from its face, but not fully. She could make out its lips, thin and chapped. A hairless chin followed, but it clung to its animal body. It should have unnerved her, and yet, with the adrenaline racing through her veins, her fear stayed at bay.

It took a running start, and Molly braced herself.

CHAPTER TWENTY-ONE

A howl broke through the silence. The shapeshifter turned towards it. Molly didn't. She ran and plunged the knife into its back. It screamed into the night and threw her off. She fell hard onto her side. The shapeshifter stood over her. Its eyes were wild with delight and pain. The fur returned to its face, covering the pale skin once again. It reached out, its claw tracing the scratch he had left behind. Was it savoring its handiwork?

It pulled its hand back, about to strike, before Violet ran towards them, wielding another knife. It stepped away, in time for the other two wolves to run from the forest and step in front of Molly. Their growls echoed through the empty park.

The shapeshifter fell back further, staring at the sight before it. The werewolf versions of Chris and Mark didn't let it stare for long, as they both leaped and chased it from the park.

"Molly, are you okay?" asked Violet, helping her up.

Molly didn't answer. She ran to Henry, falling by his side. His eyes were closed, and she placed her fingers on his neck. There was a pulse. She breathed a sigh of relief, but the relief didn't last. His abdomen lay shredded. Bite marks peppered his neck. Molly turned him onto his back to take better stock of his wounds. His arm appeared broken, too. But he would heal just like he had that first night.

Molly gasped as a hand grabbed her shoulder, but it was only Mark. He stood naked, along with Chris. They stared at Henry, worry etched on their features.

"It's pretty bad," said Molly. "We need to take him back to my house. It's closer."

Mark nodded, stooping to lift him up. He placed him on the truck bed, and Chris stayed behind with him. Molly tried to ignore the worried expressions on both their faces. Something didn't sit right with her, but she wouldn't allow herself to wallow in unhelpful fears. Not yet.

Mark sped and ran red lights to get to Molly's house. They made it there in record time, and Molly got to work.

"Place him on the table," she instructed Chris as he walked into the dining room with Henry in his arms.

She gathered what she needed. She wanted to set his arm and clean the wounds. Although his healing would take care of the infections and set his bones, Molly felt sick knowing the shapeshifter had Henry in its teeth. She had to clean it off him. Of the stink that clung to his flesh.

Amid the chaos, there was no room for fear. Worry would have to wait, as would the images of the shapeshifter that no doubt would haunt her dreams that night. There was only Henry, and so many things to get done. If she focused on that, she wouldn't fall apart.

She walked past Chris and inspected the wounds again. They looked just as bad as when he had been at the park. Blood still poured out of his abdomen when she removed the towel. She ignored it, thinking she had been too stressed to accurately assess the wounds earlier. She cleaned the wounds, fighting the urge to cry as he bled on her kitchen table. And yet, the bleeding wouldn't stop. The superficial scratches on his face didn't scab over.

"Why is it taking so long? It was faster before."

She turned and noticed Mark and Chris mumbling to each other.

"What's going on?"

They looked at each other but said nothing.

"What's happening?" Her voice came out raspy, as if she had been screaming for hours. "He's not... healing," she said. Realizing it made the fear poke through her concentration, cracking what little strength she had left.

"He's weaker, Molly," said Chris with as much softness as he could muster.

That alarmed her. She hadn't known Chris for long, but he'd never been gentle with anyone. "What do you mean, weaker?"

"He'll heal," Mark assured her.

She felt so desperate she wanted to tear out her hair, frustrated with their delicate approach. "What are you guys not saying?"

"He's weaker," said Mark, walking towards her, "because you two haven't claimed each other."

"What?"

She looked at Henry's still body. His chest moved, but only by a centimeter. Mark's warm hands wrapped around her arms. His thumbs ran over her skin, trying to soothe her. His touch felt so wrong to her.

"Fated mates are stronger together. But apart, they grow weaker. The longer a wolf waits, the weaker it will get. Until... until they can't shift."

"He didn't tell me." She wiped away her tears with the back of her hand.

"I know. This isn't your fault. Henry didn't want to tell you. He wanted to wait until you were ready to make the choice."

"He will heal, right?" she asked.

"He will," said Mark, but she couldn't tell if he was lying.

She turned away from them, her hands shaking. "Well, if he's going to heal slowly, then I have a job to do. Chris, the bathroom by the library, has bandages and gauze. Mark, I need you to go to my room. It's the third door on the right upstairs. In my closet, I have a shelf of scarves. He needs a sling." They left without saying a word, and Molly started on Henry.

Molly wondered how she had found herself in the same position, taking care of a werewolf. Before, there was a sense of curiosity and annoyance. Now she did it out of fear.

She was only half-aware of the others. She hardly noticed Chris handing her bandages. Or Mark's hands as he helped turn Henry on his side for her. With a task at hand, she could push some of the fear away. Henry consumed everything.

When Henry's torso was completely bandaged and his arm rested against his chest in a makeshift sling, Molly asked for Mark's help to carry him upstairs. They settled him in the guest bedroom. He looked peaceful in his sleep, and at the very least, that gave her some comfort.

"He'll be okay, Molly," said Mark.

"Have you ever seen a wolf take this long to heal?"

"No, but he has something I've never seen before."

"What?"

"A witch who cares about him."

Molly turned towards him. He had a perceptive look, and Molly wanted to ask him more. Did he think her selfish for waiting so long?

"I didn't mean for this to happen. I didn't want to hurt him."

"He won't think of it like that. Chris and I should stay. We can watch over the house."

Molly shook her head. "Don't be silly. We're well protected here, and anyway, I'm sure you're both exhausted."

"Are you sure?"

Molly turned back to Henry, sleeping peacefully in bed. "I'm sure."

She drifted to her room once they were gone, barely aware of what she did. Her mind was too wrapped up in Henry to pay attention to the blood she washed off her hands. The image of him lifeless on the ground wouldn't leave as she tried to get comfortable under the covers. The bed was too cold.

She woke up with a start every time she got too close to dozing off. Her thoughts drifted back to Henry. She thought of their conversation the day before. Henry wanted to carry her burdens, but he didn't realize that she had already begun to carry him too.

Chapter Twenty-Two

The first thing Henry noticed was that his chest burned. Ragged breaths made the pain worse. His eyes refused to budge for the longest time. He had no clue where he was, but there were slow and methodical footsteps by his ear. An icy hand pressed against his forehead, making him shiver. He didn't recognize the 'tut-tut' of the woman's voice, but he thought it oddly comforting. When he finally had the strength to open his eyes, he found the room empty.

Heavy blue curtains hung on the window, letting in a few slivers of moonlight onto his bed. The bed frame looked old, wooden. It creaked as he sat up. He groaned as he moved. The pain was almost unbearable. He didn't remember the last time he had been in so much pain. He tried to stretch, but the makeshift sling on his arm stopped him. The scarf bore Molly's familiar scent, and it centered him. A piece of her, no matter how small, set his mangled body at ease.

Molly.

He would have jumped out of bed if he could have. The night came back then, broken pieces he tried his best to make sense of. The last thing he remembered was howling. Letting it grow from somewhere deep in his chest, it left his mouth in a scream. He knew that no matter where Mark and Chris were, they would hear him. Given Henry's state now, they had gotten to him on time.

The shapeshifter didn't look how he'd first seen it. It no longer cared to appear like an animal, taking the shape of something unnatural. A mismatch of parts from different animals. Whatever it needed to create the perfect killing machine.

Henry remembered a mix of fear and anger coursing through his veins as he bit into its fur and as his claws dragged across the thing's body. He wondered how much damage he had inflicted on it because the shapeshifter had done a number on him. His abdomen ached, and no matter how hard he attempted to move, he couldn't.

He'd been too careless, especially with Molly and Violet. He should have called in reinforcements immediately, but at that moment, all he saw was Malcolm. His body was torn to shreds. His brother gone from this world, and haunting him until he destroyed the thing that killed him. But the shapeshifter was hungry, and it leaped through the streets with its teeth bared to bite Molly, ignoring any damage Henry had caused.

Henry stood up from the bed, his body swaying as he did. The ground beneath his feet was unsteady and treacherous, but that didn't stop him. Anger and determination ran through him. The shapeshifter tried to attack her tonight. He wouldn't rest until he knew she was safe.

He stumbled down the stairs, each step sending shoots of pain through his nerves. He made it to the front door, but unlocking it proved to be difficult. His fingers shook as he wrapped them around the doorknob. But he didn't let any of it stop him.

He stepped onto the porch and breathed in hard. The air was fresh, without a hint of the shapeshifter in the wind. He tried to will his wolf. Stir it awake so that his senses were better attuned. The silence inside his chest scared him.

"Henry?" He turned to find Molly standing behind him. Her arms wrapped around herself as the cold cut through her deep purple velvet robe. "What are you doing out of bed?" Her hands were icy on his shoulder blades.

"I didn't protect you."

"What? Stop it, come inside." Her fingers grabbed his good arm, and she tried to force him back.

"I can't. It wanted you tonight," he repeated.

He closed his eyes and willed himself to shift. His bones barely moved. The wolf in his center lightly stirred. It frightened him, panic beginning to close in around him. He tried it again, straining against the part of his soul that he had never needed to coax. His knees gave out, and he fell to the floor.

"Henry!" She tried to help him up, but he was too heavy. He tried to lift himself up, but he trembled as he did. He didn't want to leave the porch. Everything in him demanded that he stand watch and protect Molly.

"Stop it! You're in no condition to be running after the shapeshifter tonight!"

She helped hoist him up, and he grunted as he swayed on his feet. He held on to her, but he worried she would fall under his weight. The warmth of the house welcomed his shivering body, but his teeth wouldn't stop chattering.

"Do you think you can make it upstairs?" she asked him.

Henry couldn't answer without his voice shaking. He let her lead him. Each step was more difficult than the first. By the time they made it, Henry saw black spots in his eyesight.

They entered the same room he woke up in, and he crashed on the bed. Molly drew open the curtains, letting in more moonlight, and turned on the lamp by his bedside. Henry stared at her through the spots in his vision as she assessed the damage. She had a determined manner about her, but he saw an undercurrent of worry in her eyes. She sucked in air as she looked at his torso.

"You're bleeding again," she said.

"I'll heal."

"Slowly," said Molly.

Her voice cracked, and he reached his hand towards her. He wanted to feel her. She was the center. If he clung to her, he would be fine. But she left the room. He didn't have the strength to stop her.

She came back with more gauze and a bottle of something. She replaced the bandages on his torso, her touch light but firm. The room continued to swim in his vision, although he lay still.

"You're running a fever too," Molly's voice quivered.

Silent silver tears in the moonlight left wet trails on her lovely dark skin. Henry's guilt consumed him seeing her like this. He'd caused this. Brought the shapeshifter into town and put her in danger. His eyes fell on a long scratch across her cheek.

Whatever strength he had left made him sit up. He reached his hand to her face, and Molly didn't admonish him to get back into bed. He traced the cut. He didn't protect her. What good was he as a mate if he couldn't protect her?

"Lay back down, Henry." Her voice was steady even between sobs.

"Stay with me," he begged.

She wanted to fight it. He saw it in the way she avoided his gaze. He wasn't sure how horrible he looked, but he thought it was the reason she said yes. She took off her robe and slipped under the duvet next to Henry.

He trembled with the cold, but her warmth steadied the shivers of his fever. He laid his head on her chest. The scent of her skin was intoxicating between her breasts. The heavy perfume engulfed him, lessening the sharp stings in his body. Her heart beat beneath his ear, strong, steady, his.

He could sense sleep coming, enveloping him in a welcomed peace, but Molly's stable strum changed. She started shaking. His head bobbed with each of her sobs. He sat up and noticed her tear-striped face.

"Molly?" he asked, reaching to wipe each tear as it fell. "What's wrong?"

"I'm sorry," she said, wiping away her tears with the back of her hand. "I'm not normally like this. It's just been a long night."

"Molly, what is it?"

"It's because of me. You're not healing, and it's my fault."

"I will heal," he assured her.

"No, you won't. Mark told me. You're weak because I haven't claimed you."

Henry wanted to kill him. She didn't need to know. He didn't want her to know. Her decision would become tainted now.

"Why did you lie to me?" she asked.

"I want you to choose me because you love me. Not because you feel guilty about me becoming weaker. It's not right."

"What if I claimed you? Now? Would you heal?"

Henry smiled. He smoothed out the hair on her face, pushing back the tight curls so he could see her better. Her beauty stole his breath every time. Strangely, even crying, she was beautiful.

"I would heal," he said, the mere thought of her claiming him making his penis stir. "But I won't let you do it. Not like this."

"But look at you." Her eyes passed over his arm in the sling.

"I can't, not when you're so close."

Molly looked like she was about to protest, but he didn't want to hear her take the blame anymore. He pulled her face to his and kissed her. He tasted the saltiness of her tears on her lips. The shivers that ran through her body as his tongue entered her mouth excited him. He moved his good hand to her neck, letting himself relish her warmth. He kissed her deeply, and Molly shifted next to him, her hips pressing on his abdomen.

It happened again. That pull. The same one he had enjoyed at the club. A feeling so ancient it mingled with his instincts. A voice somewhere in his soul telling him to claim her. To fill her with him and never let her go. Even now, as he kissed her deeply, and her hips moved sharply against him, the pain in his arm vanished. Not only would he heal, but claiming her would fill him with power. More power than he had ever felt before. His wolf nearly jumped out of his skin at the sensation.

She pulled away, her breathing heavy. "I could claim you," she whispered.

"But is that what you want?" His wolf growled in his chest. Angry that he would question her.

"Will you be upset with me if I told you I wasn't sure?"

"I will never be upset with you," he said. She looked as if she didn't believe him.

"Go to sleep," she instructed, and shifted to lying down again. Henry followed, his head nestling in the crook of her neck. He breathed in deep, and he swore the heady scent of her worked as a sedative on his pain.

Her fingers smoothed away his hair from his face and traced the outline of his jaw. He relaxed into her hand. His eyes grew heavy, and for once, thoughts of the shapeshifter weren't the last images in his mind before he drifted off.

CHAPTER TWENTY-THREE

Molly woke up to a steady drum beneath her ear. The scent of herbs underneath Henry's gauze was strong, but he smelled woody and crisp, as if he had just come back from a run in the woods. She was glad the stench of the shapeshifter hadn't stuck to him.

The darkness remained, but dawn tinged it with a gray hue. She saw the hazy outline of a ghost by their bed, but on seeing Molly stir, they dissipated with a faint gasp. Henry stirred at the noise, but he stayed sleeping.

Molly was unsure when they had changed positions, but she enjoyed lying on his chest. He felt so sturdy beneath her. Like a tornado couldn't push him. She liked that about him.

She stretched, but Henry's arms wrapped around her. His arm seemed healed enough from how tightly he held her. She wanted to wake him and examine his wounds, but she was too comfortable to move. Exhaustion from the past few weeks adhered to her bones, and in his arms, she relaxed. She didn't think of the shapeshifter, or the night before, or of the choices in front of her. She thought only about how comfortable she felt. If she wasn't careful, she would fall asleep again.

But his hands moved, rubbing her back and massaging her muscles. He melted the tension out of her body, and she sighed in contentment. His hands idled on her ass and they tightened on her cheeks, giving them a firm squeeze. She laughed into his chest. Did he do that in his sleep? She was sure that the conscious Henry would have at least asked.

Her laughter shook him awake, and he stirred beneath her. A big yawn followed as his arms tightened around her again. He peered down at her and smiled when he saw her laughing.

"What's so funny?" he asked, his voice groggy and raspy.

"Did you just squeeze my ass while you were asleep?"

"What?" He started sitting up. Despite Molly's attempts to move, his arms remained wrapped around her, keeping her nestled on his chest as he sat up in bed. "I didn't squeeze your ass," he insisted.

"Yes, you did," she laughed harder.

"Are you telling me I got to squeeze your ass and I can't even remember it?" he groaned, and it made Molly laugh harder. She pulled his arms from around her waist and sat up. His hand went to her face, smoothing away the tangled curls. She liked the warmth of his hand and how gently he rearranged her hair. His fingers traced the cut on her cheek, and he sighed, frustrated with himself for not preventing it.

"Your arm's better," she said.

"So it would seem." He flexed his hand.

"Are you in pain?"

"Only a little."

"What about the rest of you?"

Henry pulled the gauze off his chest, like he was unwrapping a present. After he brushed some of the dried herbs, Molly examined the skin, raw and red but otherwise intact. She touched the skin beneath his belly button, where the largest laceration had been. The skin was hot to the touch, and as she brushed her fingers on it, Henry shuddered under her touch.

"Still sensitive?" she asked.

"Something like that."

Molly grew hot, a little embarrassed. She longed to run her hand against it again and see him shake beneath her fingertips. Something was wrong with her.

"You should go to a doctor. Make sure everything is okay," said Molly.

"I don't need a doctor when I have you."

"I'm no doctor."

"No? What are all these herbs for?"

"Ginger and cloves to stop infection. Yarrow, comfrey, and plantain aid in healing. It's not the same thing. And you're trying to change the subject."

"Doctors and werewolves don't mix. They'll send me to some secret government lab where they keep the aliens."

"You really think that's possible?"

"I'm not one to risk it."

His hand drifted back to her face, cupping it in his palms. "You had nothing to worry about," he said, pointing to his healed abdomen. "Good as new." He smiled, but Molly narrowed her eyes. She pressed her fingers against the spot beneath his belly button, and he hissed in pain.

"Good as new?" she asked. "You're still healing too slowly."

"But I am healing."

"That's not the point, Henry."

"Last night was not how I wanted you to find out."

"How did you want me to find out? With you dead?"

Henry grabbed her hand, caressing the skin, as if he wanted to buy himself time. "I was never going to tell you."

"Why? I don't like secrets, Henry. I deserved to know that."

"I realize that now. I'm fighting my instincts everyday waiting. My need for you, for your touch, it overpowers everything, and I forget I need time too. I want to know everything about you." His hand traveled up her arm, massaging her all the while. Molly closed her eyes as a strange, almost magical calm flowed through her. His touch softened something in her. She didn't even want to pull herself away from him.

"What do you want to know?"

"What's your middle name?"

Molly laughed, unable to help herself. "Jasmine."

"Molly Jasmine," he repeated the name slowly, tasting every syllable.

"What's yours?"

"I don't have one."

"Why?"

"My parents didn't see the need for one."

"What is your favorite thing in the world, then?"

"Besides you?"

"You cannot say me."

"Fine," he sighed. He stared off into space for a moment. The sun's rays illuminated his face, and his eyes had never looked more welcoming. "I love big family reunions. I have family in different parts of the country, and once every couple of years we all get together for these giant gatherings. Everyone comes, and my parents' house turns into this mess of people. It's just nice having everyone together."

"That's very... lovely." Henry grew sad, and he looked away from her for a moment, taking away the warmth she had gotten used to. "Are you thinking about Malcolm?" she asked.

"We can't read each other's minds yet, love."

Hearing his term of endearment made her heart flutter. Molly ran her hand through his hair, unable to stop herself from comforting him. He watched her with a sadness she hated to see.

"I know grief well. It's not something anyone can take away, but I wish I could," said Molly.

"I would never put that on you. My grief is just a part of me now. I don't think it will ever leave."

"One day it won't hurt as much."

"You know, I hunted the shapeshifter for three months. It was the longest time I had spent as a wolf. Something changes when you spend so much time in that state; you become more wolf than human. Some nights, I thought I was turning like the shifter, driven by instincts and hunger alone. But then I met you."

He cradled her face in his hands again, and Molly wanted to lean in. She wanted to feel his lips on hers again. Would it be as electric as before?

"You made me want to be a man again," continued Henry. "You made me see there was more than hunting. The shapeshifter is still there, but I'm not consumed by it anymore."

"You don't have to do this alone. You have the coven now. With all of us together, we'll find it."

A sad smile passed over Henry's lips. "You may not fully understand it, but my wolf made the right choice. You're perfect for me."

Molly couldn't stop her next movements, and yet Henry moved with her so smoothly, it was as if he had made the same decision in the exact moment she did. His lips crushed hers in an almost painful embrace. He was so solid against her, and yet his lips were incredibly soft. But Henry was voracious, as if was making up for all the days he hadn't kissed her. She didn't complain. The kiss left her breathless until she wasn't sure where he ended and she began.

Her hands wandered down his chest. His skin burned her fingertips, and yet she couldn't quite stop herself from touching him. Now that she had crossed the line, there was no going back.

No time for shyness. Or the voice in her head to tell her to slow down and stop.

But he hissed as she accidentally brushed up against the skin where last night's laceration had left him bleeding.

"I'm so sorry." She pulled away. "Did I hurt you?"

"It hurt a little, but, uh, that reaction wasn't because I was in pain." He cracked a mischievous smile.

"No?" asked Molly. The blood flowed down her body as she grew hotter. She should stop. She should get up and make breakfast. Find out what the coven was doing today and come up with a new plan. She shouldn't press her fingers on the spot again.

But her hand moved of its own volition. Her hand lingered lightly on his abdomen again, and he held his breath. She held it there, never taking her eyes off Henry. He looked incredulous and awed, wondering what she would do next.

"Do you want me to press it?" she asked.

"God, yes," he said.

She pushed down on his abdomen hard, and Henry winced.

"Okay, that hurt."

Molly couldn't help laughing, but that broke the spell. She got up from the bed, but Henry reached over, grabbing hold of her wrist. As much as she wanted to stay, the previous night's events were quickly catching up to her. Lying in bed with Henry got them no nearer to getting the shifter. They had no time to lose, and if she was going to figure out her feelings for Henry, she needed one thing off her plate.

As if the universe knew she required an out, Henry's phone rang on the bedside table. He reluctantly let go of her wrist and turned over, only to groan after reading the message.

"What is it?" asked Molly.

"It's Chris. He wants to meet up to plan for tonight. He didn't even ask me if I was feeling better, but that's Chris for you."

"You should go. We have a lot to do."

Henry stared for a moment, making her feel uncomfortable under his gaze. "You're right."

Henry stood only for Molly to remember that he didn't have any clothes. She whipped around instinctively to stare out the door.

"Sorry," he mumbled as she heard him scrambling for the sheets. When she turned back, he'd wrapped them around his waist in a makeshift skirt. "You wouldn't have any pants, would you?"

"I'll see what I can find."

Molly left the room quickly, and once in the hallway, took a deep breath. She made her way to the basement, where she was sure she would find some men's clothing. It offered enough of a distraction from the realization that she almost did something that she thought she wasn't ready for. She was getting closer to saying yes faster than she'd expected.

CHAPTER TWENTY-FOUR

I f Henry expected Chris to treat him kindly after almost getting eaten by the shapeshifter, he was sorely mistaken. All afternoon, as they pored over their plans in the cabin, Henry got the sense that his near miss to take out the shifter was bothering Chris. He knew that trying to get him to talk would be impossible. Chris liked to bottle everything up, but there was one person who would have been able to help.

Malcolm.

Every time Henry thought he had found the limit of what Malcolm did for them, something new popped up.

The forest around the cabin was still, and Henry could hear the birds singing as if nothing terrible was happening. The couch in the livingroom looked inviting, but he stood next to Chris staring down at the kitchen table, ignoring the ache in his legs.

Mark circled the area he assigned Henry for the night, but he couldn't help but wonder if it was pointless. The previous night had left him shaken, no matter how hard he had tried to play it off with Molly. His mortality shocked him. He'd gotten so used to never dealing with pain for long, and the strength his lycanthropy afforded him, that to feel sore even hours after the fact was strange to him. He hid it well from Molly, but he couldn't fool the pack.

"You okay?" asked Mark.

Henry stopped massaging his arm, not realizing that he had spent the past ten minutes trying to soothe the ache in his muscles. He wanted to sit down, but felt inclined to stand, not willing to show them how much pain he was in.

"I'm fine."

"You don't look fine."

"Yeah, well, I didn't appreciate you telling Molly the truth."

Mark bit his bottom lip. "I'm sorry, but what was I supposed to do? You looked dead, Henry. Molly was freaking out, and she knows you heal, and you wanted me to lie to her?"

"No, of course not. I'm sorry."

Chris scoffed, rolling his eyes, but he went back to the map without saying a word. Henry wanted to punch him.

"What?" asked Henry, making Chris finally turn to him. "Say it."

"I have nothing to say."

"Yes, you do. You've been acting like a child all day. What?"

"I don't want to say it. I don't want to cause more problems."

"When has that stopped you? You think I don't know about Rosie? Tell me, how was shifter hunting last night? Must have been awkward." Chris squeezed his fists, but Henry didn't care anymore. It felt good to let go of some of the smoldering anger for the shapeshifter and use it on someone else besides himself.

"It's almost like you don't even care about Malcolm."

A sharp sting in his chest knocked the breath out of him and colored his vision black. The anger, minuscule before, grew so large Henry expected he would burst.

Mark seemed to notice too as he placed himself between them. "Stop it. Don't do this now."

"I'd like to. I want to know why he would say such a thing." Henry's voice wasn't his own. He sensed his wolf peeking through his anger, overpowering him.

"Forget it," said Chris.

"No, finish it!"

Chris breathed through his nostrils. "You only care about Molly. You didn't even call us last night until it was almost too late. Why? Did you wanna appear like some sort of hero to your girlfriend? You're not looking anymore, are you? You're just with her."

"You have no clue what I've been through these past months—"

"It's not just about you, Henry! Malcolm was my family too!" Chris stepped back, shaking his head all the while. "You're not even taking this seriously."

"Of course I am. I can do both. I can hunt for the shapeshifter and be with Molly. Last night showed me that if I don't, I'll never be strong enough to kill the shifter."

Chris shook his head, and Henry realized that no matter how hard he tried to explain, Chris's stone heart would never understand. Not until it happened to him.

"You're wasting your time with Molly. It'll take her months to claim you, and by then it'll be too late. Either the shifter will leave this town, or it'll kill you."

Chris turned and left the cabin, and with him, Henry's anger left too. "He's wrong," said Henry, although he wasn't sure if he said it for Mark or himself.

Mark stared out the door, as if waiting for Chris to return. He pushed his dark blond hair from his face and returned to the map on the table.

"You're not going to say anything?" asked Henry.

"It's not gonna help either way."

"You agree with him."

"Not fully. I'm glad you found Molly. If anyone deserves a mate in this world, it's you."

"But..."

"But she's a weakness. Hopefully, the shifter didn't notice last night."

"Why would it have noticed?"

"Oh please, Henry, of course it noticed. Everyone sees how you're with her, and this thing is smart. It would be better if you stopped hunting with us."

"What?"

"At least until Molly claims you."

"I can't believe it."

Mark sighed, pushing his hair back again, unable to control his nervous habit. "Henry, be reasonable. Chris lacks tact, but he has a point. You almost died last night, and for a moment, I had to figure out what I would have to tell your mom. About how fucking devastated she would be after losing Malcolm to lose you, too."

"That won't happen."

"You don't know that. And believe it or not, Chris cares about you. That's why he's so upset, because he thought he would lose you, too."

Henry felt like he'd been punched in the stomach. Guilt flooded all his anger, extinguishing it and leaving him hollow. "I'm sorry. I never expected Molly to be so complicated."

Mark smiled softly to himself. "Of course she's complicated, Henry. She's yours."

"Not yet."

Mark turned back to the map, and Henry noticed him re-drawing the lines, erasing him from them. Henry stopped him, pulling his hand away from the map.

"Give me one more night."

"Are you sure you can? You still look... weak."

Henry tried not to let it show that his observation bothered him. "I'm fine. I'm not giving up on Malcolm."

Mark sighed, but Henry knew he wouldn't fight him on it. He would prove them wrong.

"Are you okay?" asked Violet, and Henry loosened his grip on the steering wheel.

"I'm fine," he said, but she gave him an expression like she didn't believe him.

The windows were all rolled down, giving Henry the ability to take in all the scents outside. Although with Molly near, his senses were incapable of detecting anything else but her.

He took another deep breath, trying to concentrate and not let his earlier argument with Chris cloud his mind. But it only half-worked because she pushed her curls away from her neck, engulfing the truck with another hit of her intoxicating scent.

Henry breathed in again, not giving himself the chance to let Chris win. Then, as if rising from the sulfurous depths of hell itself, the shapeshifter's scent wafted through the window. Henry stopped the truck abruptly.

The forest surrounded them. A popular hiking trail nearby meant that if they were lucky, they wouldn't bump into too many people this late at night. But Henry didn't think the shifter cared whether there were humans near.

"Where is it?" asked Violet.

"Not sure, but we should get out and see if we can follow the scent on foot."

As soon as the words left Henry's mouth, he wanted to take them back. The previous night's fight replayed in his head. The fear of leaving Molly unprotected choked his lungs. But it was too late. They were both already out of the truck.

Henry unbuckled his seat belt and followed them outside. The stench was so strong it made his eyes water. Henry sensed his wolf in his chest, and for the first time in his life, he wasn't sure he could shift. He felt much better than he had that morning, but he wasn't fully healed. His abdomen still hurt, and his arm was sore around the elbow. If he came face to face with the shifter, there was no way he was sure the night wouldn't end with Molly crying over him again.

They made their way through the woods, dodging branches and shrubbery until they found the path. The scent was overwhelming. Henry saw it in his mind. The elongated arms helped the creature swing from branch to branch. Its teeth were not unlike a sabertooth's canines pointing out of its face. Its arms wrapped around Molly while he was too weak to stop it.

Henry didn't realize that he had stopped walking.

"Henry?" asked Molly. She walked back towards him, her worry clear on her face.

"It's not here."

"What?"

"I... I thought it was here. It's not."

"Are you sure?"

"Yeah. It must be somewhere else."

"But—"

"It's not here," he said a little more forcefully. Molly pulled back an inch, and Henry hated himself for scaring her. "I'm sorry. I was wrong. It's not close."

"Okay, we'll keep driving," said Molly.

"No. Uh, we should stop for the night."

"Why? Don't we still have some territory to cover?"

"No, we got it. Let's go home."

Violet and Molly shared a concerned glance, and Henry got the sense that they weren't sure what to make of his sudden change of plan. As they made their way back to the car, he shot off a quick text to Mark, telling him where he sensed the shifter, but it wasn't enough to rid him of the guilt.

Chris was right. Faced with the choice of killing the shapeshifter or protecting Molly, he chose Molly.

He abandoned Malcolm.

Chapter Twenty-Five

When they reached her house, Molly realized she didn't want the night to end. She'd been so nervous all night that they would have to fight the shifter again that she wasn't able to speak for most of the ride. She was relieved when Henry said they could return home, and yet the anxiety wouldn't quite leave her.

He pulled into her driveway, and he got out of the car before she could stop him. Molly followed him to her door, and he waited for her to unlock it. She didn't try to stop him as he made his way inside, and she only realized after he started sniffing that he was making sure her house was clear.

Satisfied, he turned to leave, but Molly surprised herself by grabbing his arm. "Do you have to go so soon?"

Henry stared at the hand that held him and smiled. "I can stay."

"Is my house safe?" She had the answer to that, but she wanted to hear him say it.

"No shapeshifter here." He narrowed his eyes and, with some hesitation, pushed back the curls from her forehead. "What is it?"

Molly felt herself growing warm. She wasn't sure where this shyness had come from. "Can... can you stay? Here I mean. Tonight."

"You want me to stay over?"

"You don't have to—"

"But I want to."

"Okay."

"Do I have to sleep in the guest room?"

Molly smiled. "I guess not."

She led him upstairs and into her room. He didn't walk in right away, entering as if her room commanded reverence. Once inside, she found the same shyness taking hold as he took in all her stuff. Her belongings were all over the house, but her room felt more intimate. He took stock of her makeup and perfumes on the vanity, the paintings on the wall, and the small makeshift altar she kept for her ancestors by the window.

"I'm not sure what I was expecting," he said.

"It's a bedroom."

"It's your bedroom." He continued looking around, but something about his demeanor made her worry.

"Are you okay?"

"I'm great."

"You've been kind of off all night. You didn't even crack a joke with Violet."

"I've had a lot on my mind."

Molly wasn't sure whether to continue prying. A part of her wanted to; it almost felt like a right. Shouldn't she know what her *mate* was feeling? But maybe that wasn't something that belonged to her, not until she claimed him.

"Why did you ask me to stay?" he asked after a moment.

"I've been anxious all night. I'm really glad we didn't bump into the shapeshifter tonight because..." she stopped before she revealed more, but it was too late as he studied her.

"Because why?"

"I don't know," she said quickly, hoping that he would move on.

"Well, I have a confession to make."

"What?"

Henry sat on the bed and motioned her forward. Molly sat next to him, and before she questioned him, he kissed her. It took her by surprise, and she froze before she let herself kiss him back. The anxiety that had glued itself to her all day finally disappeared. It was as if everything that wasn't Henry faded into obscurity. He kissed her like it was all he had wanted to do since he had picked her up. Both urgent and hungry, but tender.

He pulled away a little too soon for her liking, and it surprised her how much she wanted to keep kissing him. With the desperate expression Henry gave her, she realized he wanted to do the same. It took a second before she remembered what he had said before.

"What did you want to confess?"

Henry released her hands, and the sudden chill shocked her. "I smelled the shapeshifter tonight. It was near us. Probably in that forest."

"What?"

"I lied to you."

"I don't understand. We could call reinforcements or cornered it. Done something."

"No, we couldn't."

"Why?"

"It was too close to you last time."

"But I'm better prepared today because of it."

"No. I can't let you do that."

"You were the one who got hurt. Not me."

"And if it weren't for Mark and Chris, you would be dead."

"That's not true."

"Molly, can you seriously tell me that there wasn't a moment last night where you thought you were going to die?"

She didn't reply. If she did, she knew the truth would hurt him. But her silence seemed answer enough for him.

"Tomorrow I'll meet the pack and tell them we'll hunt as wolves."

"Henry, that's dangerous in this town."

"I don't care. I put you at risk, Molly. I was completely unconscious, unable to help, and if I had woken up and found you dead, I would have never forgiven myself."

"You don't need to do this alone, Henry." Molly pushed his hand away and stood up, wanting to pace or do something with her anxious energy. "I want to help. Sure, there was a time when I would've loved for you to do this on your own, but..."

The words got stuck again. Why couldn't she bring herself to say it? It was so simple, but every time she got too close, an unknown fear gripped her throat. However, he gave her a look that told her he wouldn't let her get away with it again.

"What is it?"

"I... I care about you."

Henry blinked a few times, like he hadn't quite believed what he heard. "You care about me?"

"Yes."

"Molly..." The tenderness in his voice made her want to sit next to him, but she needed to stay standing and away from him if she was going to get this out.

"I care about you, and you weren't the only person worried last night. I thought you were going to die. You weren't moving or healing, and I had the worst guilt in the world knowing that I could have prevented your suffering."

"That's not what I want."

"I know."

"I want you to claim me when you're ready. I don't care how weak I get."

"But I do. I want to say yes, but something just isn't right yet, and I'm not sure why."

"I know." Henry walked over to her. She expected him to appear angry or sad, but he smiled at her as if what she said hadn't hurt him. "You're waiting until you love me."

That's what it was. She needed to love him. How did she not see it before? "I'm sorry."

"There's no need to apologize. I get it. I loved you from the moment I saw you standing in that kitchen talking to me like I was a dog."

"Well, to be fair, I thought you might have rabies."

Henry laughed, and that made her relax a little. "I won't lie to you anymore. Things are getting more... complicated. But I need you to stop hunting with me. You're a weakness for me, Molly, only I was too proud to admit it. As long as you're with me, I'll never be able to track the shifter and kill it."

"I don't think I can relax, knowing you're out there by your-self."

"I'll have the pack."

"It's not enough."

"Trust me. I'm not going anywhere."

Molly swallowed hard. What was scary to her was that she didn't want him to.

Chapter Twenty-Six

The night didn't last long after their conversation. Molly didn't realize just how exhausted she'd been until she was under the covers. If she had expected Henry to sleep on his side of the bed, she was wrong. As soon as she was in bed, he pulled her close until her back was on his chest. She liked it. His warmth acted like a sedative, and she fell asleep in record time.

With the morning light, Molly had to come to terms with what she had told Henry the night before. She lay in his arms for a while, thinking while he slept. He always looked peaceful asleep, and that was a comfort.

Did she need to love him to claim him? She wanted to say that she didn't. That she could fix everything with one quick decision. It's not that she didn't want to sleep with him. There were so many moments where kissing him felt so electric that she was sure she was about to push him down and straddle him. It was a small miracle that she had held out this long, but the weight of claiming stood in the way.

Henry stretched, finally releasing her from his chest, but she stayed put. He popped one eye open and smiled groggily. "Good morning."

"Sleep well?"

"Mm," he murmured, wrapping his arm around her again.

"Are you feeling stronger?" Henry stilled before squeezing her tight, as if that's what she meant. "Henry?"

He sighed, peering down at her. "I feel less sore, but not stronger."

"Right," she pushed herself up, and he let her go.

"It doesn't matter."

"Are you still going to hunt tonight with the pack?"

He sighed, rubbing his hands together awkwardly, as if all he really wanted to do was hold on to her again. "Yes. I'll see them later today, I'm sure."

"There's nothing I can say, is there? That would change your mind?"

"No."

Molly was about to argue, but Henry didn't let her as he pulled her into his arms. She wanted to fight him on it, say anything to alter things, but she knew it was useless.

"Stay with me," he said.

"It's not like I can go anywhere with your iron grip."

He laughed into her hair. It had been a while since she had wanted to impress someone, and she worried about what she looked like after sleeping so soundly. But Henry looked at her as if she had woken up looking like a goddess. He kissed her. The urgency from the night before was gone, and in its place was a gentleness she didn't quite expect from someone so strong. The longer they kissed, however, the more Molly felt her skin alight.

It was there again, that surge of power, flooding every nerve ending in her body until she was sure the house would explode if she weren't careful.

She pulled away for air and saw his eyes glowing gold. She caressed his face, letting her fingers trace his jaw. Henry shuddered beneath her touch, and she wanted to do more. Much more.

Her hand moved from his jaw to his throat, and he swallowed hard as she traced his veins. She continued her trail as her fingers traveled even lower on his chest. He licked his lips as his eyes fixed on her, dancing with curiosity about what she would do next.

Her hands swept against his marked abs, making her hand undulate as if they were waves. Henry's breath came harder, but he didn't question her or ask her to stop. She smiled and brought her hand lower. He stopped breathing as her hand slithered beneath the blankets at his waist. The heat of his skin burned as her fingers brushed against his pubic hair. Henry waited, and Molly moved centimeter by agonizing centimeter down until she touched his hot and hardened shaft.

Henry hissed as her fingers wrapped around it, and it excited her to imagine it inside her. She pumped a few times, taking stock of his length and girth. Henry's eyes rolled to the back of his head. Molly bit her bottom lip, her own need rising in her.

She wanted him. The fear of losing him still consumed her every thought. Her desperate attempts to heal him a few nights before made her realize just how much he mattered to her. It was strange, because apart from Granny and the coven, she never thought she would care about anyone else. And yet, here he was.

Molly pumped his cock faster, and he sat up straight. His hands reached for her face, to clutch her, but she leaned towards him to kiss him. He smashed his lips onto hers, unable to do much else. Watching him writhe and groan in pleasure made her happy. Each moan made her pump faster, wanting to caress him until he came. His cock twitched in her hand then, as his hot cum erupted in her hands. He lay back, his breath heavy. Molly watched his chest moving with each deep breath, and she fought the urge to kiss him.

"Fuck, Molly," he managed out.

He looked at her as if she were the most beautiful thing he had ever seen. He pulled her face to his and kissed her so deeply she realized that whatever resolve she had left was soon going to melt away. Her sex was heavy in her underwear. As she shifted, the slick wetness coated her underwear. She wished she could claim him. She needed more of him. More than one touch or one kiss. She wanted him inside her. Moving and pumping his hips until they were both covered in sweat and tangled in each other.

She pulled away after a moment, trying to let her thoughts catch up with her body. Could she do it? She wished to, and it terrified her. There was no taking it back after that. There wouldn't be a fight and a messy breakup. No ignored messages and mixed signals. They were as good as married, and it freaked her out.

Henry brushed the curls from her face again. He sat up and kissed her cheek on the cut that still stung. "Stop thinking," he said.

"I'm not thinking," she lied.

"Your mind is going a mile a minute. I can see it on your face." She looked away. "I can tell you want something, Molly. I can tell because you keep licking your lips. Your heart," he placed his hand above her left breast, and the touch was like a shock to her, "I can hear it. It's beating so fast. You're nervous. It's sweet. My beautiful Molly, scared."

"*Your* Molly?" she asked, a smile sneaking through the corners of her mouth.

"Do you hate that?"

"No," she whispered.

"Tell me what you want."

"I don't know what I want."

"Do you want me?" his eyes pleaded with her. She knew the answer that would hurt. The answer she would have said a few days ago. The answer she couldn't bring herself to say now, because everything had changed.

"Yes." Her heart hammered painfully. Henry smiled, caressing her neck with his fingertips.

"It scares you."

"It does."

"I'm not going to hurt you, Molly. I'm incapable of doing it. I'd sooner die than hurt you."

"What if I'm more scared of hurting you?"

"You can't hurt me."

"I'm hurting you now, aren't I? You're weaker because of me."

"Already forgiven," he said, kissing her on the base of her neck, and Molly's eyes shut.

"I could hurt you more," she protested. "I could never claim you. You would die."

"Already forgiven," he repeated, kissing her further down, his tongue in the valley between her breasts.

"Henry, be serious," Molly tried pulling him up by his chestnut hair.

He sighed and reluctantly pulled away from her chest. He pushed himself up until he was level with her face. "Everything you've already done, anything you could do, I have already forgiven it. You have hurt me in ways I didn't know someone could hurt me, and I have forgiven you. There's only one thing I would never forgive."

"And what is that?" she asked.

"Leaving this earth without me. I will never forgive you for that."

Before she said more, Henry kissed her again. This time, his kiss came laced with hunger. He pushed her down on her back and he kissed his way down. Each kiss was so hot against her skin she wondered if he still ran a fever. He moved further down and kissed her breasts, pebbling her nipple in his mouth and pulling her further from the excuses that piled up in her head.

He didn't linger there, as if he understood that her mind battled against her heart and he needed to keep her focused on the sensations in her body. Away from any thoughts that would pull her from him and this moment. She needed it. Needed him. She was far too excited to be scared anymore.

He kissed further down until he settled in between her legs and lazily planted kisses on her thighs. The cool air hit her as he pulled her pesky underwear aside and made her blush.

His hot tongue licked a path up her thighs. "You've bloomed for me," he said as he parted her with his fingers.

She shuddered as his hot breath replaced the cold air on her core. His tongue entered her, and she hitched her breath. He languorously licked her. From her entrance to her clit. He seemed to relish her taste. She grew even hotter at the idea and was a little embarrassed. But then she let go. And with every touch that jolted through her body, and every tender kiss that melted her further into the mattress, her fear disappeared.

Henry started circling her clit with his tongue, slow at first, but he quickened his pace as she made more sound. Each moan seemed to urge him along until she felt she was truly on the brink of her climax. He followed her lead. As she tightened her thighs around his head, he kept the pace. She pulled his hair. Not that she meant to, but he didn't seem bothered. Finally, she felt something at her entrance, sending her heart rate skyrocketing.

Two hot fingers slipped in and dragged on the upper wall. Molly moaned, and it only took a few strokes until she erupted. Henry licked her through her climax. Making sure he drew out her orgasm out as long as he could.

Chapter Twenty-Seven

Molly had to pull him off by his hair, but Henry followed, chuckling all the while. He collapsed next to her, breathless.

"They were right," he said. "Sweet as honey."

She covered her face and laughed into her palms. She wasn't sure whether she liked the comment. Henry moved, dipping her body closer to his. He pulled her hands from her face and kissed her. She smiled during the kiss, unable to help herself.

He lay down next to her, his fingers grazed her collarbone over and over. Molly blissfully stretched in his arms, but then her mind raced. She wanted more, much more. Why couldn't she just do it?

"You're thinking too much again," said Henry in her ear.

"Why do you always assume I'm thinking?"

"I swear I hear your brain whirring in that pretty head of yours."

"My heartbeat is one thing, but I doubt you can hear my brain."

Henry sat up, and she noticed the gold in his irises. "One day, Molly," he said, moving the hair from her face. "One day I will fuck you so good, you won't be able to think after. You will be too exhausted from pleasure for your mind to function."

Molly should have laughed, but she was excited. She didn't doubt he could.

"There you go." His fingers brushed her bottom lip stuck between her teeth. "Biting your lips again." Molly released her lip, and he smoothed out the creases imprinted by her teeth.

She was about to kiss him when a soft knock at the door interrupted her. *Oh no,* thought Molly, *the girls are here. How much did they hear?*

She felt mortified and pulled the sheet over Henry's chest and made sure her shirt covered her torso as she told the person knocking to come in.

Lenore popped in, her eyes covered by her hand.

"We're decent, Lenore," said Molly. "You don't have to cover your eyes."

"Can't be too careful after what I just heard," said Lenore. Henry laughed and tried to pull Molly closer to him. She pushed him away and sat further from him.

"What is it, Lenore?" asked Molly, growing hot with embarrassment.

"So, not sure if you've checked your phone, which I'm guessing you haven't because, well, you know..."

"Lenore!"

"Right, sorry." She giggled, still covering her eyes, and Molly wished she would open them already. Goddess only knew what she imagined right now. Probably Molly and Henry splayed out mid-act. "Ellie said River has a sample. They're coming over soon."

Henry turned to Molly, a fierce look in his eyes. This was it. They could find the shapeshifter.

"Okay," started Molly. "First, is Rosie home?"

"No, she's on her way to school."

"We can't risk it. Ask her to come back."

"I'll call her."

"Second, I need you not to tell the group chat what you heard this morning."

"Cool, well, I can do the first thing. Um, but it might already be too late for the last bit."

Molly groaned and rubbed her face with her hands. "Just go." Lenore giggled on her way out as she closed the door.

Molly sighed. Now the entire coven was onto them. Although it seemed like Henry was as subtle as a bear in her kitchen when he was near her. She didn't know how she was going to face them. By now, Violet and Lenore probably already had a running joke in the group chat about Henry's penis.

"You're great at that," said Henry. His smile was so wide it surprised her. He leaned over and grabbed her arm, pulling her closer. Molly went along, settling on his chest. "The way you take command over everything. It's so sexy."

"Sexy? Most people would say I'm bossy."

"You're not bossy; you're their leader."

"Yeah, well, clearly I'm a little too lenient on them, because they're going to tease the hell out of me because of this. I should be scarier. The kind of leader who is feared and respected."

"Nah, you're perfect. They respect you and love you. That's better than being feared."

"Was your brother feared?" she asked. His heart skipped a beat beneath her palm.

"No, he didn't have a mean bone in his body." Henry stayed silent a moment as his fingers glided over her arm.

"Stop thinking," she joked. Henry chuckled, pulling her hand up to kiss her open palm.

"How did you realize you wanted to be the leader of your coven?" he asked.

"I don't think I ever made the choice. It kind of just happened. Lola and I were friends before the Exclusion Act was passed. We realized it would be safer for us to practice our magic together. They caught Lola's mom. She was one of the first. Lola was really fragile after that. She needed my help to care for her and keep us safe."

"I can't even imagine what that must have been like."

"It was hard. But I took care of Granny. I could take care of Lola, too. It was the two of us for the longest time, and then we met Margaret and Violet. Margaret was the one who approached me first. She used to come into Books & Beans a lot to study when she was in college. And she saw me mix a little something into a rude customer's drink."

"About a year after, Rosie and Lenore popped out of nowhere. Lola met Lenore while she was doing her hair, and they joined too. Ellie is the most recent addition. We met her six months ago."

"So, did they choose you? To lead them?"

"I'm older and more experienced with magic, so they all kinda fell in line. I never chose to be a leader. But it fell on me."

"They trust your judgement."

"They're my family. Even though they all have their moments when they drive me up the wall, or cause truly disastrous consequences sometimes. I love them. And no family is perfect. But they're mine. They reach out to me to help them. They lean on me to protect them from this shit world that wants us dead. And the truth is half the time, Henry, I'm terrified." The idea made her voice falter for a beat, and he cupped her face.

"You *can* keep them safe."

Molly shook her head, and tears welled in her eyes. She couldn't pinpoint exactly what was causing the fear that brought her to tears. She pulled his hands off, but he laced his fingers with hers, unable to let her go.

"They're so sure of me," said Molly. "They're so sure that I can handle everything and anything that comes our way. But I'm not sure I can. I'm afraid of the day when I can't protect them because I understand what that's like. When you have no one to care for you. When there's no one to turn to for help."

"That day won't come."

"You don't know that."

"No, but I know you. And you made me realize something."

"What?"

"What happened to you, I think, happened to my brother. Malcolm was the first to shift. He was the oldest out of all of us. We flocked to him, and he enjoyed being the leader. He was so good at it. Whenever we needed guidance or someone to listen, he was there. And when he died, it felt like I lost more than a leader, or a brother, or a friend. I lost the person I trusted to guide me in the right direction. I've been so lost without him. And I keep wondering about what he would do if he were still here. And I always think he wouldn't be afraid. He would know exactly what to do. He wouldn't be second-guessing every move he made. But now I realize that's probably not true. He might have been afraid this entire time, and he hid it from me."

"Being a leader doesn't make you immune to fear," Henry continued, his finger running over hers. "If it did, you would stop being a good leader."

"Maybe you're right," sighed Molly.

"My offer still stands. I'll take care of you. The way you need. And I understand you say you can handle it. You don't need my help, but no one should do it all alone." His hands drifted to her face, wiping away her tears.

Goddess, why couldn't she accept it? Why was she hesitating?

"Let me take care of you. Let me carry your burdens. Let me be that person for you."

"It's kind of a lot."

"Not for me."

Molly opened her mouth to answer, but she couldn't figure out what to say. She didn't have to answer because the doorbell rang through the house. Three rings, a coven member.

"Come," she said, pulling herself away. "Ellie and River are here." He dropped his hands after a moment. Hurt by her non-answer, but Molly couldn't give him what he needed. She barely understood what she needed anymore.

CHAPTER TWENTY-EIGHT

Henry reached for his clothes on the floor, and he followed Molly out of the room. He wobbled a little on his feet. Molly had been a great distraction from the pain this morning, but he couldn't ignore the throbbing ache of his muscles, or the sharp twinge of every step as he walked downstairs. Although his wounds had healed, his body overall was taking longer to get better.

He found River and Ellie chatting with Rosie and Lenore. Lenore quieted as they entered the room, and Henry got the sense she had been talking about them. Not that he cared; his happiness was all-consuming.

It had been ages since he had last experienced such bliss and contentment. Molly hadn't claimed him, but what they shared only moments before felt much closer than a claiming. She had let him in. It was just an inch, but he would take it. Every new revelation entrusted to his undeserving ears made his heart hurt.

How he wished he had met her sooner. They'd already lost so much time, and he wanted nothing more than to turn back time and live every moment with her. He could see it in his mind. Molly, ten and lanky, with her hair curled about her head. Sixteen, and the edges of her beauty blooming. Twenty-one and enjoying the beginning of her freedom. He saw himself always there, and it pained him he wasn't.

Sometimes Henry thought his friends with mates had lied to him. Exaggerating their stories to make him and the others jealous. The morning proved them right. Every touch had felt electric to him. The mere memory of it made him want to steal Molly away from the coven and take her into his mouth again. Savor the nectar that coated her and drink it like a man dying of thirst.

"Henry, are you listening?" asked Molly.

Henry snapped out of his thoughts and nodded, but he had no clue what they were talking about.

"I should have given the sample to the cops, but I was able to sneak it away from the body before Brian noticed." River pulled a plastic bag from his pocket. Henry made out a few wisps of black-gray fur in the bag.

"Where did you find this again?" asked Henry, taking the bag to examine the fur against the light streaming from the window.

"It was embedded in a wound on a body the police brought in last night. The victim was a thirty-year-old man. Half-eaten, like all the others."

Henry felt his blood run cold. What if he had stopped it instead of running away with Molly? How many more people would this creature kill before Henry had the satisfaction of its foul blood dripping from his muzzle? He wouldn't give it another chance to kill again.

"Rosie," said Molly, handing her the bag.

Rosie stood up from the couch she slumped on. She dragged her feet and snatched the bag from Molly. Her fingers fumbled for the fur, and Henry worried she was going to drop it on the carpet.

He wasn't sure what he was waiting for. Rosie closed her hand over the fur and shut her eyes. It took a second, almost two, for her to open them again.

"You got the wrong guy," she said curtly.

"What?" asked Ellie. "You barely looked!"

"I don't have to look that long. It's not him."

Molly took a deep breath and in the most even voice Henry had ever heard her use said, "Rosie, what did you see?"

"I don't know some old guy." She rolled her eyes as if this were the most tedious task in the world.

"Why are you being so difficult right now?" asked Ellie.

"Difficult?" asked Rosie.

"Don't, Ellie, she's hurt and..." Lenore's words trailed off as Rosie shot her a warning glance, silencing her.

"No, don't you understand how much trouble River might be in if they found out that he's stealing evidence for us? And you won't even use it."

"Whatever, I was on my way to school to study for the MCAT before you guys decided it was so important for me to drop my future for a stupid game of hide and seek. I'm over it."

"Rosie, I'm sorry I called you over here. I know you're busy with school and stressed about it. But I need you to look again." Molly's voice was even but had an air of authority, and although Rosie glared at her, Henry knew she wouldn't disobey. But he read on the other's astonished expressions, this wasn't like Rosie. He wondered whether Chris was to blame for her sour attitude. He had an unnatural talent for putting everyone in a bad mood.

"Fine." Rosie huffed. Her eyes moved beneath her eyelids. The silence of the room pulled at Henry's nervousness as they waited. "It's not the shapeshifter." She opened her eyes and stuffed the hair back in the plastic bag. "All I saw was an old guy, like sixty, maybe seventy. He's living on an old, rundown boat. You know that lake by the graveyard? Close to where Margaret lives? That's where his boat is docked. Are you done with me?"

"Go," said Molly.

Rosie left in a hurry, not bothering to say goodbye to anyone.

Henry noticed Ellie looked upset, but River just ran his hand over her back, soothing her. Henry wanted to do the same for Molly, but he wasn't sure if his touch would be so welcome.

"What's her problem?" asked Ellie to Lenore.

"I wish I could tell you, but she told me not to tell anyone," said Lenore.

"Should I be worried?" asked Molly.

"No, it's just fuckboy stuff."

So it was about Chris, thought Henry.

"Well, that was useless," said River. "I'm sorry, guys. I thought the fur was the shapeshifters."

"It's still the only lead we've had this entire time," said Henry. "I've never seen the shapeshifter's human form. If I'm honest, I've long suspected that it's been an animal for too long and it can't shift back into a human. But maybe it's this person? We should still investigate it."

"The way Rosie described him, he might be too old and weak to have run across the country for months," said Ellie.

"But Henry's right," said Molly. "Even if it turns out to be nothing, it's all we have."

"Any information before we shift tomorrow can help us catch this thing."

"I'll come with you," said Molly. Henry's heart leaped with joy. "But, uh, it would be a good idea for you to call one of your boys over."

"Right," said Henry. He fought the urge to kiss her in front of the others. "I'll call Mark."

Molly, Mark, and Henry climbed out of the truck and approached the gates of the graveyard. Before they stepped over the threshold, Molly moved her hand across Henry's chest and stopped him from crossing. She reached into her pocket and pulled out three nickels and placed them on the grass by the gate.

"What's that for?" asked Mark as Molly led them in.

"I have enough spirits in my home. I don't want anything following us back."

"Coins will stop them?" asked Henry.

"Any small offering will do. I just used what I had."

The cemetery was long overgrown and neglected. Although there were fresh flowers over the newer graves, most of the gravestones bore dates from the eighteenth century. The moss on the stones obstructed most of the names and dates, but Henry could make out a few.

He kept his guard up, sniffing the air. The stench of the shapeshifter wafted faintly through the air. It stank no more than it did everywhere else. Perhaps Rosie had been right, and it was a dead end.

He sidestepped the grave of a man named Thomas Allman and followed Molly until they reached the lake nestled amongst the forest. A macabre journey to such a beautiful sight, but Henry doubted the pilgrims who chose the graveyard's location would have thought too long about the outcome of their planning. Just as the rich people who built their homes on the other side of the lake were completely at ease, having ghosts as their neighbors.

"Didn't you check this area?" asked Henry to Mark.

"Yeah, we did a few days ago. We didn't find anything then."

"Do you think that was the boat?" asked Molly, pointing to an old boat tied near the middle of the dock.

"Must be," said Henry. The rest of the boats on the lake were much newer. "Come on," said Henry, leading them forward.

The dock beneath their feet creaked with their combined weight. Henry worried it would break and wrapped his arm around Molly's waist. She pulled away a little, glancing back towards Mark, but Henry kept her close.

Henry knocked on the rusted door when they arrived at the boat. They waited as the boat swayed in the wind. Henry knocked again, but heard no answer. He tried to look through the dirt-caked windows, but that proved useless.

"Rosie was right. There's nothing here," said Mark.

"We can't leave yet," said Henry. "This is all we have." Henry walked back to the rusted door and heaved it. The door's hinges gave way, sprinkling red rust and crackled white paint into the water.

"Henry! This is someone's home!" said Molly.

"If he's not the shapeshifter, I promise I'll come back and fix it for the old man free of charge," he said, climbing into the boat. He heard a sigh behind him, but they still followed him inside.

The boat was tiny, with barely enough room for the three of them. Henry and Mark had to lean down to fit. Takeout containers, broken rope, old newspapers, and plastic tubs filled with clothes filled the space. There was a small makeshift bed in the corner by a dirty window. Piles of clothes littered every corner, and it was hard to move around without stepping on a pile.

"I don't think this is the shapeshifter," said Mark.

Henry couldn't smell a shifter in the place. It smelled of the dirty lake water and rotten food. He thought it strange that the shapeshifter stench saturated the outside, but it didn't permeate the boat or its belongings.

"Rosie had a point," said Henry. "We have the wrong person."

Henry sighed, frustrated. This was their only lead before the full moon, and it led nowhere. He couldn't understand how a creature only concerned with hunger could outsmart a pack of wolves and a coven of witches.

A small, sharp inhale made him turn to Molly. Her heart pounded in his ear. He hastened to her, making the boat sway with his weight.

"What is it?"

"Nothing," she lied.

"What?" he asked. Why was she lying to him?

"You're right; there's nothing here."

"Molly, what's wrong?"

"Nothing's wrong. Let's just go. You broke this man's boat, and I don't want him to catch us in here too."

He wanted to argue, but he noticed Mark shuffling uncomfortably, watching them. Whatever troubled Molly, he knew she didn't want him, let alone Mark, to know.

"Fine," he said.

He emerged from the boat and helped Molly off. He observed her anxiously as they rushed out of the graveyard. Molly walked faster than the rest of them. She didn't just want to leave the graveyard; he realized. If he and Mark hadn't been there, he was sure she would have run out.

He had been patient with her. Too patient. Every secret, every lie, put her in danger. He didn't understand what she could be running from. How many lives had his Molly lived? How many of those lives would she ever let him enter? Henry had hope, but it slipped from his grasp, and with it, his patience.

CHAPTER TWENTY-NINE

Molly locked her bedroom door, leaving a confused Henry and Mark downstairs. The only lie she scrounged up in her panic was that she needed to take a nap. It wasn't very convincing, but she had little else to protect her now.

Each breath in the car had hurt her lungs, and she tried hard not to glance at Henry. One look from him and she was sure she would break beneath her secrets. He might hear her heart, but thankfully not her mind. The last thing she wanted to do was answer questions. Questions led to dark places she had long left abandoned.

With shaky hands, she pulled a photograph from her back pocket. It was old and dirty, just like everything else on the boat. Although frayed and yellowed, the image was clear enough for Molly to make out.

Her.

Eighteen and with a smile that had yet to experience the worst pain in her life. She wore a purple prom dress, with a corsage from her date wrapped around her wrist. She had styled her hair in braids, piled atop her head in an elaborate updo. Her two friends, Sadie and Monica, flanked her on either side. She hadn't spoken to them in years. Seeing them again filled her with sadness, but she couldn't focus on that.

He was back. The photo proved it. Bruce. It had to be him. Who else would have the photograph? Who else knew the tune he would whistle from some forgotten show from the fifties?

No matter how many times she tried to erase Bruce from her memory, every interaction with him seemed embedded in her mind. Wriggling maggot-like memories she wished to squash if only she could reach inside her brain to do so.

She remembered this day perfectly. The hot Arizona heat as she and her friends posed outside of her dad's home in their dresses. She even remembered the joke Monica had made about her date. Something about the size of his feet that caused her to giggle. But then the whistling started.

It sent chills through her now, just to remember it. He said he was passing through. Molly didn't believe it. He glanced at her while her dad wasn't looking. His sinister eyes roamed the tight fit of her dress. His pale skin looked sickly, and she never understood how someone who lived in the same sunny city as her never got a tan.

Goddess, she hated him even then. But he was just a gross, creepy dude back then. He hadn't yet done the worst. He hadn't yet slithered into her life. No, that would happen two years later.

The air felt thick, so Molly ran to the window to let in more air. But the room was still too stuffy. The incense from her offering to her ancestors lingered from the morning, and she breathed in too much of it.

"Fuck, fuck, fuck," said Molly, unable to stop her tears.

It couldn't be Bruce. He was dead. He was supposed to be dead. Was he looking for her? Her breath came even quicker at the thought.

She assumed she had left it all behind when she and her grandmother ran away. But it never left. She realized the scared, nervous girl had burrowed inside of her, like a second skeleton shoved into her body. It threatened to jump out of her skin, erasing the years of work she had put in to rebuild her life.

Molly fought against seeing it. From acknowledging the part of herself that she had kept hidden. A part of herself she liked to pretend didn't exist. It screamed at her.

A soft knock on her door made her jump. Her heart rate shot up so painfully high she was sure her heart would squish out between her ribs.

"Molly," Henry said behind the locked door. "Molly, open the door," he begged.

She couldn't. Her hands shook on either side of her body. Tears welled up in her eyes. Fear, genuine fear, gripped her, and her muscles seized.

"Molly?" he called again, his voice desperate.

She opened her mouth to speak and choked out, "I'm fine." She didn't recognize her own voice. It croaked frog-like in her throat.

"Then open the door. Let me see your face when you lie to me."

Molly couldn't think of anything worse than Henry seeing her this way. "Leave Henry," she said between gasps for air.

"No."

"LEAVE," she screamed. That did it. All the air disappeared, and Molly gasped. She stumbled to her bed, trying to remember how to breathe. It came so easily before. Why couldn't she do it now?

"Molly!" yelled Henry through the door, but it sounded so far away. Nothing could reach her.

She gripped her sheets, struggling to steady herself, and closed her eyes to better concentrate. It didn't pass. But through her labored breathing, she heard a crash. She turned to see the door off its hinges and Henry running towards her.

He gently pulled her onto his lap. He smoothed the hair away from her sweaty face.

"Molly, breathe for me," he said. Desperation laced his voice, and Molly tried, but somewhere between her lungs and her throat, her breath stalled. "Breathe with me," he instructed.

Henry took a deep breath, and Molly tried to follow it. She took a small breath. Small, but it helped. She tried again, following his breathing as his hands ran through her tight body, soothing it away.

"There you go, love. You've got it." Molly followed his breath until her own breath flowed smoother. She shook in his arms. Her chest hurt, and exhaustion made her eyelids heavy.

Henry laid her on his chest, and she appreciated the steady thrum under her ear. Her heart slowed, following his own. She breathed with him until they were one. One breath, one heartbeat, one body. His hands roved beneath her shirt, warming her cold, clammy skin.

Her eyelids closed of their own accord, and Molly fought it. She didn't want to sleep. She needed to plan her next move, figure out if Bruce was even alive. But she couldn't. A combination of Henry's heat and his steadying whispered hum pulled her under.

CHAPTER THIRTY

Molly jolted awake at the sound of a car honking down her street. She shot up, her heart in her throat, but a pair of hands next to her drifted to her waist, pulling her back down on the bed. Henry pulled her into his chest, giving her a tight squeeze. Molly melted into his embrace, sleep threatening to engulf her again.

"How'd you sleep?" asked Henry as he pushed the curls away from her face.

"Okay."

Henry said nothing and nestled her against him.

"Have you been here this whole time?" she asked.

"I left for a bit. I had to repair your door." He sighed. It sounded like any second away from her had been a serious sacrifice. "I did what I could with what I found in the garage, but I'll fix it later."

He didn't ask her about the boat or about the panic attack, and she was grateful for it.

"You didn't have to stay with me," said Molly. She barely made out Henry's face in the dark. He had wasted an entire day of hunting, and it filled her with guilt. They only had so much time left before it would strike again, and yet he didn't look at all annoyed to be there with her.

"I promised I would take care of you," he whispered. His finger trailed the outline of her hips. "I couldn't leave you."

"Did I scare you?"

"God, you don't even know." He pushed himself up, and his eyes glowed gold before returning to their usual brown. "I... I thought you were dying. I'm not apologizing for your door. I've already told you what I can't forgive and when I couldn't get to you... I thought I had felt pain before, but nothing compared to the fear I had in that moment."

Henry cupped her face, and his warmth made her relax further into him. She felt embarrassed by her panic attack, but understood he didn't care about that.

She'd done it. She'd hurt him. Yet, there he lay in her bed. Her head was trapped in his gentle hands. The secrets that Molly kept in the darkest and long-abandoned parts of her heart were urging her to speak. She wanted them out. To be freed of them. Freedom came with a price, or so she had thought. As she met Henry's warm gaze, she knew she wouldn't have to pay. He had no use for it.

She realized then that her secrets only kept her safe while she remained alone. She lived on borrowed time. Her life was fuller now. With a coven full of women who loved her and depended on her, and a werewolf pack she was starting to like. Her secret endangered her and her life, but she would never let it endanger the coven and the man she recognized she loved.

She loved Henry, and the force of it knocked her breath from her lungs. It had no beginning. No place she could pinpoint and say that was when things changed for her. Henry didn't see it. Not as he worried over her and caressed her nerve-wracked body. Or as he planted soft kisses on her forehead. But each touch of care made the feelings in her rise.

"Molly?" Henry's hand traveled down to her chest, and the skin over her heart grew hot. "Why is your heart beating so fast?"

"Kiss me."

Henry gave her a perplexed look, but Molly pushed herself up and met his lips with hers. He was apprehensive at first, unsure where she led, but he followed anyway. Soon his hands wrapped around her, pulling her in closer. The air surrounding her crackled.

Power. That strange, overpowering electric charge she had felt in the club now unleashed itself in the room, and it encased her like a blanket.

His lips parted, and she slipped her tongue in, tasting him. He shuddered beneath her, but his hands held on to her steadily. The power continued to swell with each breath. Molly sensed it at her fingertips. Afraid it would hurt him. Afraid that she would burn him, but Henry didn't seem to notice, or if he did, he hid it well.

He coaxed her shirt up, and his fingertips grazed the underside of her breasts. He turned her around until her back met the bed. Half of his body covered hers, careful not to squish her beneath his weight. Treating her like a delicate flower he might crush if he moved too fast, or was too forceful.

She pulled away, and Henry placed his head on her chest. Listening, she thought, to her unsteady heart. He kissed the top of her breast and opened his mouth to nip the skin. Molly winced, but the soft pain was exquisite.

She tried to calm her breathing, her heart, but nervous energy caused her blood to quicken. She grazed her hands across his chest, over his shirt. Not happy with the fabric in the way, she almost ripped it off him. The power surging in her body made her more impatient than she realized. If what she was feeling was anywhere near what Henry had resisted since he met her, she had no clue how he had lasted that long.

She fumbled with his shirt until her fingers brushed against his scorching skin. She planted her hand over his heart and almost laughed at the sensation. It drummed as unsteadily as hers.

She let her hands rove along his body as he kissed her harder. A hot ache grew between her legs. His hands clasped her body tighter, as if she would sneak away if he loosened his grip. But Molly was going nowhere.

She dragged her hands down his chest until her fingertips touched the cool metal belt at his hips. Her hands were surprisingly steady as she unbuckled him, even though the magic flowed like a broken dam from her.

Henry's breath hitched in her ear as her fingers grazed his cock. His kisses grew frantic as she pumped his full length into her hand. His size still surprised her, but it also delighted her, making her impatient to experience him inside her.

She was sure now that the magic that flowed through her was affecting him too. He appeared larger. His muscles expanded almost the same way they did before he shifted. His hands gripped her tightly to him. She sensed it radiating from him. Rivulets poured from every inch of his skin. Molly worried about what the power swirling from them could do. Destroy the house or the neighborhood, but Henry wouldn't let her mind remain on it for too long.

He moaned as her hand continued its movements. He couldn't focus enough to kiss her, but she didn't mind. Watching his desire play on his face and hearing each tormented groan melted something within her. When he pushed her hand away, she realized what melted were the last vestiges of her wall.

"Claim me," said Molly. Henry stiffened next to her. He cupped her face again, and she watched as his eyes glowed again. The gold didn't disappear. She couldn't go back now. She didn't want to.

"Claim you?" he asked, as if he had misheard her. As if it couldn't be true.

"I want to claim you, Henry. Will you claim me? After everything I've done. After making you weak, and keeping secrets from you. Will you claim me?"

"Is it what you want?" he asked. He shuddered in her arms, and the wood creaked beneath them.

"It's what I need."

Henry pressed his lips to hers and crushed her to him. He grasped her hard, but Molly liked it. Her gentle giant could destroy a man's throat in a second with his teeth, but would only nip at her neck. The hands that could crush a skull, yet gripped her firmly without leaving a bruise. His strength measured and yielded just for her enjoyment.

She pulled her shirt off and unhooked her bra. He dove in, his lips capturing her nipple. She arched her back as he licked the pebbled bud. But his fingers traveled down while she was distracted. He unbuttoned her jeans and yanked them off. Her underwear went with it. She gasped as his fingers parted her and entered her. The gentle massage sent currents down her spine.

The power increased tenfold. She sensed it around her. Not a distraction, but an accompaniment, making each touch, each kiss, each sensation more. Just more. More than she had ever felt with anyone else. She could drown in it.

Molly didn't want to waste time. She wanted nothing more than to have him inside her. She grasped his wrist, trying to pull him away, but Henry didn't pay attention to it.

He would claim her agonizingly slow. She made him wait long enough. Now it was her turn.

A soft whimper slipped from her lips as Henry continued, worshiping every part of her he kissed. Molly squirmed beneath him. Her hips bucked into his hand, rubbing her sensitive clit on his wrist. Henry stopped kissing her breasts and moved up to kiss her lips.

Henry smiled during the kiss. With each soft movement of his fingers, a fire ignited in her until getting her release was all she could think of. When his thumb circled her clit, she bit his shoulder. He grunted in pain, and Molly pulled away, afraid she had hurt him. But the awed smile on his lips told her he liked it. She planted a light kiss on the bite mark to make amends.

But her patience was running thin. Even though his every touch sent currents of heat through her, she needed more. She needed him. Henry seemed to understand as he pulled his hand from her center.

She felt his hardened shaft against her stomach as they kissed. He glided it against her, and she wanted to force his hips down. No matter how hard she tried to move him to her wishes, it was like trying to push a mountain.

He pulled away, and Molly noticed his eyes didn't return to their usual warm brown. They stayed golden just for her.

"I'll stop," he said. His words came out breathless. "If you want me to. If you've changed your mind." Even this close to what he wanted, he would stop for her. But the pain in his voice rang in her ears. It wouldn't be a simple task, but he would do it. She had no doubt about that.

She caressed his face, her fingers running over his bushy eyebrows. He closed his eyes, leaning into her palm. "I claim you, Henry. You're mine."

His eyes snapped open, and before she said anything else, he kissed her so deeply she thought she had stopped breathing. His hands traveled down her arms and grasped her wrists. He guided her hands down to his cock, and Molly wrapped her fingers around it.

Henry melted at her touch, kissing her all the while. He pulled away to align himself with her hips.

"Guide me in," he whispered. He wrapped his fingers gently around her neck. "Take what's yours," he said.

Molly wasted no time guiding the head in. He stretched her around him, and she moaned as she impatiently pushed him in further. Henry stayed still, relishing the sensation of her squeezing and relaxing on his cock.

He started moving, pulling in and out with little rhythm in order to feast on her. Her own movements were more hurried. The magic threatened to flash from her fingertips towards him. She needed to feel him, to feel every inch as it slid in and out.

Her desire grew ravenous. Soon, she noticed Henry gain a pattern. A steady thrust that followed his heart. She gripped him tighter as her clit rubbed against his body with every push. She shifted her hips up as he moved, and it shot straight power through her body, leaving her shaky and gasping.

Henry thrust his hips harder against her. Her body tensed, her climax cresting on the edge. Henry kissed her, but it was nothing more than a pressured peck because he groaned as she tightened around him. She gasped as her orgasm shook her body. She closed her eyes and felt Henry's mouth on her throat as the waves of pleasure rolled through her.

"You're mine," Henry whispered as he hitched her hips up to plunge his cock even deeper into her. Molly only nodded her head as he continued pounding against her.

He was losing control, and that aroused her more. She bit his neck, and he hissed. A part of her wanted him to lose control. She could take it. Each hard push deep inside her made her crave it. But Henry was steady and firm, unwilling to push his luck.

He pulled her lips to his again as the restrained rhythm of his hips brought her close again. He hitched her leg up, holding it in his strained biceps. Her body surrendered to the bliss as another wave rocked through her. Henry's warm hand covered her mouth to stop her from crying out, but it was too late. Her sudden outburst must have startled even the ghosts.

Molly didn't care anymore. She didn't care what the people and spirits in her home heard. She was nothing but magic. It enveloped her and Henry together until she wasn't sure what power was hers and what belonged to him. They were one in body and power.

Henry moved faster, and her old creaky bed cracked and splintered as Henry's body was unrelenting. With a guttural moan, he came inside her. He didn't move for a while, and Molly kissed his neck as he lay on top of her, breathing hard. He squished her, but she liked it. His body acted as a shield. Nothing could get to her. Not the fear that crept into the corners of her mind. Or the worry nibbling at her nerves. With Henry, she was safe. She had never felt that way with anyone before.

He pushed himself off her, and Molly was sorry for it. The cold made her shiver, but he pulled her back in. His body was so hot she almost didn't need a blanket. His breathing steadied with her touch. It was strange magic indeed, and she was curious to see what else changed now that she had claimed him. His eyes grew heavy, and he kissed her forehead before a deep sleep dragged him away.

CHAPTER THIRTY-ONE

Henry heard footsteps near him. They were heavy, like someone was dragging their feet on the red Persian carpet on the floor. When he opened his eyes, he saw the faint outline of a man. He startled awake, standing up and grabbing the lamp by the bed. But the man disappeared as he turned. He looked frantically around the room, finding it empty except for Molly wrapped in the light blue duvet.

"Henry?" she asked, turning over to look at him. Seeing the lamp in his hands, she sat up. "What's wrong?"

"There was a man here. I saw him. But he... he's gone."

"Tell me, was he old? Maybe sixty?" she asked, laying down again and bringing the blankets up to her nose.

"I think so? I didn't get a good look."

"That's Peter. He's harmless. He knows a lot about insulation, though. So he's helpful to have around." She yawned, stretching out.

"Wait, that was a ghost?"

"Yes, they're just curious about you. Come back to bed. They can't hurt you."

Henry put down the lamp and climbed under the covers. Molly drifted to him. He settled behind her, bringing her in closer to his body. Her back nestled comfortably against his chest.

He felt a little silly for getting scared. After months of hunting the shapeshifter, a ghost was nothing. He mostly resented it for waking him up from his dream.

Malcolm had been there. He remembered Molly sitting in his childhood living room. The seventies wood paneling behind her looked both nostalgic and outdated.

Malcolm and Molly talked, but Henry didn't remember what they said to each other. What he recalled was joy. Pure joy at seeing them interact and talk.

Malcolm would have loved Molly, and the truth of it made Henry's heart hurt. His hand drifted to his chest, and on the left side, he met his own heartbeat. Steady and familiar. He moved to the right side and smiled as an unfamiliar sensation greeted him. Molly's heart beat slowly as she slept. That would take some getting used to.

He nestled his nose in her neck and kissed her soft skin. She claimed him, and while she had, Henry felt his wolf leave his body. It had drifted out; he was sure of it. His wolf had left him, and Molly filled the emptiness. Her mouth, her legs, her eyes. Every contented sigh and whimper filled the space. Every bite from her lips, and scratch from her nails, caused his soul to leave faster, until he found it again in his release.

None of it made sense to him. His pack mates had never told him about that. Never told him that his center, his wolf, would disappear, and for a moment he would no longer be a werewolf, but a human again. A vulnerable, trembling human worshiping on the altar of his lover, who took the curse away from him. Lycanthropy was a curse, a dangerous one, and Henry had learned to live with it. But the knowledge that Molly could take the lycanthropy, even if only for mere moments, and he could be human with her, made his veneration grow.

Molly turned in her sleep and cuddled into Henry's chest. He smiled in the dark, pulling her in closer. Her perfume flooded his nostrils. With Molly in his arms, he was complete. He couldn't imagine anything being better than this.

Molly shifted, rubbing her eyes, yawning and stretching beside him. She smiled, settling on his chest again. He traced her spine beneath the covers. "How did you sleep?" he asked.

"I wasn't trying to sleep, but you're like a furnace. You're going to be impossible to sleep with during the summer."

Henry chuckled, squeezing her even tighter. He looked towards the door, noticing the cracks he had left behind. Right, he needed to buy her a new door. He hadn't wanted to leave the house, let alone leave Molly unprotected in her room. She had passed out wrapped in him. Her breathing and heart calmed after what felt like hours of pure panic, but it pained him to pry himself off her. He had done his best to put some of the larger pieces together again with wood glue he found in the garage, but it wouldn't do.

As much as Henry wanted to stay in bed kissing and fucking Molly until he died from exhaustion and hunger, he had a job to do. He watched her serene face and kissed the thin, soft skin of her eyelids. He didn't want to disturb her peace, but they were running out of time.

"Molly," he started, "what happened in the graveyard?"

Immediately, his second heartbeat picked up, thrumming anxiously against his chest.

"I..." She sat up, worry on her face. Henry smoothed the fallen tight curls, and she relaxed at his touch. He grabbed her hand and placed it on his chest. Molly's eyes grew wide.

"You can't lie to me now," he said.

She leaned against the headboard. With a heavy sigh, she turned from him, preferring to stare out the window. Henry's hands drifted to hers, and he held them up to warm her palms.

"I just ask that you don't judge me for what I did back then." Her heart beat even faster as she turned back to him. Her eyes pleaded for a mercy that Henry would never withhold from her.

"Never," he assured her.

"My dad died when I was nineteen. It was really hard for me because, well, after my mom passed away, my dad and grandmother raised me. After he died, I was scared, but I had Granny, so I knew I would be fine. I can't say that I was always happy, but life got back to normal. But when I was twenty, Granny started getting sick. I found her in the bathroom one day. She had fallen, and she was bruised and dehydrated because she had been there all day. I was so afraid she was going to die and leave me all alone, but she pulled through.

"Granny needed a lot of care afterwards, and we couldn't afford it. So, I dropped out of college and I got a job to help cover everything. Even then, we were still struggling. And that's when... that's when Bruce entered my life again."

"Who's Bruce?" Her heart leaped when he said the name, and her fear made Henry grow angry. Who would dare hurt his mate? Where had he been during that time? If only he had known her, he could've prevented this.

"He was my dad's friend and was always around when I was growing up. He was harmless when I was younger. But I never liked him. I always got a weird feeling about him, but my dad liked him, and I trusted my dad. But he changed the older I got. He became creepier. I would notice him staring at me. He would leer. I'm not sure if my dad ever noticed.

"But Bruce disappeared after he died. He came back about a year later to visit us. He talked to Granny most of the time. He wanted to help and told me my dad had been his best friend and would have taken care of Bruce's family if he had been in the same position.

"I think about that day a lot. Sometimes I want to strangle my younger self for saying yes. I have dreams where I'm in our house in Arizona, but my younger self doesn't hear me scream at her. She just says yes. Back then, I remember being relieved, thinking that I had some help. I could return to school, finish my degree, and I would have some time and not have to work two jobs. And I would be free. Granny felt like such a burden, and I feel so guilty even now saying it. She did everything for me when I was a kid, and I was so ready to give her off to someone else, so that I might live like a normal twenty-year-old."

Henry reached up to wipe a tear as it fell from her face. Molly looked away, as if afraid to see his reaction. He kissed her knuckles to reassure her. Her hand was so much colder now.

"At first, it was fine. Bruce owned a couple of restaurants, so he would bring us groceries. He paid some bills. Our bathroom needed repairs. He paid for that as well. He used to come to our house for dinner, and he was kind, you know. The lurid look was gone. He was a normal guy, or maybe I was just telling myself that. He told me he would pay my college tuition in the fall when school started again. And he had given me the key to his house. He had a pool and invited me to come over whenever to use it. Not that I did, but he wanted to be helpful. And my life was going back to normal. Until..."

Henry's hand flew to his chest. Molly's heart raced so fast, he was afraid for her. He cupped her face. The worst scenarios ran through his head. Her eyes had tears in them, but she wiped them away, as if frustrated with herself if she let them fall.

"He invited me to his house one day. It was July and ridiculously hot. And I wasn't sure why he wanted me to come over. Until this point, he had always come over to our house, but I felt like I couldn't say no. I remember being so anxious on the drive there. I didn't know why, but something was off. I went anyway, and he wasn't there, so I let myself in with the key he gave me.

"I sat on his couch for about thirty minutes, and the whole time I wanted to leave. Something inside me was screaming, but I ignored my instincts.

"Before I could work up the nerve to do so, he came home. He was so excitedly happy. We talked for a bit. He asked me about my classes and how Granny was doing. And then... he touched my face. His hand was sweaty, and it left a wet trail on my cheek. It took everything in me not to run to the bathroom and wash it off. But I laughed it off, pretending it was fine. He offered me a drink, and I took it. I don't remember why I did. I was so uncomfortable."

Henry grew still, his muscles tensed. His wolf stirred in his chest, anger coursing through every cell of his body.

"But that's when everything changed. The room swirled, and my eyes were heavy. I remember him walking towards me, and lifting me up, but I tried to fight him. My muscles moved as if I were swimming in molasses. My punches didn't hurt him, and that made me furious. But his next move confused me.

"He placed one sweaty hand on my forehead, and it felt like I was dying. Like every inch of me, every cell pulled towards him. He was draining me, taking my magic and, by extension, my life. I was weak, and my blood burned under my skin. I could sense it traveling to my head, into his hand. All the while, he looked more alive than I had ever seen him. Younger.

"I was strong. Maybe that's why he targeted me. My magic has always been strong. He must have sensed it all those years. Maybe he was waiting for the right moment to steal it from me."

Henry squeezed her hand, urging her to continue. He needed to know what had happened. He needed to know how much he would torture Bruce if he ever saw him.

"I struggled to get out of his arms, and in the scuffle we must have knocked over a candle. There wasn't enough wax, or even a large enough flame for what happened next, but the flames grew. They covered the carpet and took hold of the curtains. He tried to stamp it out, and I think he threw water on it, but it continued to grow. He dropped me on the floor, and the tiles were hot, but I couldn't move.

"Finally, he gave up on fighting the fire and started running out the door. He was leaving me there. He was going to let me burn. But I started crawling towards the front door." Henry watched in awe as the sadness in her face faded, replaced by a focused rage. "And I willed it. I willed him to fall. His legs broke in front of me, like they were twigs snapped in two. He fell with a horrible cry. I've never been able to do it since."

"How did you get out?" asked Henry, his voice strained. He wasn't sure how much longer he could contain his wolf. He had to remind himself that Molly had survived. She was here, safe in his arms, and away from the past that dared hurt her. But his anger thundered as if it were occurring right in front of him.

"I crawled out literally just dragging myself across the floor. He grabbed onto my leg, but when he touched me, he screamed.

I don't know why, but he let me go. He tried crawling after me, but it was like he couldn't leave. He was stuck there. The flames reached him, and I watched as they consumed him. I would have stayed, but I heard sirens. By then, some of my senses were coming back, so I got into my car and drove home.

"Granny never asked me what happened, but I think she knows. I think she helped. There was no way that tiny candle could've caused such a huge fire, or that I alone snapped that man's legs. I still shouldn't have been awake. When I got home, she came to me, and smoothed the singed hair on my head, and she said, 'You're safe now. We don't need anyone else. We have each other.'"

Her heart slowed down, and some of Henry's anger dissipated with it. He pushed back the curls from her face and kissed her cheek. Molly melted into him, her hands reaching for his arms.

"I'm sorry," said Henry. The weight of her past made him ashamed of himself.

"What are you sorry for?" asked Molly, with a soft smile on her lips.

"Here I was thinking you were just too proud to accept help. Or you were too stubborn. Why would you trust me? After everything?"

"You showed me I could. I know you won't hurt me."

"Molly," he sighed into her hair. "What happened yesterday? Something scared you. You weren't having a panic attack about the past, were you?"

Molly shook her head no. She pulled away and reached into the bedside table beside Henry. She grabbed a photograph and handed it to him. He saw a younger Molly, still beautiful even then, with a familiar smile etched on her face and looking radiant in a purple prom dress.

"I found that picture in the boat yesterday. He was there when my dad took it. Do you remember the night at the club, when I asked if you heard whistling?" Henry nodded. "He used to whistle that tune every single time I saw him. We left Arizona two days after the fire. I was afraid that they would tie the fire back to me. All this time, I thought he had died, but maybe he didn't."

"Did you search for the records? The obituaries?"

"I did. I didn't find any, but I also found no sign he was alive either. All of his restaurants closed or went to new owners. He didn't have a close family, so I found nothing from them. I was so sure he was dead. He was burned to a crisp."

"Do you think it's really him?"

"I'm hoping it's not. My protection spells have kept him away from me, but I'm not sure how long it'll take for him to find a way to me. It's not like I can stay locked up in my home forever."

"He won't harm you. I would never let him."

"I know," she whispered. "What if he's the shapeshifter?"

"Shapeshifters are born, not made. Did you ever see him shift?"

"No, he was power hungry, but I'm not sure that he would've shifted in front of me. He would've wanted to hide that."

Henry held her closer, trying his best to soothe her. Her heartbeat in his chest steadied. He wouldn't let Bruce within a mile of her. He sensed a fierce protectiveness of her growing inside him, steadily gaining strength like the fire that consumed Bruce. Only he would do a lot worse if Bruce was back.

"I will never let him touch you again. I will keep you safe. My soul, my love, my life."

Molly pulled away, her eyes meeting his, and he read the love in her gaze. He didn't think he had done anything yet to deserve it. But he had time to live up to her love.

He would kill the shapeshifter first. Then, he would stop at nothing to burn down every corner of the earth until his teeth sunk into the crinkled old flesh of the man who hurt his beloved.

CHAPTER THIRTY-TWO

Hours later, and with more difficulty than Henry thought possible, he left Molly's house. His wolf growled and whined in his chest, upset at leaving her behind, but he had a job to do.

Henry strode into the cabin and found Chris and Mark already there. A heavy air hung in the room, and Chris didn't even turn to look his way. Henry didn't expect him to have forgiven or forgotten their fight, but he hoped they could move past it for just one night.

"Where were you?" asked Mark.

"At Molly's."

Chris stiffened at that. "We were supposed to meet last night and talk strategy."

"I was needed elsewhere."

"We needed you, Henry. This isn't a joke. This damn shapeshifter has been ruining our lives for months, and you wasted our time with Molly?" asked Chris, ready to pick up the fight again.

"I couldn't very well hunt if I was weak."

"Oh?" laughed Mark, clapping Henry on his back. "So you finally did it. You owe me twenty," he added to Chris.

Henry tried not to let the bet make him angry. He could already sense a restlessness in bones, and he needed to save it for the hunt.

"I'm stronger now. I can feel it."

He reached to feel Molly's heartbeat. Calm and strong, he imagined her at work, in her apron. Chatting with customers as she poured them coffee. He wanted nothing more than to leave the woods and go to her.

He ignored Chris' pissy attitude, focusing instead on the night before them. There was too much riding on tonight's hunt to let their hurt feelings get in the way.

"There's something else. We might know who it is."

"Really?" asked Mark.

"A man named Bruce. He was obsessed with Molly's powers when she was younger and tried to steal her magic."

"Does this have to do with the boat we went to?"

"Yes, I'm not a hundred percent sure it's him, but it's the only lead we have."

"We're going on whims now?" asked Chris.

Henry ignored the pointed anger in his question. "It's better than nothing. If it is him, we need to lead the shapeshifter away from Molly's house."

"Always about Molly," said Chris.

"It's all we've got," said Mark, trying to diffuse Chris. "And anyway, the further we chase this thing from its intended path, the more we might catch it off guard."

Henry was grateful that Mark understood him. "What time is the moonrise?" asked Henry.

"In twenty minutes," said Chris. He didn't appear calmer. Henry knew the full moon was affecting his temper, just as Henry's own anger brimmed over his self-control.

"So, what's the plan?" asked Henry.

"Kill the thing," said Chris.

"We follow the strongest trail. And we split up, attack on all sides," said Mark.

"Sounds good to me," said Henry, pulling off his shirt.

They waited at the edge of the woods. The forest was empty, impossibly so. No birdsong, no little chatter from squirrels. The only sound was the rustling of leaves on the trees. As if the animals understood what dark creature lurked under the canopy. Henry's eyes were closed, breathing deep, the stench reached his nostrils.

A rumble inside him made him open his eyes. The world appeared sharper, the colors more vibrant. His bones rattled beneath his skin, his muscles screamed as they expanded, and his bones stretched with a crack. He fell forward, his front paws falling on dried pine. Chris walked forward, his coat dark black and bigger than both Mark and Henry. Mark stretched as the moonlight reflected off his gray, speckled coat.

Henry growled as he picked up the scent, his instincts pushing him to tear the shapeshifter limb from limb. His anger finally found a release. Mark ran first, his gray fur blurring with his speed, with Henry and Chris close behind him.

Henry's adrenaline rushed through his veins, making him feel inpatient to see it again. Without Molly near, he concentrated better. The sound of his pounding heart and his paws hitting the ground flooded his ears. The scent grew in intensity. Henry could taste it. He wouldn't let it escape.

An ear-splitting scream echoed through the forest. Henry looked up and saw the shapeshifter on a branch, swinging with long arms resembling a monkey, but a body akin to a wolf. Its eyes glared down at the three of them. It pulled back its lips, exposing the razor-sharp teeth inside. It lunged from one branch to another, but Henry didn't move. He followed it as it tried to balance on the next branch.

Mark rushed the tree, his claws scratching the trunk, a low growl emerging from his snout. The shapeshifter jumped to another tree and almost lost its footing on the thin branch. It screeched, a little dribble from its mouth falling on Henry's paw.

It was starving. Henry knew it was only a matter of time until the thing had to climb down. It needed to feed, to satiate the gnawing in its vacuous stomach. They followed it for what seemed like hours, as it jumped from branch to branch, snapping a few, until they cornered it.

It had nowhere else to go. It could keep hopping on trees, but eventually, the forest would end. The hunger scratching at its insides would overpower everything. It seemed to know that as it hopped onto a lower branch, swinging back and forth, as if it debated its chances. Chris took a running start, jumping close enough to bite its ankle.

It screamed, its clawed paws reaching down to swipe at him, but Mark jumped next, his mouth closing down on its wrist. Mark pulled the shapeshifter off the tree. It swiped again, and Mark had to let go as bright red lacerations appeared on his fur. The shapeshifter didn't let the opportunity pass. It ran through the forest on two legs, with Henry and the pack running close behind.

Henry ran fast, his breath coming out in white puffs. He was so close now. Its heels were at his eye level; the calloused and bloody skin left prints in the dirt. Mark veered to the left and Chris' right. They tried to get in front of it, but they couldn't catch up. Henry tried his luck, lunging with a powerful kick of his back legs. He opened his snout, the stench of the shapeshifter in his mouth, but then a shot rang through the air. Henry landed with a heavy thud on the forest floor, with his back burning.

Henry got up and saw Mark and Chris standing near him. He growled. What were they doing? Why hadn't they continued chasing it?

Another shot burst through the still night. The shapeshifter's steps grew fainter with every second they waited. Mark motioned with his head, pointing to an overgrowth of shrubs and fallen tree trunks. Henry followed, even though his entire being screamed at him to keep running. The fur on Henry's back singed with the hot sting of the bullet lodged between his shoulder blades.

Shit, not again, he thought

They waited, and soon enough, the rustle of heavy boots and fumbling human voices approached their hiding spot.

"I saw it here," said one man. He carried a hunting rifle and night-vision goggles.

"How many did you see?" asked another man. He wore camouflage and wheezed as he tried to catch up. He pulled out an inhaler and took a shaky breath.

"Four... I think."

"You think?"

"I... I saw three wolves. But I... I need to buy new goggles."

The second man stooped, inspecting the ground. He dipped a finger into the earth, and Henry made out a liquid on his finger when he brought it back up.

"Well, you hurt one of them. It couldn't have gotten too far."

The men continued northward, leaving behind the pack in the shrubs. Henry didn't move until their footsteps faded. He stretched out his muscles, noticing his back didn't hurt anymore. It was impressive that the bullet hole had healed so quickly. Normally it would have taken at least an hour, but it couldn't have been over ten minutes.

He turned to Mark, whose head lay on his paws, falling asleep. Chris stayed vigilant, his ears perked. Henry huffed, a bright cloud of vapor obscuring his vision. He walked out of the hiding spot. The shapeshifter's scent lingered, but it was long gone. He wanted to howl, but he couldn't attract more attention.

As the forest grew brighter, the early dawn light cast shadows on the pines. Henry's bones shook. He closed his eyes, letting his body take care of the transformation. When he opened them again, he found human Chris and Mark staring back at him.

"I can't believe it," said Mark. He didn't sound mad. Every word reflected defeat, and Henry felt the same. "How do we keep fucking it up?"

"It's Malcolm," said Chris.

"What?" asked Henry.

"We're not the same since he died. We're useless; we always were, but he made us into what we are. But now? Freddy and Brandon won't even leave their mates to come hunt this creature, and we fail every time!"

"Stop it," said Henry. "It'll continue to kill. It'll continue to beat us if it thinks we're weak."

"It can't hear us, Henry, what does it matter?" asked Mark.

"It matters because I'm not giving up. Malcolm wouldn't. We have one more night, and this time we'll get it. We almost had it tonight! If it weren't for the stupid humans, it would be dead! It can't beat us. Not again."

"One more night," said Mark. "We can't fuck it up this time."

"We won't," assured Henry, but Chris didn't seem convinced.

Henry stretched, his back popping. He wasn't tired. His adrenaline still pumped through his body. His disappointment faded as another thought took firm root. Somewhere out of this forest, Molly lay asleep, her warmth inviting him in. He placed his hand on his chest and found Molly's heart frantic. Beating unsteadily against his palm.

Something was wrong. She should be asleep. Henry looked up to see Mark and Chris staring at him. Worry on their faces.

"What is it?" asked Mark.

"It's nothing," lied Henry. "I have something I need to take care of, but this afternoon, we get ready."

Henry turned to run, but didn't return to the cabin. He wouldn't waste anymore time. Instead, he ran through the woods, hoping the dense forest would cover his nakedness.

His senses were keener during the full moon, and he ran south until the fragrance of gardenia reached his nose. He followed it, a smile stretched over his lips, thinking of the night he had done the same thing. Followed the scent that intoxicated all his senses. Unsure of what would be on the other side. Now he knew what awaited him. He had tasted her arousal and heard her moan in his ear. Felt the supple skin of her breasts on his mouth, and it made him run faster, inpatient to be near her again.

He ran out of the forest, jumping her backyard fence. The sun was just peaking over the horizon. He hoped that none of her neighbors were too observant or had cameras. He made it to her locked back door and knocked. Molly's heart beat faster in his chest. The uneven rhythm thumped against his own fast-beating heart. He knocked again, and as his hand pulled away, Molly thrust open the door.

Her velvet purple robe ruffled with a gust of wind, acting as a pull for Henry. The scent of her sweet arousal reached his nostrils, and he crossed the threshold in a single step. His mouth was on hers in a heavy crush. He heard the door close behind them, but it wasn't him.

He couldn't think of anything else but Molly. Her lips. The way her body bent beneath his weight. The way she softened in his arms.

He pushed her against the wall, pressing his body against hers. Molly gasped in surprise, but drew him in closer. He roughly pulled the robe off her, exposing her blue pajamas. He struggled with the shirt buttons, the need for her making his hands unusable. In frustration, he growled and tore the shirt open. The tinkle of bouncing buttons on the hardwood floor was the only noise in the sleeping house, other than their panting. He expected Molly to be angry, for her to push him away, but she pulled him in for another kiss.

"Spread your legs," he whispered in her ear. His hand traveled downward, slipping it inside her underwear. He cupped her warm and wet sex, a sharp breath hitching in Molly's throat.

Henry kissed her neck, his teeth lightly grazing her pulse beneath her skin. He kissed downwards, his lips nibbling her nipples, underneath her breasts, her stomach, and her hips. He pulled down her pajama bottoms, his hands raking across her thighs. Henry got on his knees, hitching one of her legs over his shoulders. Molly placed her hands on him, bracing herself.

Henry's tongue parted the soft folds, and he flicked it against her sensitive clit. He heard Molly hiss in a breath, her fingers digging into his shoulders. His tongue moved roughly, the circles around her clit building in pressure all the while. The pleasure-pain of one of her hands pulling on his hair while the other dug her nails into his flesh made him go faster. He needed her to come on his tongue. Needed to erase the night's events. Molly could take everything from him. Her arousal filled his nostrils, a much sweeter palate cleanser after smelling the shapeshifter all night. He wrapped his hands around her thighs to keep her from bucking into his face. His own desire built, his penis heavy.

He was relentless, letting the pressure build until she tensed around his mouth. Her thighs clutched his head, but he didn't let up while she came in his mouth. Her release on his tongue tasted sweet. He kissed her thigh, his eyes stuck to her chest as she tried to catch her breath. He stood up, towering over her. Placing his hands on either side of her face, he pressed his lips to hers.

It was an odd sensation to feel her heart in his chest. The thrum built as he licked. The unmistakable rhythm as he gave her everything she wanted. She could never lie to him again, but he knew she wouldn't.

Molly moaned as his fingers reached for her ass, giving them a tight squeeze, pushing her hips up to meet his. She braced herself, holding on to the door frame. Henry reached down to lead his cock into her. He groaned into her neck, nipping at the flesh.

He thrust into her, the framed photos falling to the floor with a crash. Molly moaned in his ear as his cock slipped in and out. It drove him wild that she could take him so well. She truly was made for him, and the idea forced him to hold on to her tighter. His hands wrapped around her hips, keeping her steady as his release neared, but he needed her to finish again. He wished to feel her clench around his cock with her orgasm. His hands trailed to her breasts, massaging them. Molly held on to him tighter, her nails digging into his flesh. He groaned. His back burned, but he didn't care.

His wolf left as Molly kissed him. It slipped from the cavernous confines of his soul. The pain in his back returned, as did a new sharp sting from Molly's nails. His shoulder blades ached, the bullet wound throbbing. He was nothing but a man. Desperate to hold on to the woman that made him lose his wolf.

Molly stiffened around him. A moan escaped her mouth, and Henry kissed her through her climax. His orgasm followed soon after. With each pump of his hips, trying to prolong the deep pleasure in his cock. His wolf returned, slinking back into his body, settling near Molly's heart.

Molly's head leaned on his shoulder. Her soft lips pressed small kisses onto his skin. Everything had gone wrong, except for Molly. Unable to still fathom, she was his.

Chapter Thirty-Three

"What was that?" asked Molly, trying to catch her breath. A cold draft from somewhere made her shiver, and Henry reached over, grabbing her robe and blanketing her with it. He kept her close as they both lay on the floor, unable to move.

"I don't know," he laughed. "It's never been this strong before."

"What do you mean?"

"My need for you. All I could think about was sinking my cock deep—"

Molly placed her palm over his mouth. "Stop it, or you're going to start again."

Henry laughed against her hand, nipping it with his teeth. "Can't take anymore?"

"I think if we don't get out of this kitchen, Rosie and Lenore are going to want to move out."

"Isn't that what you wanted?" he asked.

"No, I like them here. They fill up the space."

"It is a big house. How many bedrooms does it have?"

"Seven."

Henry whistled. "Well, you have two roommates, a couple of ghosts, and now a werewolf boyfriend."

"Mm, you do take a lot of room," she said, kissing his chest.

"I'm sure we can find a way to fill out the other rooms."

"What are you suggesting?"

"I want five."

"What?" She sat up, but Henry's smile lessened the shock of his statement. "I hope you mean five cats."

"Is that too many?"

"Way too many," she laughed.

"Well, how many kids do you want?"

Molly bit her lip. Henry cupped her face, and she leaned into the warmth. Having him near her again set her at ease. The night had been terrible, and she hadn't slept a wink. "Maybe three."

"Three? I can work with that."

"My ideal is two."

"Whatever you want is perfect for me."

Molly laughed. "You're easy to please."

He pulled her closer to his chest. She sighed at the crushing weight. She could do this, create a life with someone. Build something with him. Tangible and theirs, it filled her with so much hope she didn't know what to do with it.

"What happened last night?" she asked.

He stiffened beneath her. She pushed her head up to see him. He didn't look happy. He brushed her hair out of her face, and he was about to answer, but stopped.

"Someone's waking up," he said. Molly heard nothing, but before she protested, he swooped her up into his arms and stood up. He carried her out of the kitchen, and she snuggled into his chest, breathing in the earthy smell of him as he led her into her room. He gently placed her on her bed, and she reached for his hand, pulling him in.

Henry kissed her, laying his body across hers. He pulled back for a moment, his warm brown eyes lingering on hers.

"I love you, Molly," he said. Molly's heart stopped, and Henry laid his hand on her chest. Right, he could feel it. That still took some getting used to.

"I love you too." He kissed her deeply this time, his body pressing more urgently against hers. She bucked her hips up, rubbing against him.

"Wait," said Henry, pulling away.

"No. No wait," said Molly, trying to pull him back down onto her lips.

Henry pressed his face to the pillow, taking a deep breath. "I promised the pack I would check up on you and meet them again to plan a strategy for tonight."

"You didn't get the shapeshifter?"

"No, we were close. Closer than we've ever been, but..."

"But what?" He hesitated. "Tell me, Henry."

"I got shot by animal control."

"What? Where?" She sat up straight, scanning his body in a panic.

"I'm okay. I've already healed. The claiming will speed up healing." He traced her jaw with his hands, tapping his fingers on her full lips. "Don't worry. I was okay. There's nothing to be worried about."

"A murderous shapeshifter, a rabid police force, and a desperate animal control? Why would I worry?"

Henry smiled softly, but wouldn't meet her eyes. "I'll be fine."

"Let me come with you tonight. I can cast or do something. Staying in this house just waiting for you to return was torture. You don't know what ran through my head last night."

He didn't respond, but kissed her. He pulled away much too soon for her liking. "I know you want to help, but I can't risk you like that. This is my fight. My pack's fight. We were close. We only need one more night. The boys and I will plan our attack tonight. I won't let it escape again."

"One more night?"

"I promise."

"I'll wait up for you." Henry seemed like he was about to argue, but he stopped himself. Molly already knew what kind of night awaited her. No sleep, no rest, not until Henry was back in her arms.

"So anyway, I told Scott that there was no way I got a seventy on that test! My professor got it wrong, but try to make that pretentious tenured asshole see reason? You might as well wait until hell freezes over, and—Molly? Hello Molly?" Violet waved her hand in front of Molly's eyes.

Molly shook her head, coming back down to earth, and placed the coffeepot she had been holding back on the counter. "Sorry," she said, grabbing the napkin dispensers to refill them.

"Are you okay?" asked Violet. Her textbooks were spread over the counter, but Molly hadn't seen her study once since she had come into Books & Beans. She was very busy chatting.

"I'm fine."

"Awful night?"

"The boys didn't catch it."

"Shit. Well, they have another chance tonight, right?"

"In theory, but animal control shot Henry again."

"It'll be okay, Molly. Henry's strong. Those werewolf genes will keep him safe. They'll catch it."

"I don't even know what I'm more afraid of, the shapeshifter, or animal control."

"Did you cast?" asked Violet, lowering her voice. Normally, Molly would have frowned at any mention of magic in public, but she was desperate to talk to someone.

"Of course I did. But he can't carry a charm with him. He can't carry anything. We even tried a necklace, but it slipped off him while he was running."

"It's all going to work out. It always does."

Just then, the door chimed, and Rosie walked in, textbooks in hand. She glanced at both Violet and Molly before walking towards a table in the back.

"What's with her?" asked Violet.

"Don't worry about it. Go back to the studying you said you were going to do."

Molly took a mug and a fresh pot of coffee and strode to Rosie. With her black hair in a high ponytail, she smiled tightly at Molly as she poured. It took more than a surly attitude to make her back away.

"Are you okay, Rosie?"

"I'm fine."

"Do you want to talk about it? Or are you going to be in a bad mood until the wolves leave?"

Rosie rolled her eyes, but Molly could tell her temper wouldn't last. "How long until they go?"

"They're hunting tonight, but Henry won't leave."

"Of course he's not. I knew he wasn't going to leave that first night we all had dinner together. But what about the others?"

"I don't know what Mark and Chris will choose. Did something happen between them and you?"

Rosie put on a fake smile. "Nothing happened. Everything's fine. Can I study now, please? I have a big test coming up."

"Okay, but I'll be here. When you want to talk."

Rosie sighed, and even though she wouldn't say a word, Molly understood she appreciated it. She knew there was more to the story, but forcing anyone to give away more would only lead to problems. Rosie would tell her, in her own time, and Molly had bigger things she needed to focus on.

No matter how much Violet tried to convince her, it didn't stop her worrying. She felt off for the rest of the day. She dropped a mug, splitting it in half. A customer found a toad in the bathroom sink. The pipe that Henry had fixed a few weeks ago burst again. She couldn't help but think of them as omens. Something was going to go wrong tonight.

Henry wouldn't come to see her before he went hunting. She wondered how much he hid from her. If his nonchalant attitude was more for her sake. The shapeshifter had evaded them this long, and Molly wasn't able to resist biting her lip into a bloody pulp, waiting to learn how the night ended.

Molly paced around her room, just as she had done the previous night. Her feet walked the same path over and over. If she thought she would sleep easier tonight because of her insomnia the night before, she was wrong. She tossed for an hour before she turned on her lamp again. She lit some incense for her ancestors, and asked them if somewhere out there in the ether, they would protect him and keep the shapeshifter's claws away from her man's throat. She checked her phone. No messages, but worse yet, it was still too early. Henry would be a wolf. He wouldn't be able to text or call.

She walked downstairs, her eyes stuck on the kitchen door leading to the backyard. Imagining him on the other side like the previous night.

Henry's eyes glowed gold. His body shining, covered in a light sweat. His breath coming out in heavy gusts, leaving condensed clouds by his mouth with every exhale. She needed to go to sleep. It would all be fine.

And then, as if conjured from her own mind, Henry appeared at the edge of the wood.

"Henry?" she called out loud.

He looked muddy, his nakedness hidden by the dark shadows of the forest. But those warm eyes called to her, and Molly opened her door. She didn't wait for him to come to her. She ran across the backyard. Her bare feet didn't sense the cold.

She crashed into his arms. Her relief was so palpable, she didn't even care that he was dirty. His arms wrapped around her tightly, and she felt a kiss on her head.

"Henry," she sighed into his chest.

His arms encased her tighter, a little too tight. Molly squirmed, but he didn't seem to get the message as he squeezed her.

"Henry, it's too tight," she mumbled, but he didn't let up.

"Found you."

The voice made her skin crawl. That wasn't his voice. It was devoid of warmth and laced with a disturbing sneer that scared her.

Her heart rate shot up painfully. Molly tried to pull away, but his arms crushed her to his chest. Panic gripped her as she struggled against him. But then his hand moved to her scalp, grasping a fistful of her hair, and forcing her face up to him.

Henry smiled, but then his face morphed. Melting, transforming, leaving Molly to wonder how much time she had before the shapeshifter would take his true form. And how long she had left before she became its next meal.

Chapter Thirty-Four

Henry's back ached as he shifted out of his wolf form. His hand settled on his chest, where Molly's heart beat steadily. Something was wrong. Her heart had been hammering against his ribs only moments before, taking over all of his senses, and distracting him from the hunt. It thumped against his palm now, calm like when she slept.

"Something's not right," said Henry. Mark walked up behind him, and Chris hobbled out of a bush, shifting mid-step.

They hadn't had the advantage they had the night before. The shapeshifter had learned their moves. It had prepared for the situation. It knew how to elude them better. What was worse, it had run too close to Molly's home for his comfort.

The humans were no less blundering, but they still caused their damage. Mark pulled out a bullet from Chris' leg. He hissed in pain, but once the hot metal hit the dirt, he straightened himself up.

"Something's not right," repeated Henry, massaging his chest like he could pull Molly from there.

"What's wrong?" asked Mark.

"I'm not sure. Molly felt strange."

"What do your senses tell you?"

"Is she safe?" asked Chris.

"Her heart is fine, but something was happening to her."

"I thought I heard her calling your name," said Mark.

"I need to check up on her."

"Are you serious?" asked Chris. "We're running out of time. Who knows where the shapeshifter ended up? If we lose it now, we won't find it again for another month!"

"We're not too far from her house. It'll take two minutes, tops. I need to make sure she's safe."

Chris and Mark exchanged a quick glance, their shared frustration palpable. Mark was too much of a nice guy to say it, but he waited for Chris to explode.

"Fine," said Chris through gritted teeth.

Henry ran, not bothering to shift. Molly's scent lingered in the forest outside her home. The fig and gardenia played with his senses. But there was something more. Horrifyingly, the shapeshifter's stench intermingled with her perfume.

He reached her backyard gate, finding it open. The back door stood ajar, and the lights from the kitchen flooded the porch. She had locked the door the night before. Nothing felt right to him.

"Molly?" His voice boomed through her still and quiet house. Nobody answered, not even Lenore or Rosie. He wanted to call someone from the coven, but he didn't have his phone.

He cursed under his breath. Why didn't anyone have landlines anymore?

"Is she here?" asked Mark.

"The back door's open. Molly wouldn't just leave it unlocked."

"Maybe she's with the coven?" reasoned Chris.

"No, she said she would wait for me. She was too anxious."

Henry's mind raced, unsure of his next step, or what to do. His wolf thrashed uncomfortably in his chest. He oscillated between anger, panic, and an indescribable sadness that threatened to kill him.

Something drifted past the corner of his eye. Quick enough that if he had blinked, he would have missed it. He whipped around and came face to face with another woman. He bristled, his hair standing on end. She walked towards him; her body glowed beneath the moonlight. He noticed Chris stiffen next to him while Mark stared at them, confused.

"Do you see that?" asked Chris.

"See what?" asked Mark.

"What is your name?" asked Henry, ignoring them. He had no time to explain.

"Camilla, you need to hurry."

"Where's Molly?" Hope fluttered in his chest.

"I don't know. She ran out of here after you came."

"I wasn't here."

"Yes, you were. I saw you. Naked in the woods."

"That wasn't me," he said in disbelief.

His ears rung and he placed his hand over Molly's heart. The steady beating told him she was still alive. But for how long? His mind raced. What could he do? What should he do? Where could they go?

They would lose the night. The shapeshifter would go free, but he didn't care about that anymore. Malcolm would have despised him if he had sacrificed Molly for revenge.

The shapeshifter's scent wafted through into the kitchen, and Henry's eyes snapped open. It came close to her house. He thought of its methodical path over the past few weeks. Of the concentric circles that shrank every night. It wasn't circling the town.

It circled her home.

"We need to check the boat," he whispered under his breath.

"What?" asked Chris.

"We need to go to the boat. The one we went to the other day."

"The one in the graveyard?" asked Mark.

"Yes."

"Why?" asked Chris.

"Molly's there."

"How do you know?"

"I just do."

"We don't have much time left. We can't go chasing whims, Henry. The shapeshifter—"

"FUCK THE SHAPESHIFTER!"

Camilla disappeared with a faint gasp, leaving them alone to figure it out among themselves.

"So you would abandon Malcolm and the pack?" asked Chris.

"Malcolm would have hated this. He wouldn't have cared if we got revenge. Not if it was hurting us! Not if we were hurting the ones we loved! Face it, Chris, at some point, this stopped being about Malcolm, and was all about us. Our egos and our grief. This has all been about what we needed to feel better. He would have hated to see us like this. To see me like this."

Henry's body swelled. His skin felt hot, even to him. Something strange happened. As he stood straighter, he noticed Mark and Chris cower. Their heads bent, unable to look him in the eye.

He remembered this. The unyielding obedience. The way he wouldn't be able to look Malcolm in the eyes after getting in trouble. Bowing his head and waiting for instructions, not afraid but faithful.

Something new coursed through his veins. A power he never dreamed of having, but now that it blazed within him, he had no clue how he had survived without it.

"We're going to the graveyard," said Henry, testing it out.

"Okay," said Mark.

"Fine," gritted out Chris.

Henry stormed out of Molly's kitchen, followed closely behind by his pack. The dried grass was itchy beneath his feet, but he paid no attention to it. His mind focused as his newfound power flooded his veins. He howled and hoped it reached Molly.

CHAPTER THIRTY-FIVE

Molly woke up underwater. Dirty water filled her throat, burning her lungs and eyes. Disoriented, she flailed as she struggled to kick back up to the surface, but someone kept her pinned to them. The murky water obstructed her view, and she couldn't make out the face of her captor.

Her head broke through the surface, and she coughed violently. She retched and tried to raise herself up, but she fell. Someone grabbed her up again and shuffled her inside somewhere. Her lungs heaved out the last of the water, and her vision blurred. Consciousness slipped fast, but she had to stay awake. She needed to fight whoever or whatever this was. The land beneath her rocked, and it only took a moment for the horrifying realization of where she was to sink in.

She looked up to see Bruce's face inches from hers. She didn't move. Like a striking snake, his brown eyes hovered over her body, taking it all in as if savoring every morsel. He was naked, though it didn't seem to bother him. He looked older than she remembered him. His pale face sagged, and he was bonier than before.

He reached for her neck, but she slapped his hand away with the little strength she had left.

"Now, is that anyway to treat an old friend?"

Molly didn't answer. Her head spun. He really was alive.

"How long has it been, Molly? Thirteen years? Thirteen years since you abandoned me to burn in that house?"

"You... seem... fine." She said through coughing fits. He flexed his arm; the burned skin healed. She expected to see a reflective sheen from scar tissue. Instead, his body appeared perfect. Untouched. As if there had never been a fire at all.

"How did I survive?" he asked, as if reading her mind. "No, we're not there yet, Molly. But look at you. You don't have a single scar on that pretty face of yours, well, except the one I gave you. You look grown." The word sounded lurid in his voice, and she wanted to run. "Did you miss me?"

Molly kept her mouth shut. It was getting to him as his eyebrows knitted together in frustration. He wanted a game. She wouldn't play along.

He turned away from her, grabbing an ashtray from the windowsill. He threw it, and she flinched away.

"All an act. You're still afraid of me, aren't you?"

"No," she finally said. "I'm not."

"No?" He passed a clammy hand over her arm. Molly tried to shove him away, but his hand wrapped around her arm tight enough to make her cry out. She had no escape route. His body covered the only way in or out.

"I'm tired of this. How did you survive the fire?" she asked.

"You mean after you left me? I must admit, I didn't a hundred percent understand what happened. I thought I was dead, but if that was death, it was more painful than I expected. No, your plan didn't work. I was in the hospital in the burn unit, but something was keeping me alive. A hate. You were always a pathetic little thing. I took care of you. You owed me. And you tried to kill me?"

"I didn't owe you my magic!"

"You owed me," he repeated.

Bruce lunged forward, grabbing her throat. His eyes glowed blue, and an unmistakable stench filled the room. Molly watched in horror as his skin morphed. His sagging face tightened as his hair grew long from his scalp. His jawline lengthened, and his eyes turned brown like Henry's. But they were devoid of all love.

"You're a mimic," said Molly. Everything clicked into place in her head. The strange animal combinations, the way he was able to look like Henry, to lure her from her house. A shapeshifter could take the form of an animal. But a mimic could only copy, and poorly at that. Driven by hunger for human flesh, they stopped at nothing to get it.

"Don't skip ahead in my story," he smiled, making Henry's face appear sinister. "The hate kept me alive. But I didn't realize that it was attracting something to me. Something more powerful than a pathetic witch and her old grandmother. Something that not only gave me back my strength but made me much more powerful."

"The mimic," choked out Molly.

"Yes. I didn't get it at first, but I felt better. The doctors didn't understand, but I knew. I felt it. Crawling under my skin. Its fingers would push through my stomach, like a fetus in the womb. It used to claw at my insides. Hungry. Always hungry. It took a while to learn how to feed it. How to keep it happy so it would stay. I couldn't always focus my energy on you. Some days, I had to prioritize the monster. But it made me strong enough to find you."

Molly didn't know what to say. Bruce's hands shifted, turning his nails into claws that dug into her neck.

"Your powerful charms hid you from me for years. You must have known then, no? You realized I was alive. Why did you think you could hide from me? I couldn't get at you directly, but come to find out you were chasing me!" He laughed and some of his spittle landed on Molly's cheek.

Molly had enough. She pushed him away. His claws dragged across her neck. Bruce laughed, undeterred by her feeble push. All he wanted was control over her. To take her magic and make her weak enough to destroy her. She wouldn't let him.

Bruce lunged forward again, but this time Molly was ready. She swiped the broken ashtray across his face. He fell backwards, his hand grasping his cheek. The boat swayed with the movement. His back still covered the door. He stood up, angrier than before, and she watched as his skin got harrier. He grew about two feet, his neck bent as his head reached the boat's ceiling. His arms elongated, the claws sprouted longer. But he kept his face stuck as Henry.

Molly looked for a way out. She settled on the grimy window, but she couldn't be sure that it opened. Bruce's eyes followed her. He let out a high-pitched screech, and she had to cover her ears.

Molly took a deep breath, letting the frantic energy inside her settle in the pit of her stomach. She thought of him falling. His limbs torn from their sockets. His jaw broken and his belly hungry. She closed her fist over her warming palms. The tingling grew to a painful crescendo.

Bruce pounced towards her, and Molly outstretched her hands. The cold, clammy skin of his face touched the hot skin of her hands. He screamed as he was thrown back. His spine crashed against the helm. She ran to the door, but the unsteady rocking of the boat made her crash into a pile of garbage. Two icy hands closed around her ankles. She turned to Bruce's sunken face by hers, as if he couldn't hold on to Henry's face. His empty eyes were full of hate and hunger.

Bruce opened his mouth wider, exposing three rows of teeth. Molly fought to pull back her legs. His grip tightened. She flinched away, waiting for the inevitable. But his hands loosened around her ankles.

She opened her eyes and watched as Henry gripped either side of Bruce's mouth. Henry yelled as he struggled, sending shivers through Molly's body. His jaw made an uncomfortable crunch as Henry tore his mandible from his face.

Bruce screamed as his jaw fell to the other side of the boat. Blood flooded his neck and chest and pooled at his feet. He clawed at his chest. As if to hold on to something pouring out. He screamed loudly enough for her ears to pop.

The flaxen complexion disappeared from Bruce's body as the mimic slipped from him. He crawled away from Henry, desperate and pleading.

Human.

Henry didn't let him languish for too long. His fingers wrapped around his neck. Molly looked away before he tore Bruce's head clean from his neck.

Chapter Thirty-Six

Even though Molly sat in front of him, Henry couldn't sit still. He assessed the damage, his fingers lingering on the fresh cut on Molly's throat. He breathed in hard, growing before her eyes, but the mimic was gone. Bruce was dead. The anger had nowhere to go. Molly sat on her kitchen counter, a kettle already boiling. A mug filled with passionflower and lavender was ready to steep.

"It's over," said Henry, assuring her. She wanted to believe him, but her thoughts hurled doubts. Hadn't she thought Bruce had died before? "He's dead," said Henry, as if reading her mind

Bruce's body had lain in a heap once he fell to the ground with no mimic to bring him back. Molly couldn't look anywhere else, trying to convince herself that it was really over. Mark and Chris picked up the pieces as Henry swooped her up into his arms. He carried her away from the graveyard, but the unmistakable scent of lighter fluid followed them out.

"Are you okay?" asked Henry for the twentieth time since they had arrived home.

"I will be," she answered. She sat on her hands to stop them from shaking. He wouldn't judge her for it, but she hid it anyway.

"I thought you were—" started Henry.

"It was stupid. I was so stupid. I saw you. He looked just like you."

"You weren't stupid."

"I shouldn't have run out; I should have waited. I put us all in danger."

"He's dead now. He's never coming back." She could only nod. Henry's face twisted with worry, and his fingers caressed her cheek. "What do you need from me, Molly?"

Molly didn't hesitate. "I need you to hold me."

Henry pulled her into his chest. His strong arms curved around her body and, for the briefest of moments, Molly's mind shut off. The shakiness in her eased; his heartbeat steadied her. Henry's hands ran down her back. He whispered in her ear, but she didn't register what he said. It was enough for him to be near.

The smell of bacon woke Molly up. She reached out in her half-awake state but touched cold sheets instead of the feverish body she was growing used to. She shuffled out of bed, wrapped herself in her favorite robe, and headed downstairs to the kitchen. Henry stood in front of the stove in her apron, cooking breakfast. She watched him for a moment, taking in all of him. The apron was too small for him to tie it. He hummed, so relaxed that he didn't seem to notice her.

Her man.

"If you keep staring, I'll turn into stone."

Molly laughed and stood on her tiptoes to kiss him. "How did you know I was behind you?"

"I sensed you were awake." He placed his hand on his heart.

"I didn't know you could cook."

"Just wait, I have a few more surprises in me," he winked.

Molly wrapped her arms around him. She didn't want to bring down the mood, but a question itched in her brain.

"Is it over?" she asked.

"Yes," his jaw tightened. "Chris and Mark took care of the body. I instructed them to bury the ashes at separate locations. It might be overkill, but I needed to make sure he could never come back."

"We killed its host. He was possessed by a mimic. He wasn't a shapeshifter, not a natural one. It shouldn't be surprising. He was so obsessed with power that he would try to steal mine. But to allow yourself to be possessed by such a malevolent being, it's idiotic."

"That explains why he always looked like a combination of animals. Sometimes I'd see it as one, but it changed at will."

"A mimic only pretends. It's pretty tough for it to keep a perfect copy from what I've read. The mimic will live on. It'll find someone new."

"But the host wanted you." His fingers brushed her neck. "And the host killed Malcolm. It's enough for me. Plus, I'm not sure how to locate that thing's spirit again."

"How are you doing?" she asked.

Henry smiled widely. "I feel free and so unbelievably happy." He kissed her hand before turning back to the stove.

Just then, Mark and Chris walked in through the kitchen door, smelling strongly of smoke.

"Everything's taken care of," said Mark. "We burned the boat too, for safe measure."

"Did the cops or firefighters say anything?" asked Molly.

"Well, we didn't stick around long enough to find out, but there was an old groundskeeper who seemed upset by it," said Chris, grabbing an apple from the bowl on the island. "We might have singed the dock a little."

"So what now?" asked Mark.

"We need to contact the others and tell them what's happened. Chris will go back to school and finish that damn PhD, and I'm staying here with Molly."

"I'm not sure Brandon and Freddy will want to move their entire families here," said Mark.

"And I get that. I won't force them. But we are stronger together."

"And if the alpha says..." said Chris, rolling his eyes.

"Alpha?" asked Molly.

Henry rubbed the back of his head. "You missed a few things last night."

"Yeah, I can tell."

Chris and Mark took their orders without saying a word. Henry waited for her to say something, but all she could do was kiss him. He would be a great leader. He always had it in him, and she was glad that he finally saw it for himself.

After breakfast, Mark and Chris said their goodbyes as they left to obey Henry's instructions. Molly helped Henry clean up and found as many opportunities to kiss him as possible.

Following months of chaos with Ellie, Violet, and the mimic, the sense of calm she felt was strangely new. Some chaos was beneficial; it led to her meeting Henry. And her life would never be the same.

"Is it really over?" she asked.

"Not for us," said Henry, pulling her in closer.

EPILOGUE

"This won't work," said Molly as she tied her shoelaces.

"Sure it will," said Lenore. She stretched her hands above her head and yawned. "Look, all we need to do is take a quick peek into the attic and see if we find any bats. Or raccoons, or Derek resurrected back from the dead," she laughed, but none of those things were laughing matters to Molly.

The scratching had started late the night before, and she would've asked Henry to check the attic himself, but he was gone at four in the morning. He'd been so secretive all evening about what he was up to, and he had slipped out before she could ask more questions.

"Okay, but just one quick peek. But if we find nothing, we wait for Henry."

"Come on, your house is crawling with ghosts and you're more scared of bats?"

"Ghosts don't have rabies."

Lenore stopped her trek up the stairs. "I didn't think about that."

"You see, we should wait."

"He might take forever, and I need to be at work in like twenty minutes. A quick look, and then we'll let Henry get it out."

"Fine," agreed Molly. The scratching had only gotten worse in the hours since he had left, and trying to guess what creature lived in her attic made her anxious and curious.

They opened the hatch at the end of the hallway. Dirt and dust fell as the stairs descended. Lenore pointed her flashlight up, illuminating the old wooden framework covered in spiderwebs.

"After you," said Lenore.

"What?"

"You can check first," she said sheepishly.

"I'm sorry, what happened to brave Lenore just now?"

"Brave Lenore didn't realize how dark it was going to be."

Molly sighed heavily. "Fine." She tucked her flashlight into her overalls and climbed up. Once at the landing, she pulled out the flashlight and waved it slowly through the perimeter. She saw the Christmas and Halloween decorations closest to the hatch. But the further she illuminated, the less she could make out. Nothing showed an animal was living up there until a pair of eyes flashed at her.

Molly screamed as her heart leaped into her throat. She descended the stairs in a panic, but her foot missed a step and she fell straight on her back.

"Are you okay?"

Molly laughed at first when she realized nothing was broken, but groaned as she moved to her hands and knees.

"Well, what did you see?" asked Lenore, helping Molly up.

"I don't know. I just saw eyes, but something is living up there."

"MOLLY!" They jumped at the sound of Henry's voice.

"I'm fine," she said as Henry cleared the hallway. His worry fixed on his face as he reached for her. His hands drifted over her body, and when they touched her back, she winced.

"What were you doing?" he asked.

"Checking to see what the scratching was about. I'm fine really; I just got scared." Molly felt embarrassed. All this fuss over a raccoon or a bat.

"You have to be more careful," pleaded Henry.

"Never."

He sighed but still held onto her tightly, as if she would break with every step she took. He supported her downstairs, but he refrained from carrying her. He knew she would hate it. Lenore didn't stay, and she rushed out the door.

"I'm fine," she repeated as he eased her onto the couch. "Anyway, there's something up there, and I need you to take care of it."

"I will," he promised. "I told you last night that I was going to do it."

She didn't like the tone of his voice, as if he were reprimanding a child. "Well, I was only going to assess the situation. Where did you go off to so early in the morning, anyway?" she asked.

He looked her once over. "Do you think you can walk to the front door?"

"Yes," she said with a huff.

"Okay then," he pulled her up, and she shuffled to the door. He left her standing on the porch, her hand holding on to the wooden railing.

Henry hopped into the back of his truck and lifted something up. Molly couldn't make out its shape.

"Close your eyes."

"This is so silly," she said, but she closed them anyway, unable to keep a smile off her lips.

"Open them," he said after a moment.

The first thing Molly noticed was color. The deep red of the rose cast a shadow on her railing. The bright green of the vines and leaves reflected in the sunlight. Rainbows danced on her skin. It was a replica of the stained-glass window in her library.

"It's not an original, I'm afraid," said Henry, bringing it closer for her to inspect. "Your house is one of a kind. But I found a guy who could recreate it, and I sent him photos of your other windows."

"Our house," corrected Molly, as her fingers traced the silver-wrapped panes. "It's beautiful."

Molly kissed him, her fingers tracing his jaw. Integrating Henry into her life had been so much easier than she had expected. Lenore didn't seem to mind that he moved in, while Rosie gradually warmed up to it. Granny was beside herself and had already given Molly her great-grandmother's pearl necklace for the wedding. No matter how many times Molly told her they didn't have plans for marriage yet, nothing deterred Granny. During her last visit, her grandmother had pulled out a calendar and asked her to choose the date so she could get a new outfit made in time.

Henry took his role as the alpha seriously. The other wolves and their partners had moved into town, although Chris was still in school, much to Rosie's relief. He filled the position which such ease; she wondered how he had doubted himself before.

"I'll install it after I take care of a couple of raccoons."

"How do you know they're raccoons?"

"I can smell them," he said, scrunching up his nose.

Molly laughed, and as he helped her back into the house, she settled on the couch with her new window as he went upstairs to handle the raccoon.

Henry came down with a box. Frantic scurrying and growling emanated from it.

"How many?" she asked.

"Just one. He's okay, though. I think he was just looking for shelter from the storm last night. I found where he crawled in through."

"Well, set him free far from here."

Henry left and came back after much too short of a moment.

"That wasn't very far," said Molly.

"I run fast."

"Henry, I don't want it coming back in."

"It won't, I promise, but I couldn't leave you here for too long. You're injured."

He stooped to pick her up, and she winced.

"I'm fine. I'm sore, but I'll be okay."

"You're lying," he said, carrying her back upstairs. He set her down on their bed, taking great care in going slow, and helped her out of her overalls. "I'll find ice," he said, turning towards the door.

"Henry, wait," she said, grabbing hold of his hand. "Come here. I don't want ice. You can be my heating pad."

He smiled and climbed into bed. He took off his shirt and settled in behind her. Her back nestled against his chest, and the pain faded away. She sighed, grateful for the pain relief, and Henry kissed her. It wasn't the urgent, hungry kisses of their past. It was light and tender, as if any movement would make the pain worse.

"Better?" he whispered. Molly could only nod.

They stayed quiet for a while until she felt something push against her thighs. The familiar pressure made her giggle as it grew larger.

"What's so funny?" asked Henry.

Molly wondered if it would hurt to reach back, but she had only one way of knowing. She reached behind and found the bulge in Henry's pants. Her fingers fumbled with the zipper, but once inside his trousers, she clasped her hand around his hot flesh. He sighed, and she found it didn't hurt at all.

"Molly," he said gruffly. "Not now. You're hurt." She didn't respond, only touched him further. His lips pressed against her neck.

"Be gentle," said Molly. Her own need intensified as his cock grew thicker in her hands. After months of being together, she knew just how gentle he could be, and how rough. Every time they had sex, she found herself pleasantly surprised by how much she still needed him, and how she had lived so long alone. He fit in so perfectly. How had she never noticed before that there was a giant Henry-sized hole in her life? She couldn't see her future without him in it.

Henry pulled her underwear down, his fingers cupping her core as he kissed her. His index finger teased her clit, caressing it. Molly couldn't move very much. A small arch in her back proved quite painful, and he stopped his movements.

"No," she protested, the whine in her voice surprising even her. "Keep going."

"Love, I don't want to hurt you."

"You won't," she said between heavy breaths. "Just go slow."

Henry continued then, and she squeezed her eyes shut as his finger entered her. She bit down on her lip, and Henry's arm snaked around her to press her more firmly into his chest. She sensed it again, that power surging between. Flowing between them like waves until she no longer knew what came from him, and what was hers. It heightened every touch and magnified the love she felt for him.

Henry moved excruciatingly slow. Each movement was planned to keep her back supported by him. But she soon grew impatient. He could tell by the way her breath came out — more a sigh than a gasp.

"Henry," she finally begged.

"No," he said in her ear. His breath made her shiver, although she was quite warm. "Slow." He pulled open her thighs a little more, and Molly wrapped one of her legs around his thigh. When Henry seemed satisfied that it didn't hurt her, he pushed her open just enough to guide his cock in.

Henry grunted as he pushed every inch in until he was fully sheathed inside her. He didn't dare move just yet, but Molly became more inpatient. She pulled away a little before pushing her ass back again. Henry groaned, making her want to arch her back.

"That didn't hurt you?" he asked.

"You can't break me," she said. "I'm not fragile."

Henry kissed her before he moved. He pulled his lips away as Molly's mouth opened mid-moan. "You are fragile, my Molly. So incredibly fragile." And yet his movements grew stronger. He pushed his cock in further and further, the steady rhythm pushing her closer to her climax.

Nothing hurt anymore. His warm flesh on hers replaced the pain. The taste of his lips and the scent of cedar in the air masked it. Molly closed her eyes as her orgasm climbed. Henry clasped her to his chest as she came. Not allowing her to arch her achy back.

He waited for her climax to fade away, letting the remnants of it languish in her body before continuing at that slow, excruciating pace. Molly came once more, and Henry groaned as she squeezed around his length. He shuddered behind her, and he held on to her tighter.

Sweat glistened on their bodies, but Henry wouldn't let her go. His lips traced her jaw. His hand cupped her breasts as he pulled out. Molly didn't want him to move.

"I'm never doing that again," sighed Henry, burying his face in her curls.

"What sex? Doubt it," laughed Molly.

"No, having sex when you're hurt." He sounded exasperated with himself.

"I wanted it," she protested.

"I need to stop being so easily swayed by you."

"You were the one who told me you would take care of me, and you did. Very well," she added with a kiss.

"I should take better care of you," he said.

"You take perfect care of me. Really, Henry, you do." He kissed her again, this time with the urgency and pressure she had grown accustomed to.

She hadn't expected a werewolf to crash through her window. She hadn't expected love to crash into her life, but it had found her anyway. And for the first time in a long time, she didn't fear facing the future alone. They had each other.

* * *

AFTERWORD

Thank you so much for reading and I hope you enjoyed it! Please consider leaving a review as it helps a lot!

If you want to know what's next for Molly and Henry, you can subscribe to my newsletter at https://www.sulaalba.com/newsletter for a free second epilogue.

I started writing Molly and Henry's story back in 2022, and it was one of those stories where I couldn't stop thinking about it until I got some words on the page. This story had so many changes before I felt comfortable enough to let others read it, but I'm so excited to continue writing about the rest of the coven and now the wolf pack.

About the Author

Sula Alba is a paranormal romance author living in the deserts of the Southwest.

When not writing, she loves to photograph her cats laying in the sun, baking and reading.

www.ingramcontent.com/pod-product-compliance
Lightning Source LLC
Chambersburg PA
CBHW032344310726
48973CB00007B/1841